Edel Coffey is an Irish journ[...] work as an arts journalist and [...] She has since worked as a prese[...] and as editor of the *Irish Independent Weekend Magazine*, and Books Editor of the *Irish Independent*. She lives in Galway with her husband and children.

Breaking Point is her first novel, and is the winner of Crime Novel of the Year at the An Post Irish Book Awards 2022.

'A gripping, compulsive page-turner about what we expect from women, especially mothers. It's going to be a massive hit'
MARIAN KEYES

'Prepare to feel devastated and enraged all at once'
HEAT

'*Breaking Point* has all the hallmarks of a future bestseller ... the tenderness of Edel Coffey's descriptions elevate this beyond the status of page-turner'
JANE CASEY IN THE *IRISH TIMES*

'A rare treat, an emotional thriller steeped in humanity. I read it in a single sitting!'
JOHN BOYNE

'Heat has been building steadily around this debut'
IRISH INDEPENDENT

'A very thought-provoking story that will no doubt resonate with parents everywhere'
SUN

'Gripping, unswerving, heart-breaking, you'll read this book through parted fingers – and learn a crucial lesson as you go'
CELIA WALDEN

EDEL COFFEY

BREAKING POINT

SPHERE

SPHERE

First published in Great Britain in 2022 by Sphere
This paperback edition published by Sphere in 2023

1 3 5 7 9 10 8 6 4 2

A CIP catalogue record for this book
is available from the British Library.

ISBN 978-0-7515-8240-6

Typeset in Sabon by M Rules
Printed and bound in Great Britain by
Clays Ltd, Elcograf S.p.A.

Papers used by Sphere are from well-managed forests
and other responsible sources.

Sphere
An imprint of
Little, Brown Book Group
Carmelite House
50 Victoria Embankment
London EC4Y 0DZ

An Hachette UK Company
www.hachette.co.uk

www.littlebrown.co.uk

For David

Chapter 1

Susannah hated waking the girls so early. They were sleeping soundly in the dark nursery, their breathing long and shallow. She could smell the dry, oaty heat of their bodies when she walked in. Louise's hair – a sprig of light blonde fluff – had just started to grow and it stood on end, wafting like an underwater plant. Susannah brushed her nose over the downy tuft as she lifted her six-month-old baby out of the crib.

She crossed the room and gently woke her other daughter, Emma, who was four years old. She was half-awake already, and protesting. Susannah wanted to protest too. She was exhausted. Louise had kept her up half the night. It was only the first day of June but New York was already sweltering through a heatwave, and despite her best efforts with the air con, it was making everyone grumpy. The forecast for today was no different.

It had been 10 p.m. when she had gotten home from the hospital last night. John had been slumped on the corner couch, an iPad propped on his knee, 24-hour news playing silently on the TV. He had stood and stretched stiffly, his long body still slim and boyish, his thick silver-grey hair flattened where he had been lying on it. He always took Susannah's return from work as his cue to go to bed. And these days he was always asleep by the time she joined him.

Susannah changed Louise's diaper quietly and quickly in the soft glow of the morning light. She measured her weight as she carried her downstairs for breakfast. She knew Louise's weight by feel, to the ounce, gauged it in her arms every day. She inhaled Louise's hair deeply. So soft and silky, and that smell. *How did I get this lucky?* Then . . . *If I'm so lucky, why am I so frustrated all the time?* She tried to chase away the doubt, the *guilt*, shoo it like a fly from her mind. But it was persistent. An article she had read in the *New York Times* the previous week had said women were waiting until they were older to have children. One young woman quoted in the article asked, 'Why have children if you're not able to enjoy them yet?'

Were you really supposed to *enjoy* it?

Susannah loved Louise and Emma. She had never loved anyone or anything in this way before. It was a physical kind of love – sometimes it made her feel nauseated, weak, overwhelmed – but could she really say

2

she was *enjoying* being a mother? She wasn't enjoying anything at the moment. She and John never got to spend time together as a couple. They never relaxed, never hung out, never stayed in bed laughing like they used to do. And work at the hospital was busier than ever. The more successful she became, the more she had to do. Between her increasing TV commitments as a family expert, a publishing contract that demanded a new parenting book every year, and her *actual* job as Professor of Paediatrics at St John's Hospital in Manhattan, the days seemed to run on ahead of her, like a too-fast playmate. And then the nights slipped into one another, telescoping down into mere minutes, as Susannah tossed on a dreamless sea, burrowed deep in a dark exhaustion until Louise's cries punctured her oblivion.

A familiar wash of self-loathing plumed in her, like paint in water. Why could she not just be like other mothers, love her babies straightforwardly instead of second-guessing herself about every decision she made, interrogating her choices, questioning her own identity? Could she not just be patient, put aside her personal frustrations, her career goals, even for a few years, in exchange for the blessing of having children? And it was a blessing. She had undergone IVF to have Emma, and then had an unexpected natural conception with Louise. John had not been keen on having a second child. 'We're too old,' he had said. 'We're already so busy, and Emma took so much out of you. We need to think of ourselves as well, *our* relationship. We should talk about this,' he had said. She knew exactly what he meant but she wouldn't hear of it. How could she not accept a second child so late in life as the blessing it was? In the sleepless world she now inhabited she sometimes imagined what their lives would be like if she hadn't become pregnant a second time.

She banished her thoughts with a shake of her head, fearful that bad thoughts were enough to make bad things happen. She didn't believe in prayer but she whispered one to herself anyway.

A high-pitched scream from Louise in her baby chair snapped Susannah back to the present.

'Sorry! You're hungry today, aren't you?' She scooped some more baby cereal onto the spoon. Louise was momentarily placated. Emma drew a picture whilst shovelling Cheerios into her mouth. She grinned at Susannah and Louise. 'This is Mommy, this is Daddy, this is Emma and this is Baba Loulou,' she said pointing at the crude simulations of her family members, who comprised her entire world.

After Susannah had finished putting the dirty breakfast dishes in the dishwasher, she brought the girls to their bathroom, where she washed their faces, their pink lips wobbling under the sponge (they liked that), their eyes squeezed tightly shut against the cool water (they didn't like that).

A door slammed downstairs. John, leaving for work. He knew Susannah's finely calibrated itinerary didn't have contingency for distractions like 'hellos' or 'goodbyes', kisses or hugs. Their routine was so tightly wound that there was no space for unscheduled items, spontaneity. Nobody could wake up late (Susannah always set two alarms), nobody could be sick (the rearranging it required was unthinkable), nobody could have a slow start (what even *was* that?). Still, sometimes, she wished John would say goodbye.

The door downstairs banged again.

'John? *John?* Is that you?'

Her husband's head popped around the door. She still marvelled at how immaculate John looked first thing in the morning – shower-fresh, clean-shaven, crisply dressed, his springy silver hair contained with some pomade.

'My car won't start,' he said in disbelief. 'Any chance you can give me a ride on your way to work?' He flinched a little as he said it. Susannah realised he was afraid of provoking an angry, impatient reaction. She pressed her lips together to hide her irritation and said as calmly as she could, 'Of course! Here, you take the girls and the diaper bags to the car ... I'll just brush my teeth.' She mentally calculated the extra seconds and minutes it would take to drop him to work, and how much of a kink it would put in her day. Why would he not just call a cab? John was so brilliant at his job and yet, somehow, so useless at *life*. He blithely ignored things like car servicing schedules and deadlines. Learned helplessness, she thought furiously, as she finished brushing her teeth.

Emma's Montessori school was the only one in the area that opened at 7 a.m.; it also opened on Saturdays, which Susannah didn't like to admit had played a part in her decision to enrol her there. She tried not to use it too often. She never mentioned it to anyone when she did. Why not? The truth was something close to shame, or perhaps failure, particularly as she spent so much of her time giving advice on how to be a perfect parent. What would people think if they knew Dr Sue's kids were farmed out to daycare and a nanny so she could go to work, write research papers, write and publish books and appear on TV advising parents on how to manage this very juggle? People didn't seem to realise that being the perfect mother involved a lot of outsourcing and a lot of money. And sometimes she didn't even get to kiss Louise and Emma goodnight. She was sure the people who bought her books would think she was a fraud if they knew. Louise's daycare was closer to the hospital. It wasn't ideal doing two drops every morning but on the upside, Susannah could visit Louise if she had a quiet hour at work. Or that had been the plan.

But work was never quiet.

Susannah would have preferred it if a family member could have helped out but her mom was never the most nurturing type, and it would be a huge stretch to ask her to mind the girls. She was pushing eighty and Susannah, at forty-six, knew how exhausting looking after the girls could be. And besides, they just didn't have that kind of relationship. Some of Susannah's friends had those mothers, who had moved in with them after they had had babies, cleaned the house, made dinner, sent them off with their husbands for romantic weekends. It would never occur to Susannah's mother that she might need help (and it would never occur to Susannah to admit she *needed* help).

When Susannah and John arrived at the Montessori, she dropped Emma off quickly, leaving the car running as she did so. It was blindingly hot already, and she had started to sweat by the time she got back into the car. John hung up his call and ran his hands over his hair.

'Part of the roof on the new house has collapsed.'

John seemed to be the only engineer in New York who could make glass houses stay up using nothing but a few pieces of slender steel. He engineered improbable houses for star architects with starrier clients.

'Oh, Christ – can this day get any worse? Is anyone hurt?'

'No, it looks like it happened overnight but the place

is a mess. Can you drop me straight to the site instead of the office?' He winced, again, waiting for her reaction. 'I'm really sorry, Susannah, I know it's out of your way.'

Shit. She moved the seconds and minutes around in her head. If she hit the highway now, dropped John, then looped back, she could still be at the hospital before 8 a.m. Her secretary, Roberta, had texted the night before to say she was down a doctor in clinic this morning. She could really do with getting to the hospital early but it would just have to wait.

'It's fine,' she said, shaking off her irritation. 'It's not your fault. There's nothing we can do about it now.'

She turned the car around in a large, smooth semicircle, elegantly done, just like everything she did, and headed back in the direction they had come. Louise snuggled into her car seat, drifting deeper into sleep after her wakeful night.

John called the architect and the builder, and spent the rest of the car journey on the phone. He put his hand on Susannah's leg and gave it a little squeeze. He mouthed the word *sorry* at her.

She gave him a tight, brief smile to tell him not to worry about it.

They pulled up to the site and the builder emerged to greet them. As John got out of the car, he tilted his head to look at her and asked, 'Everything okay?'

'Yes,' she said. 'I'm just thinking about clinic. I'm

down a doctor this morning and we're overbooked so I'm just trying to organise it all in my head before I get there.'

'Always thinking about the job,' he said. It felt pointed.

'Someone has to,' she retorted, then she hated herself for sounding so snippy, so martyred.

Her phone rang. 7.50 a.m. 'I'm sorry, John, I have to take this. Will you be okay?'

He rolled his eyes and smiled. He leaned back into the car to kiss her, just managing to skim the corner of her mouth as she put her phone in the hands-free cradle and hit the button on her steering wheel to answer. She waited for him to walk away before she reversed the car and floored the accelerator in the direction of the hospital. She merged onto the highway, not seeing what was in front of her, driving on autopilot as she listened to her panicked resident doctor on the end of the phone. A driver changing lanes from the other side nearly wiped her out. She swerved to avoid him, muttering 'asshole.'

'Look,' she said to her resident. 'I'm two minutes away, it's easier if I just come see the patient. Meet me at reception in two.'

The phone continued to buzz and beep, ping and vibrate in its cradle while she drove. Her mind was everywhere, on the road, on her phone, on her marriage, but mostly on the child that awaited her at the hospital. She had built a career on insightful diagnosis and she took enormous pride and care in her work, in helping children, in improving, and often saving, their lives. She took the responsibility seriously. She had seen too many times how quickly a child could flip from fine to critical.

She pulled into the employees' car park, at the back of the A&E department. She grabbed her handbag and stethoscope from the footwell of the passenger seat. She pointed her key fob over her shoulder without a backward glance and heard the double beep of the horn telling her the car was locked. It still gave her a little thrill of satisfaction. She had bought the car new a few months ago and was still enjoying its little quirks, even the souped-up spoiler John had been so against.

'You're having a midlife crisis,' he'd mumbled when she'd ordered it but she didn't care.

'At least I'm not having an affair,' she had told him. She had had suspicions about John on and off over the years but he never flinched. Either she was paranoid or he had an excellent poker face.

She strode around the block towards the hospital reception. She was the picture of composed professionalism. The sun beat down on her back and sweat beaded her upper lip as the automatic doors of the hospital parted smoothly and she crossed the threshold into the air-conditioned comfort of the A&E department. She spotted her harried-looking resident by the reception desk. She felt the sweat cool on the back of her white silk blouse and a calm descended as she switched into work mode and forgot about everything else.

Back in the car, baby Louise woke up and began to cry.

Chapter 2

Susannah tried to calm her resident as they walked briskly towards the little girl in question. She was white-faced and couldn't have been more than three, but she was conscious. Susannah was always pleased to see them conscious and alert.

Susannah got down on one knee and took out her pink stethoscope.

'Hello, Lucy, my name is Dr Sue. Your mommy told me you're not feeling great but I was wondering would you be able to help me with a really important job? I have a really sick teddy here and I need to listen to his heart but he's afraid of my stethoscope. Can you take this end and pop it on his chest for me and then we're going to listen to his heart together.'

The little girl lifted her head and smiled. They all loved the teddy and the stethoscope. Susannah had a pink one and a blue one for these situations. While the girl was distracted playing doctor, Susannah took blood samples, and hooked her up to a cannula and drip. If the blood samples confirmed Susannah's suspicions she would be able to treat the condition with medication and have this child home within a few days. Susannah loved the feeling of having everything under control, the beautiful mathematical simplicity of problem and solution that her work presented to her every day. It was why motherhood was so unexpectedly perplexing. Things never felt under control at home.

As she and her resident walked back towards the nurse's station, Susannah said, 'Paediatrics is as much about having a way with kids as it is about knowing your medicine. I didn't have a clue until I had kids of my own.' Her resident frowned and Susannah realised she had done that awful thing of saying 'you can only know how to do this if you're a mother'. She could kick herself. She had sworn she would never be *that* woman. She switched back to professional mode. 'I'll come by after clinic and do a round with you, okay?' She walked briskly towards her outpatients office in the ER.

The emergency department of St John's hospital was the usual dystopian nightmare. It was one of the busiest hospitals on the Upper East Side, with people coming in from Harlem and the South Bronx as well as up from Midtown. Some moaned, some were quiet, some were surrounded by entire extended families, others were terminally alone. She looked at the list that Roberta had emailed her last night – fifty-three patients to see. She really was overbooked. She tried to see everyone as an individual, but with such huge volumes she found it difficult. It didn't help that many of them often turned out to have little wrong with them.

'Try to get her to drink more water,' she found herself saying to one parent; 'Try to cut out sugary drinks' to another. She suspected many of them just wanted to say that 'Dr Sue' from the TV was their doctor.

Most of the time, Susannah managed not to think about the fact that she was famous until, on occasion, the parent of a patient asked her to sign a copy of one of her books. It always felt weird, and Susannah always mentally scanned back through their consultation to make sure she hadn't said anything brusque or unprofessional. She didn't want anyone telling dinner party stories about how stuck-up Dr Sue was.

As she arrived at outpatients, Susannah's secretary put her head around her door and nodded towards the car park.

'I think that's your car.'

Susannah looked out of the window at the sun attacking her car's black bonnet, its indicator lights flashing, alarm blaring. She jumped into action, rooting her key fob out of her handbag.

'Oh God, thanks Roberta. Sorry.'

How long had that been going off? She stood at the

window, squinting, as she pointed the clicker at the car. The indicator lights deactivated and the car settled into silence again. She felt irritated now. Was nothing built to last these days?

'I'm just going to grab a coffee for my desk before we start,' she said to Roberta. 'Can I get you one?'

She walked to the coffee station at the end of the corridor.

On her way back, she bumped into a colleague.

'Susannah, can I pick your brain?'

Susannah was moving at speed but she stopped and focused.

'I'm having an issue with a patient – fifteen-year-old male, we're treating him as an adult but I suspect there is something paediatric going on with him. He has high blood pressure and there is some blood in his urinalysis but nothing significant has shown up in his blood testing.'

Susannah let her mind clear.

'Is there any family history?' she asked.

'The mother said she was told she had blood in her urine once but she doesn't sound too sure,' her colleague said.

She smiled. 'Well, if the mother has had that it could be Alport Syndrome.'

Her colleague blushed. Susannah tried not to gloat. She knew she was popular at the hospital for her ability, and the positive publicity she brought, but she also knew her fame and success brought envy, jealousy and resentment too.

She walked quickly back to her office, eager to get started on the long line of patients. A siren punctured her thoughts.

Shit, she thought, not again! She frantically rooted in her bag for her keys. Not there. She panicked, shuffling papers off her table. The keys clattered to the floor and she followed them, grabbing the fob and pointing it at the car. She implored it to stay quiet for the rest of the day.

Without her car she was incapacitated. How was she supposed to do her job and ferry the children around and quite possibly be John's chauffeur too if it was faulty? She would have to hire a rental.

'Roberta! Would you book my car into the garage please? Tell them the alarm is on the blink? And book me a rental for however long the car is going to be in the garage? Thank you. And send in Mrs Olewande, please.'

She worked methodically through the list of patients, clearing one after another until, by lunchtime, they were all done. She arched her back and flexed her knuckles in an improvised yoga pose. Everything cracked. Not good, she thought. She'd get Joni to take a look at her at yoga on Wednesday. Her phone vibrated on the desk, startling her. Would this day ever end? She checked her watch. 1.03 p.m. She looked at the phone screen and saw Christina's number. Her stomach zoomed to her pelvic floor; Christina only called when something was wrong.

'Hi, Christina. Is everything okay with Louise?'

A pause.

'Hi, Dr Susannah … I'm at the daycare. They said you didn't drop Louise this morning. Did I miss a message?'

There was a deep, eternal silence, a kind of everlasting moment. Everything stopped. Then everything was destroyed. The phone clattered to the desk, to the floor as Susannah grabbed her car keys. The screen cracked but Susannah was no longer there to see it. She was gone, down the stairs, through the doors, around the block to the parking lot at the back of the hospital.

She was whispering the whole way: 'No! Oh please no! God, no! PLEASE! Louise! Louise!' The whispers turned to screams as she reached the car. 'Help me! Somebody help me!'

The car shimmered in the heat haze like a mirage. A woman asked what she could do.

'Go to the hospital reception,' Susannah screamed. 'Tell them there's an emergency in the car park. Tell them there's a baby.'

As Susannah opened the car door, she prayed, 'Please God, let her be okay. Please, God.' She wrenched the door open so hard that it recoiled from its hinges. It couldn't be happening. This could not be happening.

Despite what Susannah saw, despite all the evidence her eyes were feeding to her brain, she unbuckled Louise, laid her on the asphalt and started to perform CPR. Louise was lifeless, her face scratched, her scalp bloodied in patches from her tiny fingers, grasping for life.

Chapter 3

Adelaide Gold woke up slowly. Her alarm was set for 7.30 a.m. but she always woke before it went off. The New York traffic noise rose up from the street outside. She never got tired of listening to this dawn chorus of joggers, delivery men, garbage trucks, construction workers, car horns and jaywalkers. She loved living on the Upper East Side, just a couple of blocks from the East River on one side and a few blocks from Central Park and the best museums in the world on the other.

Adelaide never dared to believe that she would live somewhere like this and yet, somewhere inside of her, she had always hoped that she would. She had grown up the daughter of French-Senegalese immigrants, living in a community housing apartment in Brooklyn and spent her teens on high alert, always ready to make a run for it. The background noise that filtered through the thin walls of her family's apartment was of neighbours fighting, someone drunk in the stairwell, doors slamming. The elevator was permanently kicked out of service. Here, that was all a distant memory. Here, she could walk the streets calmly after dark and her building, which came with a doorman, was blissfully event-free.

She lay in bed looking at the bare ceiling, the light rippling softly on the plain white walls of her studio apartment. It was soothingly anonymous. That was one of the reasons she had first rented the place nine years ago. She had moved here the same week as she had switched jobs from working as a writer at the *New York Times* to working as a TV reporter for CNN. After a working day filled with the noise of the newsroom – ringing, texting, persuading, charming, scrolling, blogging, vlogging, tweeting, filming, arguing, shouting, reporting – the sensory deprivation of her studio felt like stepping into a decompression tank. She needed it for the noise in her head too, the constant memories, questions and what ifs that never left her alone. The calming light in the apartment had clinched the deal for her, even though the rent was outside of her budget. But this was New York. The rent was always going to be outside of your budget. And she only had herself to think about now, so she figured she could take on the risk.

She stretched and yawned, looked at the bronze-cast

baby's feet that sat by her bedside. She touched them briefly with her fingertips, then grabbed the phone that lay beside them. She checked Twitter, Insta, ignored Facebook, then moved on to her news apps. She searched for anything breaking, breathing a sigh of relief when she saw there were no catastrophes, no overnight political scandals, nothing that might ruin her morning. She hated surprises. It was better to know what storm she was walking into before she got to the newsroom than to find out on arrival and have to play catch-up.

Adelaide lived and breathed her job. She turned news stories over in her head like a Rubik's cube puzzle. It was her life, and it had become even more so over the past decade. Her radio alarm clicked itself on and WNYC crackled through the speaker. Curtis used to laugh at her quaint radio-alarm clock but she liked to wake up to the headlines. She listened to the main stories – economy, the president, shooting murder, drug death, fatberg blocking the city's sewers – and was content that she had accurately guessed what the running order would be. It was one of her favourite games in the morning.

'Still got it, Adelaide,' she said, as she stretched again and hauled herself out of her bed.

After her shower, she dressed quickly in her off-screen uniform: a crisp white shirt, skinny black tuxedo pants, ballerina pumps and a blazer. She was petite and attractive, with high cheekbones and a pert mouth, which she inherited from her mother. She wore her hair natural and short, which accentuated her fine bone structure. Her laptop bag was always packed and ready to go. She liked the feeling of travelling light. She looked around her sparse kitchenette. The silence of her mornings now was still remarkable to her. This used to be her favourite time of the day. She still enjoyed the morning, the calm before the day started, but the silence always reminded her now of how noisy and busy her mornings had once been. She pulled the apartment door shut behind her. Hopefully today would be a slow news day.

*

Adelaide had barely taken a bite out of her croissant when her producer, Jimmy, came huffing across the floor towards her. He started speaking from twenty feet away.

'Adelaide . . . Adelaide!'

She knew the drill. She re-wrapped the croissant in its paper bag. She mentally went through her checklist of notebook, pen, and phone. She had her blazer on by the time Jimmy was standing in front of her.

'I need you to get uptown to St John's Hospital now,' he said. This first sentence came as a punch to the head. Out of nowhere.

Then the second statement. 'They've got a dead baby.'

She saw stars. She physically recoiled.

'Found in the car park. They think it's Dr Sue's baby.'

'Dr Sue?' she repeated, stupidly. The name was a dark thread, pulling her back into an old abyss. Adelaide thought she could hear screaming but her face was a mask. She tried to catch her breath. She couldn't breathe. *Get it together, Adelaide.*

'Yes, Adelaide!' Jimmy snapped. 'Dr Sue. Dr Susannah. RICE. The *Oprah* doctor? The *Goop* guru?'

'Yep, yes, I got it. I know who she is.'

Adelaide knew exactly who Susannah Rice was.

'Take Luke with you. Get whatever footage you can. I want something for six o'clock.'

'No problem,' she said coolly. Inside she was in free-fall.

Chapter 4

Susannah was sitting in the bad news room. So this is what it felt like. She had been here thousands of times, speaking calmly, in the simplest terms, to frozen, numb family members, loved ones, husbands, wives, parents just like herself, breaking the most awful news. Now she was here herself. Her hands were bluish-white under the aggressive air con. Two uniformed police officers stood loosely by the door, sentries with iPhones.

Susannah was momentarily subdued, having spent the last two hours wailing and screeching, tearing at her hair in a dreadful mirroring of what Louise must have done. The noises seemed to be coming from somewhere outside of her. *Who is making those awful noises?* she had thought, before realising the screams were coming from her. She remembered thinking the same thing when she was in labour with the girls.

Louise had been taken away, but not as she had been

when Susannah had given birth to her, to be wiped clean, fingers counted and umbilical cord clamped, before being returned to Susannah's arms. Now Louise had been taken away to be wiped clean and prepared for the coroner. She would never be returned to Susannah's arms ever again. John was on his way. After a terrible period of not being able to get him on the phone she had finally managed to get through, then found she couldn't bring herself to tell him what had happened. Instead she told him that Louise was in hospital and he needed to get here immediately. How was she going to tell him? How was she going to tell him what she had done? Would he ever be able to forgive her? She desperately wanted him here but she also wanted him to take longer, to put off the awful inevitable task of telling him. Perhaps if she didn't have to say the awful truth out loud, she could fool herself that it wasn't true.

When John finally arrived, he was wild-eyed with worry and out of breath, as if he had run all the way to the hospital.

He ran to Susannah. 'Where is she? Is she okay? What's happened?'

Susannah burst into tears. 'Where have you been?' she said. 'I called and called and called.'

'I'm so sorry. I–I ... was in a meeting. My phone was back at my desk.' John crouched down so he could meet her at eye level. 'Susannah, what's happened? Where is Louise? Is she okay?'

Susannah crumpled. She couldn't say the words. If she said the words it would be real. If she said the words, how could he ever forgive her? She heard herself wailing again. She tried to say it but she was incoherent.

'Susannah, honey, I can't understand you …' he said, but Susannah saw comprehension dawn on him.

Susannah took a breath then whispered, 'She's dead.'

John whispered back at her. 'What did you say?'

His face had turned white. His jaw hung open. Susannah knew he had heard her but he couldn't compute what she had said. Language had disintegrated, detached itself from logic, the words she was speaking didn't make sense when put together.

'I said she's dead,' Susannah said.

He stood up and shook his head in confusion. 'No, no, no. I just saw her this morning,' he said, as if that counted for anything. 'She was fine, Susannah … *How?*'

Susannah was doubled over now, keening.

'I did it. I killed her. It's my fault.'

A doctor entered the room at that point.

'Mr Rice?'

John was losing control of his own reactions now, the reality of what Susannah was saying was eroding the edges of social propriety and decorum. 'Yes, yes, that's me. Where is my daughter?'

'Mr Rice, I'm so sorry, we did everything we could.'

John closed his eyes, and put his hands up to his face.

'I need to see my daughter now,' he said.

'I'm sorry,' the doctor said. 'My colleagues are just preparing her ...'

'Preparing her!?' John shouted this and the room fell silent. 'Can somebody please tell me what the *fuck* has happened to my daughter?'

The doctor only then seemed to realise his mistake, that nobody had actually informed John his daughter was dead. 'I'm so sorry. I thought perhaps your wife might have had a chance to speak to you. There's been a terrible accident. Your daughter was left in your wife's car. In this heat ...'

'No, no, no, no, no ... oh God, no, please, no ...' John was crying now.

'We tried everything to revive her,' the doctor said. 'It was just too late. You'll be able to see her very shortly. I'm so sorry.' John held his head in his hands and cried bitterly. 'How could this happen, Susannah? What did you do? *What did you do?!*'

The police officers shuffled uncomfortably and looked at each other but didn't leave. They had their orders: Susannah was not to be left alone.

The doctors had prepared Louise as quickly as possible and placed her in a pink-rimmed plastic crib, just like the one she had been put in after she was born. The room was sunlit and smelled clean, all wrong for the occasion. Susannah wanted to leave, to run away. As long as she didn't have to see this, to be in the room with Louise's body, she could pretend it wasn't real. She looked at Louise's feet, the little hat that somebody had put on her to cover the scratches on her head, her curled fingers. She could only look at Louise laterally, one tiny detail at a time, or she would go blind, or mad. She felt as if her body were being split in two. She wanted to climb out of her own body, to get away from this all-consuming feeling, this reality. And then it hit her. This was her new reality. This was how she would feel for the rest of her life now. John was at the head of the cot already, weeping, saying Louise's name, heartbroken, but Susannah was rooted to where she stood.

She forced herself to walk towards the crib. She looked in at the feet, usually restless and kicking, now completely still. Susannah put a trembling hand out and touched Louise's toes. Cool, and strangely firm. She moved her hand up the little legs, the chubbiness of her knees, the layers of fat at her thighs. Her nappy was gone and Susannah put her hand on Louise's tummy, the little curve still protruding, she waited to feel the rise and fall of her stomach but it never came. She held her little hand, the fingers no longer curled to grip Susannah's fingers. She brought her hand to Louise's perfect cheek. Susannah remembered the beautiful hair underneath the baby hat that she had pressed her face into that very morning. How could she be witnessing this and still be alive? She wanted to die herself. She was overwhelmed with love for her daughter. She picked Louise up out of the cot and held her to her chest. She pushed her face into the crook of Louise's neck. She could still smell the trace of her underneath the chemical cleanness. She rocked her and began humming a lullaby. It was Louise's favourite, the one that always got her back to sleep. She rocked her back and forth for a long time.

'Mommy's here,' she whispered, kissing Louise's head. 'It's okay. It's okay, Mommy's here.' John embraced them both and quietly cried as the awful reality sank in.

When it was time to leave, Susannah wouldn't, couldn't relinquish Louise. It went against every instinct to leave her alone, unattended in the room. It reminded her again of when she was born and the nurses tried to get Susannah to take a shower and leave Louise sleeping in her crib. As if she could leave her on her own, no more now than then. John slowly eased Louise from Susannah's arms, explaining that they would be able to see her again before the funeral. Susannah's colleagues explained that they would take very good care of their precious little girl.

Chapter 5

Adelaide stood outside the hospital. The sun filtered through the trees and made the streets feel iridescent, alive. She could smell the East River on the warm, dry breeze. Summer in New York. It could be heaven. But not today.

Her notebook and pen sat impotent in her hand, her mind looping back to the last time she had been here, at this very same hospital. It was like no time had passed. It didn't feel like *remembering*. It felt like she was there, in the day, reliving it, reliving the horror. The tsunami of pain swelled and threatened to engulf her but she couldn't go there, not now, she had to focus on her job.

She had spoken to everyone who had walked in and out of the hospital. She had found and spoken to the woman who had gotten help. She had stumbled across her, loitering outside the hospital, and bundled her into Luke's media van to keep her away from the other reporters who were gathered at the hospital. She secured an exclusive interview for her 6 p.m. report and then called her an Uber. If she was away from the hospital, the chances were less likely that she would be interviewed by another reporter. She could relax a bit now. All she really needed for her report were colour comments and something official from the hospital. She couldn't help asking herself, as always, did someone do a better job, did someone get a better story? Today she knew that she had done well enough. The only better interviewee would be Susannah and nobody was going to get that today. Of that Adelaide was certain.

It was the same when she worked at the *New York Post*, before she had moved to the *New York Times*. If somebody got more information on a story, whether it was newsworthy or not, you might as well pack up your desk. The pressure had made her an excellent journalist but she wasn't so sure what kind of person it had made her.

Her mind looped back again. Her feelings were roiling, memories rising up with frightening intensity before disappearing again, down beneath an obsidian surface. She felt them circling there, knew they would rise again soon.

Her phone rang. It was Jimmy. She felt a stabbing pain in her side. Her stress IBS was back.

'Hello?'

'Where are we with the dead baby?'

Well, hello to you too, Adelaide thought, rolling her eyes.

Adelaide could picture the slug on the news feed for tonight. *Dr Sue's baby found dead in St. John's Hospital car park*. The words held no meaning other than their ability to boost ratings. Adelaide's heart pounded harder. She could feel it in her throat, in her hands, pulsing in her stomach. Her head was hot and aching.

'We're good. No sign of Dr Sue or her husband but I've got an exclusive with the woman who called for help, eyewitness account.'

'Anyone else got her?'

Never, 'Great job'. Never, 'Well, done Adelaide', always, 'Is it exclusive?'

'I put her in an Uber myself, sent her home. I'm going to stroll around to the morgue now to see what's happening there, see if I can get any more detail on cause of death. It's not looking like homicide. Looks like she might have just forgotten the baby.'

'Ah, Jesus,' Jimmy said. 'Go heavy on the tragedy angle if so.' He hung up.

Adelaide couldn't figure out if he was disappointed that the story had become less interesting – on his scale of newsworthiness at least – murder was always preferable to accident.

But *was* it a less interesting story, less important, just

because it was an accident? This wasn't the first story like this that Adelaide had covered.

Back at the office, Adelaide put her script together for her report. There was so much archive footage of Susannah. Adelaide had always thought Susannah was a bit of a pain in the neck when it came to her parenting advice. She sounded haughty, a bit judgemental. She had the kind of rigorous expectations and standards that you can only have if you are rich. She came across as someone who thought moms who were failing were just not trying hard enough. And yet she had legions of faithful followers. Certainly, she inspired a love-her or hate-her divisiveness in people. Some mothers swore by her advice, others called her rigid and cruel. Those ones were going to have a field day with this news, Adelaide thought. Maybe Adelaide's personal feelings about Dr Sue were getting in the way.

At six o'clock, she was back outside the hospital, ready to recite her report into Luke's camera.

There were people everywhere. Locals who lived in adjacent blocks, rubberneckers on their commute home. Although really it was only the fatally idle or curious who stopped and stared for long. This was New York. Everyone had somewhere to be and something to do and news moved along quickly, like detritus on a fast-moving river. Reporters swarmed the pavement. Local and national. She spotted Julie Connerty about ten paces down and smiled. Julie was a celebrity newscaster for Fox as well as a social media star as the voice of misunderstood conservatives but despite all of this she and Adelaide had become firm friends over the last nine years.

Adelaide's smile changed to a frown as Bob Kreshner from NBC started unpacking his camera light directly behind her.

'Are you kidding me, Bob? You're in my shot.'

'Can't you just adjust your angle, like ten degrees? If you do that we both have the shot we need.'

'No, Bob, if we do that, *you* have the shot *you* want and I have the brick wall instead of the hospital entrance and nameplate that I got here early for.'

He continued to unfold his lamp. Luke stepped in.

'Dude, you're in our shot.'

'For Chrissakes,' he grumbled and moved down the street.

Adelaide hated that it took Luke's intercession to get Bob to move. *He thinks he's a fucking movie star, not a news reporter.* She stood with her legs wide apart, taking up as much space as her small frame would allow, trying to protect her territory from the swarms of reporters who were looking for the same shot. Once the red light went on, she knew she was safe. There was an unbreakable law amongst TV reporters that you didn't cross the shot when the red light was on.

'Tragedy struck this morning at St John's hospital

in midtown Manhattan when the parenting guru Dr Sue found her six-month-old baby girl unresponsive in her car. The baby was taken from the car park, which is around the block from the entrance of the hospital, which you can see here just behind me, where Dr Sue's colleagues worked on her baby in the emergency department. But tragically the baby was pronounced dead a short time after.

'New York has been in the grip of a heatwave for the past ten days. As temperatures soared to over 100 degrees today, experts believe temperatures inside the car could have risen to as much as 150 degrees.

'Manhattan resident Ms Kayleigh O'Brien was the first person to come across Dr Sue as she desperately tried to save her baby. She raised the alarm in the hospital and while paramedics were on the scene within minutes, there was nothing the doctors could do to save the baby.' As the the footage of Kayleigh ran, Adelaide tried to calm her breathing, and compose her thoughts to complete her report.

'Dr Sue rose to fame as a parenting expert and has appeared as a regular contributor on talk shows like *Oprah*, *The Today Show* and *Goop*.

'Now forty-six years old, she has a stellar career in both medicine and media and is the founder of the parenting website and app Family Ties. Dr Sue published her first book, *Growing Pains*, at the tender age of thirty, and has since published a total of twelve titles, all of which have been *New York Times* bestsellers.

'Dr Rice is married to John Rice, an engineer, with whom she has one other daughter. The couple left the hospital earlier this evening under police escort.

'There will be a coroner's report into the death of the baby and a police investigation has been opened but police are not looking to speak to anyone else in connection with their inquiry at this time.

'I'm Adelaide Gold for CNN News at St John's Hospital, Manhattan.'

As the red light went out, Adelaide noticed her hands were shaking.

Chapter 6

Susannah woke dry-tongued, a single shaft of white sunlight blazing through a crack in the curtains, lasering into her cortex. One peaceful moment before reality rushed in. Louise was dead. Life was grey ash. John was gone from his side of the bed but she could hear his voice, talking to Emma over the soft burbling of cartoons. The funeral was today. It had been a week of this awful purgatory of life without Louise. Susannah tried to brace herself to go downstairs but she couldn't muster the courage to look into Emma's sweet face as she asked for Baba Loulou again. It had taken them two full days to figure out how to tell Emma that her sister was dead. In the end, they took the easy way out, told her that Louise had gotten sick and gone to heaven to be a guardian angel. Emma didn't quite understand that Louise was never coming back but every time she asked for her sister, the pain it sent through Susannah's head and heart and stomach made her feel as if she was going to go insane. She was surprised that grief felt this physical.

At night, she was afraid to fall asleep. She didn't want to go through that awful groundhog-day realisation every time she woke up but, also, her dreams were haunted by Louise. Being awake was a different kind of hell. In the dark and quiet of 2 a.m. on the couch, the thoughts rushed in. Louise's last moments. Was she conscious? Was she crying for Susannah? She was tormented by thoughts of Louise's uncomprehending pain, her tiny confusion, by the fact that she might have been able to save her.

She took the bottle of pills from the bedside locker, broke a valium in half and swigged it down with a half-glass of dusty water sitting on her bedside table from the night before.

It hit her then, as clear and pure as her pain: she would have another baby. It was the only way she would be able to survive this. Not to replace Louise but as a companion for Emma, a balm for Susannah. And if she couldn't do that? Plan B was even clearer. She'd kill herself. Emma didn't need a mother like her. She couldn't live with herself for what she had done to Louise, couldn't live with the pain of life without her.

John came in and tried to move her.

'Susannah,' he said, touching her hair softly. She must have dozed off again. 'It's time to get ready. The funeral director said we should be there by eleven.'

'Where's Emma?' she asked groggily.

'She's watching TV.'

She looked at him. 'I just still can't believe Louise isn't here. I keep thinking I can hear her crying.' She lifted the duvet and pulled him under it, into her arms and legs.

He clung to her, fresh tears rolling down his face, into the crevasses in her neck. 'What are we going to do, Susannah?' His trousers were rough against her bare legs.

'We're going to have another baby,' she whispered.

John flinched. He pulled back.

Susannah started talking, fast.

'I can still have one, John. It's not too late. It's the only way I will get through this. But it has to be now. With every month that passes, my chances disappear.'

'Susannah, have you lost your mind? You can't just replace Louise. You can't just have another baby and think that will make everything okay.' He whipped back the duvet and stepped swiftly out of bed. 'You need to get ready. We can't be late today.' He left the room.

The past week had been hellish. Susannah had not known a moment of peace. Everything reminded her of Louise. Her bottles and sterilisers were still on the kitchen counter, her breast milk pouches were still labelled in the freezer, supplies of diapers that would never be used sat neatly stacked under the changing table. She found teething rings and chewy toys and crinkly cloth books everywhere she turned, underneath the cupboards, down the side of the sofa. Her handbags were full of pacifiers and baby wipes, tissues and sterilising tablets. Everything was still here. Everything except Louise.

She replayed that morning over and over in her head. If only John hadn't asked her to drive him to work. If only his car had started. If only she had said, no, sorry, I'm too busy, get a cab. If only she hadn't detoured to the construction site. If only she hadn't taken the phone call. If only Louise had been awake and gurgling happily instead of sleeping silently. If only. If only.

As if that wasn't bad enough, she had to deal with the press. Despite her fame, she had never been the focus of so much attention. The day after Louise died was the worst. Pictures in all the papers, pictures of that awful moment, captured for posterity. The fire services and police cars surrounding her car, paramedics rushing into the bare hospital car park, and Susannah on all fours, head hung low between her shoulders, covering Louise's body. They ran the pictures on the front page of every newspaper. Susannah couldn't believe that they could legally publish pictures like that, pictures of the worst moment of her life, pictures of her daughter's death. Nor could she believe that that was what people thought to do when they saw someone in trouble, instead of helping, they took out their smart phones and recorded the scene. Each day had brought a different report, new speculation, archive photos of Susannah, quotes lifted from her parenting books on how to keep your children safe, all coming back to haunt her now. Would she be cancelled now, her books removed from shelves and pulped, her career destroyed in one swoop?

The minute she woke up in the morning, before she even opened her eyes, before the fresh awareness of her hellscape sank in, she could hear the hum rising up from the pavement, the swarm of journalists who now followed her every move. Her phone was permanently off. Her landline was unplugged from the socket. If she turned either on, they rang incessantly. She took another pill from the bottle she had prescribed for herself, using John's name on the script. She broke the pill in half. She needed to quell the rising panic she felt in her chest.

John came back into the room. How much time had passed? Five minutes? Twenty-five minutes? She had no idea.

He sat down on the bed beside her. She put her head on his lap. Her stomach hadn't felt right since Louise had died. Empty and sick. Nothing could take away the feeling in the pit of her stomach. It was like hunger, except she wasn't hungry, couldn't eat a thing. Every muscle in her body ached and her head pounded incessantly. She had a pain in her chest that felt like she was having a heart attack. Grief, people said. Just grief. But she knew it was something else too. Guilt.

'I'm sorry for reacting the way I did, Susannah,' John said. 'We can talk about it another time but I think today we need to concentrate on Louise and getting through the funeral. It's going to be hard. It's going to be really hard.' He broke down and she pulled him towards her in a desolate hug.

She stood up and put on her black silk jersey dress, which she had taken out of her dressing room last night. She already knew she would never wear this dress again. She wouldn't be able to touch it after today, as if putting on this dress would be like putting on this feeling again, and why would she ever want to do that? This dress could only ever mean bad things now.

At the funeral, John spoke about Louise, biting back sobs, to make sure that everyone at the service knew just how much their gorgeous baby girl, their light, their joy, their gift from God was loved. Susannah couldn't even contemplate talking about Louise. She didn't know where John got his strength from but she was glad that he had done it, that he had told everyone how special their baby was. After the ceremony and the graveyard, they had planned to have a small reception at their house in Gramercy Park. It was the only way they could ensure privacy. They had stated that the funeral was for family only but the service had been thronged with media and sympathisers and the house was no different. 'Why are they *here*?' Susannah asked with despair when they had gotten back to their house and the doorbell kept ringing.

'I have no idea,' John said. 'I think they just want to pay their respects.' And so, instead of Louise's funeral being a small private affair, Susannah's house was packed full of acquaintances, people she didn't know very well and certainly didn't want to see at this point in time. Susannah felt as if she had entered another dimension. This was her baby's funeral, two words that repelled each other with such force, and yet, in this most intimate grief, she saw her agent and her publisher, her yoga instructor, John's ex-wife, Marianne, some of John's clients, including the basketball player. So many people from so many disparate aspects of her life in the same room at once. Emma darted in and out of the room like a timorous goldfish, flitting from Susannah's mum, to Christina, to Susannah and John, and enjoying all of the attention she was getting from the grown-ups. She still didn't understand that Louise was dead. Susannah still didn't quite understand it herself. The pills helped, they made everything feel like walking through a cloud – soft, gentle, buffeted. When her publisher squeezed her hand, Susannah realised she hadn't returned a phone call from a few weeks back. She gasped, 'Agnes, I'm so sorry. It completely went out of my head.' Her publisher cut her off. 'Let's not worry about it now, Susannah. I think it's probably a good idea to shelve all of our planned projects for the time being anyway, just until this all ... blows over.'

Susannah was stunned. Had she just been dropped by her publisher? At her baby's funeral? But there was no time to think about it. There were more unwelcome guests to see to. Ralph Lyons. She hadn't spoken to Ralph since he had crushed her hopeful, beating heart into pulp, just before she had met John. Could that really only have been six years ago?

At least Ralph had the decency to keep it brief. He embraced her awkwardly.

'I'm so sorry,' he breathed in her ear and then he was gone.

She wondered was he really sorry, sorry for *everything*. But probably not. People like Ralph Lyons were never truly sorry for anything.

Outside her house, the media clogged her normally quiet, tree-lined street. Reporters spoke an endless stream of meaningless words into cameras at the bottom of her brownstone steps, their performances dripping with tragi-drama, as if it was a soap opera, and not her real life, not an *actual* tragedy. She despised them all, and their grotesque appetite for the minutiae of her grief, the details of Louise's death. She called the police but they told her the media weren't breaking any laws. They sent a couple of uniformed officers to keep them off her property but that was the most they could do. Her property, and her rights to any sort of privacy, ended at the stoop that led from her front door to the sidewalk. It didn't make much of a difference to the situation but it made a difference to Susannah to know that they could not set foot on her stoop, could not contaminate her life any further by being one centimetre closer to her than they had to be.

Susannah cast regular glances through the window and watched as the reporters stopped guests arriving at her house, asking them for comments. Over the last week, the story had moved on from being a tragic accident to being the act of a neglectful, careless mother hellbent on success at the cost of her children. Then there was the gleeful schadenfreude of the headlines that delighted in a parental expert getting her comeuppance. The papers blared stories like DR SUE DIDN'T PRACTICE WHAT SHE PREACHED and DR SUE HAS A TASTE OF HER OWN MEDICINE. She made a note of those who stopped to talk to reporters on the way from her house and instantly deleted them from the list of people she used to call friends.

As the evening wore on, the news huddle thinned out. There were still a few reporters doing late reports, speaking into their phones perched on top of tripods or their TV cameras. She realised with a jolt that they were all talking about her and what she had done. Her eyes went to two women standing by the kerb. They looked so unthreatening, just two women talking. Susannah thought she recognised the black woman from somewhere but couldn't quite place her. Probably just from the news. The women both had that generic TV sheen – perfect make-up, block-coloured uniforms of blazers and tight dresses, size four figures.

She moved away from the window. The last of the uninvited guests were leaving. At least the funeral was over. At least now she would be left alone to grieve in private.

When she closed the door on the final guest, she tore her dress off. She couldn't stand to be in it for one second longer. She went out to the back yard, stuffed it into the barbecue, squirted lighter fluid on it and set it alight with a match. She had paid $3,000 for that dress. Dior. How she wanted it gone now, reduced to ashes, dispersed on the breeze, never to be seen again, along with any other reminder of this wretched day. She took off her pantyhose too, then her bra, her underwear and added them all to the fire. They were brutal mementos of the worst day of her life and she wanted them gone. Just as she considered adding herself to the fire too, John came running out of the house.

'Susannah, Susannah! What are you *doing*? Susannah, please, come inside.' He put his arm around her and tried to shield her as best he could from the neighbours. He looked around to check for photographers but there were none to be seen.

On the sofa, under a blanket, John squeezed her to him and began to cry.

'Oh Susannah, my darling,' he said, stroking her hair and hugging her harder. 'My poor darling. You cannot do this to yourself. You cannot tear yourself apart like this. What happened was an accident. It was not your fault.' He pulled her tighter to him. 'I know things haven't been great between us this year ... well, they've been pretty awful, I know, but I still care so much about you. You're still my wife. You can't destroy yourself like this.'

She felt the carapace that had solidified around her over the past week crack and her shoulders began to tremble. The tears that hadn't come all day finally broke.

'Where *is* she, John? Where is our baby girl now? I just want her to come back. Please, tell her to come back to me.'

John shushed her and kissed her gently. She and John had not made love lately, even before Louise had died. And after their conversation that morning Susannah wondered if they ever would again, but John's kisses deepened from comforting to passionate. All Susannah could think about was having another baby. She was afraid that he would read her mind and stop. But he didn't. And as John made love to her, she whispered a silent prayer.

Chapter 7

Adelaide ran her hand across her forehead. It felt cool but clammy. She rubbed at the layer of foundation and fixing-spray, thick on her skin. She hadn't slept properly since she had been put on this story, the past week already felt like a month. Last night she had taken a sleeping pill from her old stash for the first time in years.

'Ten minutes to air, Adelaide,' Luke shouted across the street. 'Oh, hi, Julie!'

'Hey, Luke!' Julie smiled back.

'Jesus, this story,' Adelaide said, shaking her head.

'I know, right?' Julie said trying to balance in her high heels.

'Got another one of those?' Adelaide asked, and Julie passed her the pack of cigarettes and lighter. Adelaide and Julie really shouldn't have been friends. On paper, they were opposites. Julie Connerty was midwestern, conservative, white. Adelaide was a die-hard liberal, raised in New York, and understood first-hand the inequities of being a black woman in white America. Julie held her fellow citizens to high standards. She posted judgemental comments underneath news articles. She got into Twitter spats. She defended herself by saying she was a dying breed: an outspoken American. She called it her inviolable right to free speech. Julie loved a cautionary tale the way some people loved the Old Testament. It was just better if bad *things* happened to bad *people*. She also liked it if bad people were punished for doing bad things. It gave life a neatness, a sense of symmetry, a sense that we weren't just chaos strapped to a rock hurtling through space.

Despite all this, she and Adelaide had become friends over the years. Camaraderie was hard to find on this beat but it was also a life-saver. Their brief only really covered bad news stories, the items that were awful enough to cross state lines and be of national interest: climate catastrophes, high-profile murders, mass shootings, gruesome sexual assaults and tragedies, just like this latest one. It was why very few reporters stayed as long on the job as Julie and Adelaide had. It wasn't pretty.

'I just don't buy it. I mean, how could you just *forget* that your baby was in the back seat of your car,' Julie said. 'Do you believe her? I mean, she didn't even cry at the funeral.'

Adelaide felt only confusion. She couldn't think about Susannah without feeling her own pain. She couldn't tell where one ended and the other began. She was suddenly exhausted. 'I think I do believe her. She thought her baby was in daycare. It could happen to anyone. It could happen to you. It could happen to *me*.' Adelaide crushed the cigarette under her shoe. She suddenly felt light-headed, nauseated. She wasn't used to smoking and only really did it now when she was nervous or agitated.

'Maybe,' said Julie, 'although there is one gaping hole in your argument.' A smile spread across her face. 'We don't have a baby between us.'

Adelaide would normally have laughed at this tension breaker. But she couldn't laugh today.

Julie leaned in closer to Adelaide as she saw Luke wave her back from the media van.

'You know what I really think? I think people who neglect and kill their children don't deserve to have them in the first place.'

People like me, thought Adelaide.

Chapter 8

Susannah and John were snuggling quietly on the couch in their post-coital calm. The pills provided a comforting distance between Susannah's thoughts and reality. Since his unexpected appearance at the funeral, Ralph Lyons had been irritatingly present in the back of her mind. She had spent the tail-end of her thirties in a relationship with him, or what she had thought was a relationship, but it turned out that their definitions of the term differed. When she had broached the topic of moving in together, getting married, maybe even having a baby, he had laughed and said, 'But Susannah, I thought we were just having fun.' It turned out that he was having fun with half the young female doctors in the hospital. Susannah was furious, devastated, not, she realised, because she loved him, but because she had wasted prime child-bearing years on him. She had never given much thought to children, only enough to assume that she would eventually have some, with the right person, when the time was right. But that time had never come. Not as a teen when it was shameful to be pregnant and not in her twenties when it was foolish to be pregnant and not in her thirties when she was on a career track and it was inconvenient to be pregnant. And so the the years went by and she was about to turn forty and still hadn't had the children she assumed she would have.

It was no wonder then, that she fell willingly into the arms of the mature and handsome engineer who was working on the architectural redesign of her home (some women cut their hair after a break-up, Susannah redecorated). She had enjoyed John Rice's calm presence at progress meetings at her house, his slim tanned good looks gave him a glamorous but laid-back West Coast vibe and he seemed thoughtful, soft-spoken, calm, everything that was different to the kind of stressed-out, ambitious, bad-tempered men she encountered at work. Men like Ralph Lyons. When John asked her out when the redesign job was finished, she said she'd love to and that was the beginning of Susannah's rebound.

He was older than her, by ten years, and divorced. He should be cynical, Susannah thought, but instead he was crazy romantic and his friends commented on how 'mad about her' he seemed. People could tell he was in love with her. Was she in love with him? It was hard to say, but she was certainly in love with the idea of a kind, admiring, supporting, romantic man, one not afraid of commitment and perhaps not afraid of having children too. Was he too good to be true? Okay, so he didn't make her fizz and spark, but hadn't she already tried that kind of man and found him to be less than satisfactory? She wasn't going to make the same mistake twice. So what if her relationship with John didn't have the same charge? Maybe that charge was destructive. Maybe this is what grown-up love felt like. And so after a few dates, when John broached the topic of dating exclusively, Susannah agreed, but as the months passed and the topic of children didn't come up, she became more and more uncomfortable until one night, she couldn't bear it any longer and had an outburst, saying that she was forty and didn't want to waste time dating someone who didn't want children. John had looked at her like she was crazy.

She put her head in her hands.

'I know, I know. We've only been dating for six months but it's something that's important to me and I want to be honest about it, I want kids. So I don't have time to mess around. I want to know if we have a future together or not.'

'Well, then,' John had said, with a broad grin, after a couple of uncomfortable seconds had passed. 'I suppose we'd better get married.'

Maybe this was the point at which Susannah should have heard alarm bells. But if she did, she ignored them. The most important thing was that she would have a baby, she would have a husband, just as she had always thought she would. It wasn't too late.

But her excitement was short-lived. Six months later, after they were married, a year to the day since they had first met, Susannah allowed two menstrual periods to come and go before making an appointment with her colleague, Dr Sharad, a fertility specialist. She was suddenly desperate, determined, she felt it was her biological right as a woman to have a baby. Or maybe just her right as a wealthy, middle-class, white woman who was used to getting everything she wanted. Either way, failure was not an option.

The phone's ring tore through her reverie. John heaved himself up from the sofa and answered.

'Is this really necessary tonight?' she heard him say. 'Perhaps you're not aware, we just buried our daughter today.'

Susannah gazed at the fire and her eyes glazed over, entranced by the dancing flames. She heard John's voice again.

'I still don't see why this can't wait until another day. It's not like we're going anywhere ... Okay. Okay, fine, I'll put her on.

'Susannah ... Susannah ...'

Susannah blinked and looked away from the fire.

John's face was serious, like he was barely controlling his anger.

'It's the police.'

All of a sudden, she was wide awake, adrenalin pulsing around her body.

'Hello?'

'Yes, hello Dr Rice, this is Detective Brian Williams from the 19th Precinct. I'm sorry to disturb you so late, I'm running the investigation into your daughter's death . . .' He left a gap for her to speak but Susannah could find nothing to say.

'I wondered if you could call into the station on East 67 and Lex at some point tomorrow, please, just to answer a few questions.' His voice had not formed a question, this was a statement, a directive.

'What kind of questions?' Susannah asked.

'Just a few routine questions.'

'Um, does it have to be tomorrow? We just buried—'

'I'm afraid so. The sooner we get this done, the sooner we can progress and close our investigation, which I'm sure is what you want. And it's best to talk about these things as close as possible to the . . . ah . . . the events, when everyone's memory is still fresh.' Susannah looked at John. She wanted him to come rescue her, to make it all go away, to cross the room, take the phone from her hand and end the call by sharply hanging up.

'I—' she faltered. 'I already told the officer I spoke to

in the hospital that day everything that happened . . .'

'I understand that this is a difficult time for you and your husband but it's better for everyone if we can bring our investigation to a conclusion in as timely a manner as possible. Let's say eleven o'clock tomorrow morning.' The house felt eerily quiet. She could hear the hiss of the gas fire.

'Okay, I'll come down at eleven. See you then,' she said, but she was talking to a dial tone.

Chapter 9

Adelaide stared into the camera and waited for the red light to go on. *You're a professional, Adelaide, you can do this.* She gripped her microphone tightly but her hand still shook. She felt her stomach lurch, sudden nausea rising like it had done when she had been pregnant.

She looked at her body from above, her hair lightly oiled, her fingers bony on the microphone. She lined up the facts from the funeral – chief mourners, eulogy, tiny white coffin. She felt faint. Luke counted her in.

'And we are live in FIVE, FOUR ...'

She sometimes wondered if she would ever freeze when that red light went on. Why did these thoughts always come into her head the second before she went on air?

Luke counted out the last three seconds silently on his fingers, then did a dramatic point at her as the red light went on.

Adelaide started talking as smoothly as if someone had pressed play.

'Mourners gathered in the upscale neighbourhood of Gramercy Park earlier today for the funeral of six-month-old baby Louise Rice, daughter of the parenting expert and TV personality Dr Sue. Amongst the mourners were celebrities from the TV and publishing worlds.

'The funeral took place exactly one week to the day since Dr Sue's baby was found dead in an overheated car in St John's hospital car park.

'The service lasted just under one hour with Dr Sue's husband, John Rice, performing a moving eulogy. In it, he said, and I quote:

'"Louise was our miracle baby. Our light and our joy. She was a gift from God. Too good for this earth, God has called her back to be one of his angels. We will always love you, Louise. You will always live in our hearts."

'A police investigation into the baby's death is ongoing but no arrests have been made. Adelaide Gold, CNN News, Gramercy Park.'

The light went off and she burst into tears.

Luke stared at her.

'Adelaide, are you okay?'

'I'm fine, thanks,' she whimpered into her chest. She pulled a tissue from her make-up kit, keeping her face averted from Luke. 'It's just ... this story. It's just so sad . . . ' She sniffed loudly, patted under her eyes with her fingers and shook her head. She took two deep breaths and said, 'I'm fine. I'm fine.'

'It's a tough story,' Luke said, patting Adelaide awkwardly on her shoulder before busying himself with packing up his camera. Luke's almost comic level of discomfort with Adelaide's emotion was enough to make her smile again.

'Thanks, Luke. I'll see you tomorrow.'

Adelaide looked at her watch. 9.35 p.m. already. She hated doing live reports for the nine o'clock news. It meant she didn't get home until 10 p.m., by which time it was too late to have dinner, too late to meet friends for a drink or a movie, too late to do anything except sit up and let her anxieties run riot. She hadn't expected to sympathise so much with Dr Sue – she had always thought of her as a bit prissy, a bit too perfect – but she couldn't stop thinking about how unfair what had happened to her was. And she hadn't stopped thinking about the baby all week. She recognised what was happening, of course. She had been triggered. How could she not be? A dead baby? St. John's Hospital? She was reliving her own nightmare.

Ten years earlier

'Welcome to Alphabet Soup Daycare Centre.' The greeting came with a side of head-tilt from the generic blue-eyed, blonde twenty-something behind the counter.

Adelaide put her best foot forward and smiled. 'Hi, I'd like to enquire about a daycare place for my baby,' she gestured at her huge seven-months-pregnant stomach.

'Oh my goodness congratu-LATIONS! So, okay, this daycare only accepts applications from people from around here, like this *specific* neighbourhood, within a six-block radius to be exact.'

Adelaide let the phrase 'people from around here' roll around her mind like a cool metal ball. It was, after all, mostly white people who lived 'around here' on the Upper East Side. Living 'around here' was to be constantly aware of whiteness, or blackness, depending on which way you were looking. She felt it from the very first day she and Curtis had moved into their little one-bed. Adelaide had run downstairs to the 7-Eleven to buy a bottle of cheap champagne to celebrate their first night in their first real home together. She paid, and left quickly, but she was stopped on the way out of the store by a security guard.

'Ma'am, would you mind stepping back inside the store with me please . . . I think you may have forgotten to pay for something.'

Adelaide had not forgotten to pay for anything. What she had done was momentarily forgotten herself. When the cashier offered her a bag for her purchase, she had declined. She had taken her receipt, however, because that's something she never forgot to do. Her mother's voice was always in her head, saying, 'Always take your receipt, Adelaide, so you can prove that you have paid.'

Adelaide unballed the receipt from the palm of her hand, politely pointed out the purchase and smiled at the security guard's apology. He *should* be ashamed. But he wasn't. He was just surprised.

She tried to loosen the tension in her jaw and smiled again at the receptionist.

'Yes, I live just two doors down actually. You know the Smith building?'

'Oh! Yes, I love that building! So nice. Okaaaaay, can you show me some documentation to prove you live there?'

Once Adelaide had rummaged in her bag, produced a bank statement and had it cross-referenced with her driver's license, she felt more than a little exhausted.

'Great, so when do you need a place?'

'I'm due in two months, so I was hoping in three months' time?'

The girl sucked the air in through her teeth and made an 'eek' expression.

'Let me just see . . .' she said as she started clicking

and tapping at the computer in front of her. Without lifting her eyes from her computer monitor, the receptionist said, 'You know, the daycare situation is really competitive in this city. People from around here usually start looking for a place as soon as they conceive.'

Adelaide felt rebuked. She should have known to apply early, like most people who lived around here.

'So, the earliest vacancy we have is six months from now. Would you like to join our wait list? There are thirty-six people on it at the moment so you would be ... ' She tapped a few more keys.

'Number thirty-seven?' Adelaide offered.

'Yes! Should I add you?'

'Yes, yes, please do. Can you recommend another daycare centre nearby?'

'Sure! But I think you might find the same problem everywhere,' she added, doing the 'eek' thing with her face again. 'You really have left it quite late.'

Back at work in the city, Adelaide went for coffee with Emily, her colleague, who worked with her at the *New York Times* and was a mother of three.

'My baby isn't even born yet! How can I be *late* applying for childcare? Can there really be that many babies? I thought New York was full of single people, not families!'

'Most parents work now,' Emily shrugged. 'Even the ones who *want* to stay home with their kids can't afford to.'

Adelaide was close to tears.

'Have you thought about somewhere down here, near the office?'

'Downtown? I was hoping for something within walking distance of our apartment, so Curtis can drop the baby off on his way to work. He starts later than I do so we thought it would be best to get something uptown.'

'Well, I know you'd have to bring the baby with you on the commute,' Emily said, 'which isn't ideal, but there are pros to having them in a daycare nearby work – you get to see them on your lunch hour and breastfeed if you want to.' She nodded at the building across the street. 'There's one just above that coffee place . . . I used it last time around, for Janie.'

Adelaide's eyes widened. She squeezed her colleague's arm.

'Emily, you are a genius!' She set off for the daycare across the street. It would be perfect, she thought, just perfect.

Chapter 10

The day after Louise's funeral Susannah woke up with the same leaden realisation. Louise was dead. Then came another realisation – the police wanted to interview her again. John was needed back at work and Christina was minding Emma so she went to the station alone. She walked west and took a cab uptown. Should she even be doing this alone? she wondered, as the cab rocked her roughly. Maybe she should call Dana, her lawyer? Was that over-reacting? Would it make her look like she had something to hide, like she was guilty? Wasn't she guilty?

Her baby was dead. She had killed her baby. How could this be happening to her? And John ... She kept putting herself in his shoes. If he had forgotten Louise in the car, if he had told Susannah that their baby was dead because of him, she didn't think she could even be in the same room as him. He must on some level be feeling some sort of resentment towards her, but if he was, he wasn't showing it.

The police couldn't possibly hope to discover anything new by questioning her again. Investigations were for mysteries, unsolved crimes. She had forgotten her baby. Her baby had died. She was responsible. She was not denying she was responsible. No mystery to be solved. The facts here were known. She was reminded of them every waking minute of every day, her mind spooling back, trying to find the exact second at which, had she done something differently, Louise might still be alive.

Susannah realised as she climbed the steps to the precinct that she had never actually been inside a police station before. The black double doors were huge, and flanked on each side by what looked like giant green Victorian lanterns. An American flag flapped in the breeze above her head. Despite the elegant dimensions of the building, the ceilings in the front desk area were low and oppressive. A harried officer behind the duty desk looked at her.

'Help you, ma'am?'

'Oh, hi, um, yes, I have an appointment to see, um, Detective Brian Williams? He should be expecting me.'

'And who might you be?'

'Oh, sorry, Susannah Rice.' Susannah turned her back to the desk while he spoke to the detective and took in the room. It was just like on TV. People in various stages of down and out, sitting around, waiting to be booked or bailed.

'Dr Sue!' Susannah spun around. The entire precinct looked up. Susannah could see recognition dawn on their faces. Did he really have to use her TV name? She looked at the detective as he walked towards her. Why did detectives always look like they had slept in their suits? 'Follow me.'

They went to another bland area, into an interview room. She was feeling nervous now. Was she under arrest?

The interview began with simple, bald questions. In her job, she too had to ask difficult and direct questions of people at difficult times. She suffered from what John jokingly called 'compassion fatigue', where the tears of family members became irritating delays, minutes stacking up in her day, frustrating bottlenecks to be inched through. To her, they were pointless; they changed nothing. They didn't save anyone. They didn't improve the diagnosis. As the years went by, Susannah had developed a trick that she felt was an acceptable way of not having to deal with patients' time-consuming emotions. After breaking the news she would gently say, 'I know this is a lot to take in. I'll give you a few minutes in private.' And then she would go and get through a couple of other patients, clear some emails and paperwork, before returning to the room. She knew she was hardened but how else was she supposed to get through her workload? If she sat with every crying relative she would see about three patients a day.

Being on the receiving end of such hardening, she realised now, was a different story.

'You had your two daughters later in life. Would you say you were coping?'

Susannah was blindsided by the question. *Coping?* What did that have to do with anything? The detective kept his face neutral. Susannah looked at him, he looked down at his folder. What was in the folder? He looked back at her, waiting. His cheeks were red and dry, a bit flaky, like he scraped them with a blunt razor every morning and considered moisturiser something women used.

'Ye–yes, I think so,' Susannah said. 'Life was busy but my husband and I are both organised people and we have our nanny, so yes, I think we were coping.'

He made a note. He held the pen the way a lion might, gripping it clumsily in his giant hand. What was he writing? It all looked like hieroglyphics to Susannah. Was he using shorthand or was his writing the worst she had ever seen? His shirt looked clean, soft, plain white cotton, even if it was rumpled. The collar struggled to contain his neck, which was the same width as his head.

'Let me put it another way, did you yourself, as an individual, ever feel ... overwhelmed?'

She paused. She took a sip of water from the small plastic cup the detective had placed in front of her. Was it possible she could incriminate herself by admitting to being overwhelmed by motherhood? She opted for honesty.

'Doesn't every new mother feel overwhelmed at times?'

He made another note in the spiral notebook. He saw her looking at it and placed one of his huge hands on top of it, obscuring her view.

'Okay, let me ask another way. Did you ever seek professional help for anything . . . postnatal?'

Postnatal? Were they trying to suggest she was depressed? Susannah looked at the other police officer. He wouldn't meet her eye. She crossed her legs and her knee jumped, rattling the metal table, wobbling pens and notebooks and water cups, a minor tremor, a warning of the earthquake to come.

'No. I didn't suffer from postnatal depression. I see a therapist every six weeks, and have done for a long time, over twenty years now, and I continued to do so after I had my children, not specifically for any postnatal issues. It's more for things like time management, organisational skills, coping mechanisms . . . '

'Coping mechanisms?'

The image of a mountain fox pouncing on some helpless prey floated into Susannah's mind. The silence crept up the back of her neck like a spider. She looked at the walls, a swampy shade of green. Was there psychology involved in the selection of paint colours for interrogation rooms? She swallowed, and it felt like her throat was sticking to itself. She took another sip of water. She wondered at how her life had changed overnight. How she longed to be back in that ignorant state of grace, rushing from daycare to job to home, complaining about how busy she was, arguing with John about whose turn it was to cook. She longed for those uncomplicated days, when Louise was alive and Susannah was not a suspect in a police interview room.

'Should I have my lawyer here with me, just for – I mean, is this a formal interview?'

Something flashed across the detective's face. Was it irritation? Anger?

'Why would you need a lawyer?'

It came out challenging. Susannah flinched. The detective softened his body language, spoke to her in a gentler tone, almost cajoling.

'We're just trying to establish some background information for our investigation, Dr. Rice. You are not under arrest and are free to go at any time.'

Susannah tasted adrenalin. Her palms were sweaty. She didn't believe him. He was trying to come across as friendly now because he didn't want her to have her lawyer with her. She had been on enough boards to know when the room was against you. The energy was not right.

'Is it okay, then, if we take five? I think I just need

some fresh air. This is . . . difficult to talk about. I'll be right back.'

She stepped outside the building and called Dana. She didn't care if they saw it as lawyering up, didn't care if she was over-reacting, or if it made her look guilty. It wasn't like being in that room without a lawyer was going so well either. At the very least Dana would be able to reassure her.

'Stay there,' Dana said. 'I'm five minutes away. I'm jumping in a cab now. Do *not* go back into that room without me.'

'Dana, I'm not sure you need to come down here. I just wanted to ask you what you thought of the whole thing.'

'Susannah, it stinks, is what I think. Stay there.'

Three minutes later, Susannah saw a cab screech up to the kerb. Dana sprang out of the car. 'Let's go,' she said, bouncing past Susannah and up the steps of the precinct like a tiny coiled spring in stilettos.

Susannah had second thoughts when she saw how wound up Dana was.

'Dana, I'm worried us charging in there, all guns blazing, will make me look guilty, like I *do* have something to hide.' Susannah was worried about John and Emma and whether she would ever get back home to them. This was all her fault.

'Susannah, trust me, I know what I'm doing. And I know what they're doing too.'

Dana talked as fast as she walked, issuing demands before she had even entered the interview room.

'I want the audio of this *illegal* interview deleted and all notes pertaining to it destroyed. And now that I'm here, you can request an interview with my client, which she politely and respectfully declines.' All she was short of doing was blowing smoke off her guns before re-holstering them.

Susannah saw the look on the detective's face turn to something between a sneer and a sinister smile, as if a suspicion of something had been confirmed for him and permission for something else had been granted. The permission to destroy her.

'We'll be in touch,' was all he said.

Chapter 11

Ten years earlier

Adelaide had been so stressed on that first day back at work. Zane was only two months old but already it was time for her to go back to work and hand her baby over to strangers like a character in an awful fairy tale. She was running around the apartment with a slice of toast jammed between her teeth. She wanted to cry but if she cried she would never get to work on time. She couldn't be late on her first day back.

She felt a prickle under her armpits, as her breasts responded to Zane's smile. She grabbed two breast pads from the bathroom and shoved them into her bra to staunch the milk. These pads were so crude, like sanitary towels, she thought. She still had a bandage on her tummy for her C-section scar, a giant green maternity sanitary pad between her legs for the seemingly never-ending bleeding, pressure stockings the length of her legs to reduce the risk of stroke and a giant elastic trainer around her waistband to try and encourage her stomach muscles to knit back together. Add the tubes and bottles of her breast pump and you had a pretty decent rendition of a modern-day Frankenstein's monster. How was she supposed to work like this? It would take her thirty minutes alone just to go to the bathroom.

She mentally went through her checklist for the millionth time: diaper bag, packed lunch, change of clothes, bottles, breast milk, cooler bag, breast pump, sterilising wipes.

'He will be fine,' Curtis said.

'I just can't believe I don't get to look after him, even for a little longer. I just don't want to leave him. How can we leave him, Curtis?'

'That's totally natural, but you will both be fine. If you've forgotten something, the nursery will have it. They *are* costing us two-thirds of your salary. He'll love it – won't you, Zaney,' Curtis said, tickling Zane under his chin. Zane kicked his legs and smiled. 'It's good for an only child to be around other babies.'

'I know. I know, you're right,' Adelaide said, blinking away tears. She put the diaper bag across her body, then strapped Zane to her chest. The bag was strangling her a little bit, but if she wore it this way she could put Zane on her chest and her laptop in the backpack on her back.

'You look like you're about to embark on a polar expedition,' Curtis laughed.

'Why does it feel like that would be a considerably easier challenge?' She laughed too. Adelaide did not feel ready for this day but she had no choice. She had taken as much unpaid leave as they could afford, had taken her entire annual holiday allowance, but it still hadn't given her more than two months together with her new baby. Even if she could afford a sabbatical, she couldn't get around the fact that without her job, they had no health insurance. Curtis worked a few blocks away at Hunter University as a contract researcher. He had been lucky to get a job there after finishing his undergrad course, but because it was contract work it didn't come with health-care or other benefits. As soon as Adelaide had Zane and realised she didn't want to leave him in daycare so soon, she and Curtis had spent almost every night trying to figure out a solution so that she could stay home with him even for a few extra months, but they could never get around the problem of no healthcare.

'Why did I have to choose such a ridiculous career as journalism?' she had asked Curtis tearfully the night before. 'Why couldn't I have done something sensible like law or finance or medicine? At least I'd be able to afford to take a few months' unpaid leave to look after my own child!'

'There are couples in much worse situations than ours, Addy,' Curtis had told her, stroking her hair gently. She knew that; she thought of the women in her mother-baby group, how some of them had been back working the day after they gave birth. This was just being a modern woman in the land of the free. Living the American Dream. So much for feminism.

And it wasn't as if she could ask her parents for help. They had returned to Adelaide's mom's hometown in the south of France as soon as Adelaide had graduated from university and started working. They said they would come visit when Zane was a little older but Adelaide knew she would have to visit them. Her friends were blissfully ignorant of parenthood, still enjoying their twenties, and they saw Adelaide's decision to have a baby so young as her own business. Adelaide had been in a rush to have a baby. When she and Curtis had married it was the first item on her agenda. Her own mother had had Adelaide late in life and made it clear she would have liked more children, that she should have started earlier. Adelaide vowed she wouldn't let the same thing happen to her. She wanted a family, and she wanted her child to have siblings, not to grow up alone like she did. Still, her friends thought she was crazy having a baby in her twenties. She saw how they had looked at her when they came to visit after Zane was born. She saw the pity in their eyes when the baby cried, or fussed over her attempts to breastfeed him. They were uncomfortable. One of them even said 'gross' when they caught sight of Adelaide's engorged breast. There was no connection between them in the way that there used to be. Adelaide had brought a new, unwelcome dynamic into the group. She had crossed a rubicon and she had crossed it alone. She was no longer one of them. She was a mother and a wife now.

The more time she spent with Zane, the more she realised she loved being his mother and with every passing day, her desire to stay home and look after him grew but there was no possibility of her doing that.

'How is it possible that we don't have any choices here?' she asked Curtis. 'How is it that my mom stayed home and looked after me on my dad's mediocre public service salary? How come we can't make it work on two decent private sector salaries?'

'Addy, we've discussed this so many times,' Curtis said, trying to hold his patience. 'The economy is different to what it was thirty years ago. Only the very rich or the very poor can afford to be stay-at-home parents now. We are what's officially known as the squeezed middle.'

Adelaide packed her laptop into her backpack and double-checked the contents. It had been two months since she had opened this bag and she didn't miss it.

'I just never expected to feel this way,' she said, zipping the bag shut. 'That's the really surprising thing. I thought I'd be dying to get back to work. Don't get me wrong,' she added, pulling the straps up over her arms and bouncing Zane with the effort, 'it's not that I want to be a stay-at-home mom for ever. I just don't want to leave him while he's still a . . . a . . . larva!'

'There is no point dwelling on it now,' said Curtis, and she knew he was trying to shut the conversation down so he could get to work. 'We've looked at every possible permutation from every possible angle and it never works. It always comes back to healthcare. We can't expose him in that way.'

'I know,' she said, kissing him quickly. 'We'll be fine.'

'You will,' he said, squeezing her and Zane. 'And you're just two blocks away from him. If anything happens, you can be there in a matter of minutes. I'll see you both later. Have a great day, baby.'

Adelaide arrived at 77th Street subway station, and threw herself into the sea of people that was rush hour. The heat was overwhelming already and a humid wind whipped up from the tunnels, hitting her with that familiar subway scent somewhere on the warm, decomposing garbage spectrum. The breeze was hot and sticky, airless. It offered no relief. She felt the baby's chubby legs, his back radiated heat through her shirt as they waited for their train and she worried she would have a sweat stain on her stomach when she took the baby sling off. When the train pulled in to the platform, the doors parted to reveal a wall of bodies. Adelaide and Zane were not going to fit. But a man behind her smiled and gave her a little encouragement: 'Just push, and they move.' Adelaide did what he advised and the bodies somehow parted to make way for her and Zane.

As the train pulled out, Zane started to screech. He had never done this on their trial runs, but Adelaide had never dared test him during rush hour. The cortisol throbbed and pulsed around her body. She jostled for space, planting her feet wide apart for balance. Zane continued to screech. A man in his sixties stood up for her and she gratefully took his seat. She turned Zane towards her so he could feed. She felt an enormous release of tension as Zane latched on. A woman to her left sighed loudly, crossed and uncrossed her legs, shook her head. Another man stared directly at Adelaide's breast. She tried to make herself invisible, to shrink into herself. She practically leapt from the train when she arrived at her stop. She just made the shuttle at Grand Central Station and when she emerged from the subway steps onto Times Square she was gasping for air.

At the daycare centre, she cuddled and kissed Zane goodbye, promising to return at lunchtime to feed him.

'It's really best if you just leave quickly,' the daycare attendant said, as Adelaide loitered.

Adelaide made it to the elevator before bursting into tears.

She called Curtis as she left the building.

'How did it go?' he asked.

'I've just left him,' she said, her voice wobbling. 'It was awful.'

'Was he okay?'

'Oh *he* was fine, he was happy. It just feels so wrong to me. Why does it feel so wrong?' She felt herself losing control again. She stood at the cross-walk and waited for a chance to dodge the traffic. 'It would be weird if it didn't feel wrong,' Curtis was saying. She could hear his keyboard keys clacking in the background. She felt bad for calling him at work. 'You're his mother. You've spent every second of the last two months together. It's totally natural that you are feeling this way.' He paused and she heard more typing. 'It's only because you're such a good mother that you feel this way.' She put her foot out onto the street but a horn blasted and she stepped back on the pavement again. 'You'll both settle into the routine and once you get back into the swing of things at work, you'll enjoy having some independence too. It will be good for everyone, Adelaide.'

She nodded.

'Right?' he asked.

'I'm nodding.' She sniffed a smile.

'Okay, well, try not to worry and have a great first day back at work,' he said. She could feel him wrapping up the conversation. He typed a bit more. 'And don't take on too much! Ease yourself back in. You have nothing to prove. I'm sure they have something nice planned for you anyway. Love you.'

'Love you too.'

Adelaide crossed the street. With each step she took away from the daycare, every fibre in her body told her to go back and take her baby. But she pushed onwards to the office.

Chapter 12

Susannah walked the entire sixty blocks from the police station back to Gramercy Park. She needed time to think. She diverted through the pretty little park from which her neighbourhood took its name. She was stunned by the morning's events, the hostility of the detective, Dana's adversarial intervention. She felt like she was going mad. Her life, once orderly and controlled, was now unpredictable and chaotic, subject to external forces. She needed to get some structure back. She couldn't keep going through her days like this, replaying that day in her head, wondering what she could have done differently, wondering what might happen with the police investigation. She needed to get back to work, even if only to take her mind off things. As she turned the key in the door to her house, she heard Emma and Christina's voices filtering through from the den. Emma came running into the hallway.

'Mommy! Mommy!' Emma said, running to her. Susannah bent down and almost fell over as her daughter ran into her arms. 'Mommy, Christina bought me a cookie in the coffee shop.'

'I'm sorry, Dr Rice,' Christina said. 'I never do that. I just felt a little sorry for Emma today. She was talking about Louise a lot.'

At the mention of her sister's name, Emma perked up.

'Mommy, when is Baba Loulou coming back to life?'

Christina covered her mouth with her hand. Susannah zoned her out. She had to face this head-on.

'She's not coming back to life, darling. She's in heaven now, she's an angel. She's your guardian angel and will always be looking after you, like a fairy godmother.'

Christina turned her back to them. Susannah could see that she was crying but Susannah needed to be strong for Emma, to show her that she could talk about her sister, that it wasn't a bad thing to say Louise's name and to ask about her. She knew this was important. She had written a whole chapter about it in her book *Childish Emotions*.

When she went to her study, however, she closed the door and allowed the grief to completely envelop her. It came everywhere with her now; she slept in it like a duvet, carried it with her, zorbing around in her self-contained bubble of despair. It did not feel unlike the time as a young doctor when her body had completely given up on her, shut down, broke down. The technical term was burnout. She was checked into a facility for two or three weeks. She still wasn't quite sure how long she had been there and she was on medication for nearly a year before she came back to anything she could recognise as herself. She had continued to see a therapist ever since, to make sure she stayed on the straight and narrow, but she had not attended an appointment since Louise had died. There was no facility for her now. Sometimes Louise's death felt so cartoonishly horrific that it didn't feel real. Denial, she supposed. Tomorrow though there could be no more denial. Tomorrow she was going back to work.

Chapter 13

Adelaide was loitering outside the hospital entrance, along with a few other hard-bitten hacks, on the off-chance that Susannah Rice would come to work. It had been over a week since the baby had died and Adelaide was working on the basis of what she herself knew about this type of grief – Susannah would not want to be alone with her thoughts, her guilt, her torment. Adelaide was sure of it, she would be back any day now. She sucked the last of her frappuccino through her straw and swished the ice around. You knew it was summer in New York when you switched from Venti cappuccino to frozen frappuccinos. She sucked the last of the cold watery coffee from her cup then chucked it in a bin.

Adelaide stared at the hospital doors. Her memory of walking through those doors still felt fresh. What would her young self, straight out of journalism school, think of Adelaide now? Stalking a hospital doorway in the hope of picking on some woman's grief? She hated this aspect of being a reporter. It felt wrong. But so did losing her job.

She was roused from her reverie by shouts of, 'There she is! Dr Sue! How are you feeling? Why are you back at work so soon? Dr Sue?'

Susannah was impossibly thin, tall and lithe in a perfect black suit, her hair glossy and bouncy, her face half-covered with gigantic sunglasses. She was so elegant, Adelaide thought, so perfectly poised. She looked more like a movie star than a doctor. She half-shielded her face from the flashing cameras.

Luke was already filming and Adelaide sprang after him shouting, 'Dr Rice! Is it too soon to be back at work? Why are you back at work?' but it was more for the camera than for want of an answer to such a stupid question. Adelaide followed Susannah and fell into step with her. She had to move fast. She knew Susannah would be lost to her the minute she crossed the threshold of the hospital. She kept pace with her.

'Dr Rice, Dr Rice! Adelaide Gold from CNN – how are you feeling today?'

'Fine, thank you.'

'Dr Rice, is the police investigation still ongoing? Have they interviewed you again?'

'I have answered all of the police's questions.' Adelaide tutted in frustration. Dr Sue's media training was almost as good as a politician's. She was well able to swerve a question whilst making it appear like she had answered it.

'Have they closed the investigation, then?'

'I have no knowledge of the status of the investigation, but these processes take time.'

'Is it true you have lost your publishing contract?'

'I have put my publishing projects on hold for the moment while my family grieve.'

'What is your plan for today?'

'I'm hoping to do my job.'

'Do you feel capable of doing your job ... so soon ... after?'

Susannah's heel scraped on the pavement as she stopped at the entrance to the hospital. The doors swished open and Susannah said in a sharp tone, 'I am eminently capable of doing my job, thank you.'

She flicked her hair and walked into the hospital. The doors swished shut behind her. The security guard padded gently back and forth behind the doors, enough of a warning to keep the journalists on the other side.

Adelaide watched Susannah's figure disappear down the hospital corridor. She looked at Luke the cameraman.

'Did you get that?'

'Yep,' he said, scrolling back over the footage. 'I'm going to take a few shots of the car park for cutaways. See you back at the office.'

Chapter 14

Inside the hospital, Susannah's hands were shaking. She hadn't expected to be accosted like that. When would they just go away? She had thought that once the funeral was over they would all just disappear.

And how did they know about the police? And her publishers? At least they couldn't get at her inside the hospital. She just wanted to bury herself in work and try to forget about the reality of her life for the next ten hours. But it turned out nothing was the same as it had been before. Work, once a refuge, was now an uncertain place. She had to endure the looks, the head tilts, the whispers, the solicitude of colleagues, the 'if there's anything I can do's. There were less sympathetic looks too, the ones who clearly believed she was somehow culpable, that she had had some deliberate part in her daughter's death, that her success and ambition were the toxic ingredients that led to her daughter's death.

There had been a noticeable exodus from the canteen when she had entered for a coffee. Nobody wanted to talk to her, or even be seen with her.

She tried to focus on patients instead but even that area was fraught. She looked at her patient list. First up a seven-year-old boy. *Thank God it's not a baby.* The thought surprised her.

The boy had a small growth on his face, nothing to worry about, steroid cream prescription, *next!*

As the boy and his mother left, the mother turned around.

'Dr Sue?'

Susannah looked up from her notes.

'Yes?'

'I'm so sorry about what happened to you, to your baby.'

Susannah felt like she had been slapped. She managed to squeeze out a 'Thank you'. The tears started to flow and she grabbed a tissue, dabbing furiously at her face. Susannah looked at the next patient on the list. A baby girl. Six months old. Suspected twisted gut.

'Good morning. What can we do for this beauty,' she said, addressing the baby.

The mother, who couldn't have been more than twenty-one, smiled carefully and described her concerns. Susannah examined the baby, her hands lingering on the baby's stomach as it rose and fell with each breath, taking in the sensation of warmth and vitality. She cupped the baby's face gently with her hand. She felt Louise looking back. She gave the baby an injection and wrote a prescription for a course of medication. 'She should have some relief from the shot and medication should sort the issue within two weeks but I'd like to see you back for review in one month.' The mother and baby left.

'Roberta, just give me five minutes before sending the next patient in.' She locked her door and shoved her fist in her mouth, biting down as hard as she could to stop herself from screaming. She took deep breaths over the sink by the examination bed and waited for the tears to stop, tried to steady herself. This was supposed to be her safe place, her haven from thoughts of Louise, not a trigger. She splashed water on her face. *You're a paediatrician, Susannah. You're going to have to learn how to deal with babies. And if you couldn't look after your own baby, the least you can do is take care of these children who need your help.*

As her first week back at work wore on, she found herself retreating behind her work, avoiding her colleagues, skipping meetings. Every conversation, even the most basic conversation with Roberta about her diary, or with a nurse on call about the dosage of fluids for a patient, was layered with meaningful looks and sympathetic faces, analysing if she was doing okay. She wasn't functioning but the busier she was, the better she could ignore her grief, the constant scrutiny and the worry about the police investigating her. It was punishing but it felt good to feel *something* that wasn't the numb pain in her head, the dead pain in her heart.

She had thought that after the funeral was over the reporters would go away, but she had miscalculated the media interest. As long as the police investigation was open she was still on the news agenda. Dana had been checking in with the police every couple of days to see whether they were pressing charges or not but she kept getting the same answer. 'Our investigation is progressing.' Meanwhile, there was a different news story on her every day since she had returned to work. She saw her own picture on the cover of three different tabloids.

One headline screamed, MOM WHO FORGOT BABY BACK AT WORK. Another said: HOT CAR MOM RETURNS TO WORK DAYS AFTER FUNERAL. Each report gave a painful recap, a medley of the greatest hits of her sorry story:

Mom ignored car alarm as baby fought for life ...

Hot Car Mom was workaholic who went back to work days after giving birth to both children ...

Dr Sue put baby in daycare SEVEN days a week ...

She grabbed the papers and her coffee each morning and pounded to her office with her head down. She locked the door and sat down. Why was this still happening? She understood how the media worked better than most people but this felt gleeful, gratuitous. She forced herself to read the reports. The papers described her 'expensive highlights', her $500 sunglasses (they had been a birthday present seven years ago), her $1,200 Prada handbag. That was a purchase she had made herself and she didn't even like it. It was part of the uniform. She wore it, and several other nearly identical thousand dollar bags, as a kind of armour. They were the signifiers that you were a smart, serious professional, earning a certain pay grade, which was how patients learned to trust you. Her media career had taught her the tricks of the trade, which meant her look was high-gloss. Her wardrobe was made up of a rotating cast of cashmere, silk, leather, suede, fine wool tweed skirts in a palette of cream, grey, beige and black. Natural, dry-clean-only fibres. Everything breathable, everything luxurious and everything tasteful. Had she not bought those items, dressed in that way, put forward that particular front, she would not have gotten referrals, business, respect from patients and other doctors. She would not have a television career, or rate so highly with the ABC1-demographic who bought her books. But while the uniform made her disappear amongst her peers in medicine and on TV, on the cover of a tabloid newspaper, as a supposedly grieving mother, it made her conspicuous. Even dressed as she had been, in the simplest black dress, black pumps, beige handbag and sunglasses, the press sniffed it all out, the brands, the prices; she couldn't understand how they figured out her simple plain black dress was Prada. It was completely unadorned, untagged, the most basic cut imaginable. Her slim, bronzed legs ended in $800 Jimmy Choo pumps. They too were as simple as you could get.

She hadn't once thought to remove what the papers described as her '$40,000' Cartier watch. It went on with her wedding ring every day. She'd bought it when she had gotten her professorship at the hospital. Paid cash, celebrated her landmark moment with an heirloom piece, which she planned to pass on to her daughters.

She could have wept when she saw the watch costed in the breakdown of her outfit in that day's tabloids. One headline dubbed the potential trial the '$50,000 Question', managing to round up her outfit to a $50k price tag.

John was offered sympathy, described as 'devastated dad', a selfless husband standing by his cold wife who was obsessed with overpriced accessories and her career. They were punishing her.

But why shouldn't they? She deserved to be punished, didn't she? She couldn't possibly make amends for what she had done, not even to herself. Perhaps a punishment would serve as a pressure valve for the guilt. She had a panic attack every time she thought about Louise's hair, the floating strands she kept finding in the car. But she couldn't bring herself to sell the car. It was the last place Louise had been alive. She looked at herself in the pictures in the newspaper, taken outside the police station. She looked cool, collected. Almost beautiful. She looked polished. She was thinner than she had ever been in her whole life, and the black made her look serious, appropriate, but she somehow still looked so glossy, too glossy. Nothing like how John looked in the photos they'd gotten of him outside the house. He looked haggard, his skin was grey and slack, his expression grim. John was the acceptable face of a grieving parent.

Later that afternoon, there was a commotion in the waiting room. Susannah edged closer to her door. She heard a woman say, 'I'd like to see a different doctor, please.'

Susannah heard Roberta explain.

'I'm afraid that's not possible. This is a busy clinic and patients are assigned to different doctors according to their needs and to ensure the most efficient running of the clinic. If you want to see another doctor, you'll need to get a referral from your practitioner to the doctor of your choice, although I assume you were referred here because Dr Rice is the most suitable expert to deal with your child's issue.'

'Look, I've seen the news stories about what happened to her baby and I'm not comfortable with her examining my child. Frankly, I don't have much faith in her abilities not to overlook something. I want my little girl to be seen by another physician, please.'

'Well, I'm afraid that might take a while to organise,' Roberta said.

'I'll wait.'

Chapter 15

Ten years earlier

The elevator doors opened onto the *New York Times* newsroom. Adelaide had forgotten the speed and the noise of the place. Couriers, porters, security guards, receptionists fielding calls, visitors, disgruntled conspiracy theorists, electronic passes swiping and unlocking security doors, turnstiles clicking, the sound of keyboards and people shouting into phones. She took a deep breath and walked through the doors.

Her boss, Max, was standing in the same place he had been when she had last left the office, leaning over some page proofs, his hand placed heavily on the table, taking the brunt of his weight. He looked up and saw her, stood up straight, put his hands on his hips, fingers under his belly and said, 'Well, there's a sight for sore eyes.' His smile was broad and he stretched his arms out as he approached her and pulled her into a bear hug. 'Boy, am I glad to have you back.'

Adelaide was so unsure of her own worth, this gave her an unreasonable surge of happiness.

'Let's get you set up with a desk and your passwords. Editorial is at 10 a.m. so we can go grab a coffee before then.'

Adelaide smiled back. She started walking towards her old desk but stopped when she saw the intern, Rachel, was sitting there – was she *touch-typing*? She didn't seem to be looking at her keyboard or her screen and yet her fingers were flying over the letters. Adelaide looked around to see where Max had gone and trotted after him, catching up in time to hear the end of his sentence.

'. . . and Heather is in Features now.' He leaned in and whispered, 'Family stuff. Current Affairs got too much for her when she had the third kid so I am down a political writer which means I might need you to pick up a bit of slack there too but you've always been a good all-rounder so I'm not worried about it, okay?'

Adelaide gulped a little. What about her own 'family stuff', she thought. Great, now I just need to brush up on American politics *and* keep on top of my old brief as culture correspondent *and* keep my new baby alive.

Max was still talking. ' . . . advertising have come up with a weekly magazine on mothers and babies and we thought, you being the expert now, who better to edit it? It's still in the pipeline but on the horizon.'

Everybody seemed to be speaking on high-speed. Their thoughts didn't need to undergo the lengthy transition period between thinking and verbalisation that Adelaide's did. She felt like her thoughts were being kept captive by her brain, each one had to fight its way out of the quicksand of her hormone-drenched mind.

'I've a few in-depth pieces I want you to pick up from last month. I have a hole in Sunday week's magazine cover story and I'd like your property developer piece to slot in there if you think you can hit the ground running?'

He saw Adelaide's surprise. 'Look, I know this might seem like a lot but I really don't want it to look like I'm cutting you some slack just because you have a baby. Bad for optics.'

'Right,' she said, and smiled. He stopped, and turned to look at her properly for the first time since they had started walking. The sensor-activated lights in the empty part of the office flickered on.

'This is you,' he said gesturing at an empty bank of desks they had stopped at. There were about eight desks, brand new, empty, waiting to be populated. She looked back at him with horror. This was *Siberia*. The whole point of a news room was you were in the thick of it. She wouldn't hear anything here. He picked up on her reaction.

'It's not permanent, Adelaide. The intern will be finished up next month and you'll have your old desk back.'

'Well, why can't she move here then, if she's leaving in a month ... ?'

'Don't bust my balls about it, Adelaide. She's young, she doesn't know what she's doing, it's just easier this way.'

He walked away, then pivoted back to her.

'Oh, also, Ryan is on leave next week, some BS about his wife needing help with the new baby – no offence! – so I need you to edit his section. Everything is commissioned, you just have to make sure it all finds its home.' He necked the remaining coffee in his cup as if it was a shot of tequila and walked off. 'See you at the editorial at ten. *Really* looking forward to hearing your ideas. It is great to have you back, kid.'

It didn't feel great to be back. Adelaide felt shattered already. Her breasts felt hard and lumpy, she could taste adrenalin in her mouth. Had she ever worked at this pace before? She knew she had. And what's more she had loved it. Thrived on it. But that was when her sleep was uninterrupted. Even if she had only gotten five hours they were *consecutive* hours. She didn't have a single idea to bring to the editorial meeting. She had thought that her first day back might involve a little bit of reorientation, catching up with colleagues, lunch with Max, catching up with news and then figuring out a work plan for the coming week and month. But she was just another body whose finger was needed to plug a hole in the dam.

She stood up. A gush of blood in her pants, a black spot in front of her eyes. She put her hand out and steadied herself on the desk. She kept her eyes closed for a second or two and her equilibrium returned. She needed the bathroom already but there wasn't time. She went to the papers station instead and picked up a few leftover tabloids for story ideas. Max seemed to be under the impression that she had just had a two-month holiday and was expecting her back revived and chock-full of the new and fresh ideas of a rested mind. He didn't seem to understand that she was reeling, in shell-shock, pining for her baby and pining for her old self, the one who was able to do this job.

She needn't have worried. The meeting was delayed, people were too busy, so Max simply assigned the news list, including the property story for Adelaide. At lunch-time she visited Zane and he fed hungrily, sucking her dry on one breast before she swapped him and started him on the second. The physical relief was immense.

Zane started to fall asleep as he fed and she tickled the back of his neck to wake him up and get him nursing again. She didn't have time to let him nap and nurse and nap and nurse like he normally did at home. She needed to pump him full of as much milk as possible within her window of thirty minutes before running back to work. And she really wasn't looking forward to seeing Max's face when she left the office again at 5.45 so she could collect Zane before the daycare shut at six. Most of her colleagues didn't leave the office until at least seven and even then they usually went to the bar down the street for a kind of informal editorial debrief with added alcohol.

As she finished the final thing on her list for the day, with an enormous sense of achievement, Max sauntered by and dropped a page on her desk.

'Adelaide, can you follow this one up for tomorrow? Just eight hundred words.' She looked at him and felt her blood pressure skyrocket. She sneaked a peek at the clock on the wall just beyond his head. Five p.m. He caught her hesitating. 'Is there a problem?'

'Oh no, no problem, it's just, I might have to file from home, if that's okay? I have to pick Zane up from daycare at six. I'll make a few calls now and I'll write it up at home and send it through. It's no problem.'

'I knew I could count on you. It's really great to have you back again.' She watched him walk away from her, take his jacket off the coat stand. 'See ya tomorrow guys,' he said as he left the building.

She wanted to explode. Or more embarrassingly, she thought she might cry. She spent the next forty-five minutes leaving messages and emails for as many people she could think of to ask for a comment on the piece, a completely vapid item on gluten-free menus proliferating in the city's restaurants. If even a handful of the people she had left messages for got back to her, the piece would be fine. She left the office at 5.45 p.m. in panic and despair, her heart pounding in her chest. How was she going to do this all over again tomorrow? And the next day. And the next day.

By the time she got home with Zane, she was exhausted by the adrenalin she had been working off all day, and the stress of worrying about everything going smoothly. It was nearly seven. Curtis had walked in the door just ahead of her and said, 'Hey, my babies! How was your day?' He kissed Zane, who gurgled happily to see his dad and kissed Adelaide before asking, 'What should we eat? I'm starving.'

Her response was not in any way rational. Really, he was just asking what she would like to eat. But what she heard was, 'Hey, after your fifteen-hour-day, will you make a decision for me about what I will eat for dinner, and also prepare and cook it?' She ended her outburst by flinging the Chinese takeaway menu at him. She unstrapped Zane from her chest, shoved him towards Curtis and said, 'Here, take him. I have to work.'

She could hear Zane's fright as he began to cry but she had to ignore him and just get her piece filed. At eight, when the doorbell went and the smell of Chinese wafted towards her in her bedroom, she had all the quotes she needed to write her piece and now it was just a case of stitching it all together. Curtis knocked on the door with a plate and a glass of wine.

'Zane is asleep. I gave him some of the expressed milk in the fridge. I'm guessing work was tough today?'

She burst into tears.

'I'm so sorry. I just don't know how I'm going to do this. How am I going to cope? This is impossible already.'

'It will get better. Come on, eat. Take twenty minutes and then file the piece.'

By ten o'clock she was done with work.

'Come to bed,' said Curtis. 'You'll be exhausted tomorrow.' But she had to prep the entire kit bag, diaper bag, breast milk and laundry for Zane.

'You go ahead,' she said. 'I'll be there in a minute.'

Chapter 16

By the end of Susannah's second week back at work, she was wrung out. She turned off the lights in her office at 10 p.m. and left the hospital. She was staying later and later each day, in the hope that the media pack would lose interest, and tonight her strategy had finally paid off. There was nobody there when she left the hospital. She looked around, breathed a sigh of relief and walked towards her car. She parked in a different car park now.

She rang John but he didn't answer. She wanted him to make food. She hadn't eaten anything since breakfast. What was he doing, anyway?

The car park was dark and abandoned. She got into her car and central-locked it quickly. She drove home in silence, with the radio off. She wanted peace, or some form of it.

When she got home the house was quiet, too.

'John? *John*, are you home?'

But it was Christina who came silently tiptoeing out of the living room.

'Mr Rice is not home yet, Dr Rice.'

'Oh, Christina, I'm so sorry I'm so late. I thought John would be home much earlier.'

'It's no problem, Dr Rice. Emma is asleep. She was asking about Louise again today and was crying going to sleep but I told her she is in heaven now and is her guardian angel, just like you said the other day.'

Susannah gave a smile and breathed out to try and maintain control of herself.

'Thanks, Christina.'

'She was such a beautiful baby. I miss her so much.'

Christina started to cry and Susannah couldn't quite believe she was comforting her childminder about the loss of her own baby.

'I know, Christina, I know.' She squeezed Christina's hand and gave her a smile as she opened the door for her. 'I'll see you tomorrow.'

She leaned her head against the door. *I can't go on like this.*

She went upstairs and checked on Emma. She was fast asleep, cuddling one of Louise's baby teddies. Susannah sobbed quietly. Emma had lost her only sibling, her playmate. Would she even remember Louise? It made Susannah all the more determined to try for another baby. She thought back to the night of the funeral, when she and John had made love. She still hadn't got her period. Could this sluggishness she was feeling be the first signs of pregnancy?

She went back downstairs and opened the fridge but found she wasn't hungry any more. She didn't have the energy to cook something anyway. Where was John?

The house was so quiet. Moments like these were the hardest, alone in the silence with her thoughts. When she had first brought Louise home from the hospital she felt that they were still connected. She liked to experiment with regulating Louise's breathing. She would take a deep breath, and the baby would follow. Then she would take three shallow breaths and the baby would do the same. It was the most remarkable thing, they were still connected, somehow, without being physically connected. If it was that way in life, surely it must be the same in death. Some essential part of her had died with Louise, of that she was sure.

Sometimes, if she listened closely, she was sure she could even hear Louise, like the sea in a shell, her chest rising and falling, the air flowing in and out of her nose, the even breathing that marked her sleep. It really felt like Louise was still here, invisible, but here, just beyond a thin veil. She wanted to travel to whatever world Louise was waiting in, find her, and bring her back.

She tried calling John again but there was still no answer. Where was he? She needed him. She was too exhausted to wait up so she climbed the stairs to the bedroom. Mechanically, she removed her make-up, layered her face with vitamin C, retinol, moisturisers, took a sleeping tablet and slipped the bottle into the pocket of her robe.

In the bathroom, she found blood in her underwear. 'No!'

She slumped forward, convinced that was her last chance, gone. She went back downstairs and filled a hot water bottle, then lay on the couch to wait for John to come home, sobbing into a balled-up tissue. *My one chance to have another baby. My one chance to give Emma a sibling.* She drifted off about 1 a.m. and dreamed of Louise again.

She was crying for Susannah.

When Susannah woke, it was hard to tell if it had been a dream or reality. It was 3.45 a.m. and all she knew was that Louise needed her. Susannah took a sip from a glass of water on the nest of tables beside the couch. She felt the pills in her pocket.

She saw her hand open the bottle and take a pill. She watched it happen like it was someone else's body. An immediate calm washed over her. She took another pill, and another. Every time she took one, she thought she felt the pain dissipating, thought of holding Louise again. She lay back on the couch, peaceful at last.

Chapter 17

Ten years earlier

Two months passed in a hectic blur and Adelaide was in a routine of sorts but it felt more like a reign of terror. She was constantly rushing. She was always late. For everything. She was always shouting at Curtis because she was so tightly wound. When she dropped Zane off at daycare and got to work it was no better. It was just a different kind of panic. A panic to try and convince everyone that she was the same solid journalist she had been before she'd had her son. A panic to get all of her work done before the clock ran down and it was time to leave and collect Zane. It was like being in some kind of dystopian gameshow.

The sense of being appraised at all times was brutal. Adelaide felt the eyes of her colleagues on her as she stood up at the same time every evening and left the office. She got as much, if not more, work done in the office than they did, because she knew she didn't have the option of staying late. But still, she knew people thought she was slacking. And it wasn't like she had the option of working at home either, if she wanted to keep her marriage intact. She could see Curtis becoming more and more alienated.

'We work all day, Adelaide, you can't work all night too. I'd like us to *be together* when we are together.'

'I'm doing it for us, for our family,' she'd say, tearful. It seemed like the harder she worked, the worse things got at home. She missed those first few months of Zane's life, where they would stay in bed, wrapped in the duvet, snoozing and feeding. Curtis would come home for lunch, snuggle them both and make some food for them to eat together in the kitchen. They felt so close, so in love, like an unbreakable unit. Now she felt criticised from all sides.

On the second day of his second month in daycare, Adelaide dropped Zane off as usual. At lunchtime, she quietly disappeared from the office, hoping no one would notice her leave. She always felt like she was stealing time from her job, even though this was her lunch break, time for which she was not paid, time which she often worked through for free. She speed-walked the two blocks to the daycare. On the walk, she thought about Zane's warm skin, about how the ache in her breasts would be relieved by a feed, how his powdery smell would fill her senses like a night-blooming flower.

There was no one at reception when she arrived. She walked through the double doors that led into the main area and then over to the baby room. Something was wrong. The security guards were gathered around a crib, along with three of the carers. Adelaide's heart was pounding. She could hear it in her ears, feel its pulsing in her fingertips. This was the confirmation of everything she had feared. A prickle of nausea crept up her neck. She said hi but nobody responded.

Adelaide noticed one of the women was on the phone, talking quietly, taking orders, repeating them to the woman at the centre who was clearly doing something to the baby. Adelaide zoned in on the familiar bodysuit with the trucks on it. She started to move but her knees buckled. Hands gripped her under her armpits and she clawed at them, trying desperately to get to the crib.

'That's my baby,' she whispered. It was like a bad dream; she wanted to scream but her voice wouldn't work. She broke free of them and made it to the crib. Zane's lips were an alarming shade of blue. Her stomach lurched. Disbelief, hysteria, terror swept in. She was dreaming, she had to be dreaming. That was why she couldn't scream, why she was frozen, silent.

But a scream finally tore through the room and broke the spell.

'What's wrong? What's happened?'

Nobody had any answers. She was dialling 911 even though she knew they were already on the phone to the first responders. She whisked Zane out of the crib and held his cool cheek to her breast. She spoke calmly to him, whispered to him that she was here, that everything was okay. She tried to latch him on to her hard breast, tried to get him to nurse. If he would just nurse, he would be fine, she could revive him.

A couple of seconds later, the paramedics came through the door then and gently took Zane from her.

At the hospital, she waited outside the room where the doctors continued to work on Zane. She called Curtis and told him Zane was extremely sick, and that he should get to the hospital. She couldn't say what she knew somewhere deep in her being: that Zane was already gone. An eternity later, a doctor emerged from the emergency room. Adelaide recognised her from the TV.

'My name is Susannah,' the doctor said. She wanted to ask Adelaide for permission to stop attempting to resuscitate Zane. They couldn't revive him but they needed her permission to stop.

'I'm waiting for my husband to get here. I can't do this without him.'

The doctor nodded, went back into the room. Five minutes later, Curtis arrived. The permission to stop resuscitating Zane, the pronouncement of death, the autopsy all happened but Adelaide had no memory of making any of these decisions. They were as inaccessible to her as if they were someone else's memories.

She did remember the request to perform a postmortem. The idea of the pathologist cutting into Zane was too much to bear. She was hysterical. She kept thinking, if they cut him, they will kill him. She couldn't absorb the fact that he was already dead.

She and Curtis were allowed to take Zane home for a day and a night before the funeral. They put him into their bed, she couldn't face putting him into his crib on his own. She didn't want him to be alone. 'I should have been with him,' was all Adelaide could say. 'He should have been here, at home with me. It should have been me who put him down for his nap. It should have been me.' People told her not to blame herself. There was nothing anybody could do. It was nobody's fault. Just another tragedy where a child dies without explanation, and his mother wasn't there.

Chapter 18

Susannah opened her eyes. She was in a hospital bed. She scanned the room and her eyes found John's. He was sitting in a chair by the bed, Emma snuggled up in a blanket, snoozing in his arms. Dawn was fading up from the city streets, diluting the indigo sky to a pale peach.

Her eyes filled with tears as the realisation of what had happened dawned on her.

'It's okay, Susannah,' John said. 'You're going to be okay.'

She tried to talk but her throat was raw. It felt as if someone had superglued her throat to itself. John looked so sad and betrayed, angry too, she thought. And he was right to feel that way. She looked away, hid in her shame.

She was propped up in bed, in a room with a jug of water, an empty glass and a push button in case of emergencies. Her stomach had been pumped and she was hooked up on ECGs, blood pressure monitors, two drips. She knew the procedure with these things. A day or two of close observation, full psychiatric assessment, and long-term outpatient monitoring. Christ, what had she done?

She would tell the doctors that she had had a few glasses of wine too many, followed by a handful of sleeping pills and that the two must have counteracted badly. She was getting good at pretending, pretending everything was fine, pretending she was coping, pretending she was dealing with it all. No need to make things worse by telling the truth. So what if the toxicology report suggested otherwise? Nobody needed to know what she had intended. John didn't need to know.

A nurse bustled into the room without any apology for the interruption. Susannah was a patient now, her liberty removed, her personal space non-existent, she was not the boss in this hospital. The nurse fussed around Susannah's bed, straightened her drips, neatened her pillows and moved the table with her water and the TV remote control just out of reach. Susannah narrowed her eyes.

'She's stable,' the nurse said quietly to John, just outside the door but within Susannah's earshot. 'You shouldn't be too worried. She's not in any danger now. She's probably feeling a bit sore and a bit silly. Try not to ask her too many questions. We have a lot of tests to get through too, so that's going to take up the next few hours. I think the best thing you can do is go home with this little one, get some rest and come back a little later.' She rubbed Emma's cheek. 'You've probably both had quite a morning.'

When the nurse left, John went back into the room to say goodbye to Susannah. He was holding Emma so closely, slumped over his shoulder, her arms wrapped loosely around his neck. Susannah had the strange impression that they were one person, a team, in opposition to her.

John spoke in an even tone.

'Emma and I are going to go home and get some rest while they do some tests. I'll be back a bit later.'

Susannah smiled weakly. She still couldn't speak.

'Please co-operate with the doctors, Susannah,' John said. 'I know you think you know more than they do, and that might even be true, but you have to let them help you.'

She nodded her head. Her eyes filled with tears and she reached for his hand. How could she do this to him – to *Emma* – after everything they had all been through already. He gave her hand a quick squeeze.

'The doctors say you just need some rest. It might do you good, Susannah. I've been saying all along that you went back to work too soon.'

You went back to work before me, Susannah thought, childishly. She was glad, for now, that she couldn't speak, that she couldn't hurt him more.

114

He shifted Emma's weight to his other arm and she roused. 'Mama!' she said and wriggled from his arms. 'I want Mama!' She climbed up on the bed, and snuggled into Susannah. 'Are you going to get deaded, Mama?'

Susannah's voice croaked and she managed to hoarsely whisper, 'No, baby, Mama's not going to die. Mama is going to live for ever and ever and ever so she can look after you, okay?'

Emma smiled and squeezed Susannah.

'Say bye-bye to Mama,' John said to Emma. He leaned in and kissed Susannah's cheek. 'I'll see you later on.'

As he reached the door, he turned back.

'Oh, Susannah? I gave the medication bottle to the paramedics and I told them how many pills were in the bottle when I filled the prescription for you a couple of days ago. So maybe just tell them the truth about how many pills you took, because they already know ... And so do I.'

Chapter 19

Nine years earlier

After Zane died, Adelaide and Curtis tried to get through their coruscating grief without destroying each other. There was blame, recrimination. They went to grief therapy and couples therapy, separately and together. The therapists told them that they would probably feel some resentment towards each other, that this was normal. But Adelaide felt *only* resentment. She despised Curtis for not having had the kind of grown-up job that came with health insurance, the kind of job that would have supported the needs of a family, allowed her to stay home and take care of Zane, even for a couple of extra months. She despised his grief too. He had no idea what *she* had lost. She had been filled up with Zane's flesh, had grown big with his body, had felt every throb and pulse of blood, every unfurling finger. She had mourned his transition from inside of her to outside of her, had carried him around like he was still a part of her for those first two months and then had handed him over like a sacrifice, as if she had always known nothing so good could happen to her.

Curtis, she knew, had felt only guilt too, guilt that he couldn't support his wife and child, guilt that he wasn't successful enough to have enough money to cover them until Zane was a bit older, guilt that his job didn't come with health insurance. But what use was his guilt?

'Did you talk about it at the time, about you giving up work and staying home and taking care of Zane?' The calm, infantilising voice of the counsellor.

'We had the conversation,' said Adelaide.

Curtis shifted, in his seat, interrupted. 'We had it a *lot*.'

'I never ever wanted to put Zane into daycare so young. I was so uncomfortable with leaving him. He was so, so *tiny*. I always felt something bad was going to happen. I begged and pleaded with Curtis ...'

Curtis jumped in angrily again.

'Adelaide, we both wanted him at home with you in an ideal world but we always agreed that we had to have healthcare no matter what. We always got stuck at that point.'

The atmosphere was charged. They were actively arguing, in front of the therapist. They were just a couple of decibels off shouting at each other. The therapist stared at them blankly, like she was calmly watching fish in an aquarium.

'I just feel like we didn't ever try hard enough, we didn't fight enough to find the right solution for our baby,' said Adelaide.

The therapist pointed her knees at Curtis. Curtis took his cue.

'We *agreed*, Adelaide. You were as adamant as I was that we couldn't put Zane in a situation where he didn't have health insurance.'

'Okay,' the therapist said, heading off what she saw as another escalation. 'What happened to Zane was a tragedy, the worst luck, but you have no way of knowing if it would have happened anyway, whether you were there or not.'

The post-mortem said the same thing. 'Inconclusive' was the useless conclusion of the coroner's court. 'Most indicative of crib death.' 'No underlying genetic causes.' There was nobody to blame so she blamed herself, and she blamed Curtis.

Adelaide bit her cheek. She was so tired of hearing this. She looked out of the office window, still listening, but letting the therapist know that she didn't like it.

'This is part of the difficulty of processing this particular kind of complicated grief. You will *never* know if this was preventable. But it didn't happen because you agreed as parents, as a couple to put your child in daycare. That's not *why* this happened. This is what most parents do when they have babies. They put them into daycare. It's perfectly normal, it's not abusive, it's not abandonment, it's not reckless endangerment. It's what we do. It's time to start acknowledging the *tragedy* of Zane's death and move on from blaming each other, start comforting each other. Let go of your anger on this because it is destructive. It won't help you, and it doesn't help Zane.'

Adelaide felt herself getting annoyed. *Acknowledge the tragedy of the death?* Did she not acknowledge that in every breath she took, every living moment? The tears came fast and signalled, as they always did, the end of any useful conversation.

'I just don't know what we're doing here,' Adelaide said, dabbing roughly at her eyes. Curtis leaned forward, his elbows on his knees, his head in his hands. 'It's been a year since Zane died and I think we're in worse shape now than when we began. We're further apart than we've ever been, we're completely at odds, we don't turn to each other for comfort, it's the opposite actually – we seem to make things worse for each other.'

Curtis looked at her, stung.

'These things take time, Adelaide,' the therapist interjected in her infuriatingly neutral tone. 'And perhaps things do *feel* worse now but that might be because you are actually confronting your feelings. Change equals progress. I would ask you to trust the process, stick with it, don't give up when you are so close.'

'So close to what? It's not like there's any solution to this problem. Our baby is dead. He's not coming back.' Adelaide had crossed the threshold of politeness. She was now in that bitter, mean, sharp-tongued attack zone. 'So what do I do now? Live life without my beautiful boy? Live in this nothing shell of a marriage where we are frozen in our grief? Is that how my life is going to be now?'

Curtis was staring at his hands. He hadn't said anything in a long time.

'How does it make you feel, Curtis, to hear Adelaide describe your relationship like this? Do you agree with her?' the therapist asked.

'Adelaide is right,' he said. 'We should be able to comfort each other and yet all we seem to do is fight. Before Zane died, I knew what I was doing and I knew why I was doing it. I had a plan. I had responsibilities, I had a *family*. Now, it's like life is fake. Everything just feels pointless.'

Adelaide looked across at him. She had never heard him talk like this. He finally looked back at her.

'I never had any doubts about us but this last year has just torn us apart. We don't have Zane and we don't even have each other.'

Adelaide was crying softly, whispering, 'I'm so sorry, Curtis. I'm so sorry.'

When they got home that night, after a silent subway ride, Adelaide told Curtis, quietly and calmly, that she thought they should finish things. She was completely wrung out by everything and she needed to offload anything that was causing her more anxiety, more upset, more sadness.

'It's *not* your fault but I can't keep going like this. It's too much, it's too painful. It's like we wake up every day and have, in each other, a constant reminder of what we have lost.'

After that, Adelaide felt like a weight had been lifted. She and Curtis were friendly and generous towards each other. Things felt good again, easy, a lightness returned to their relationship that hadn't been there since before Zane was born. Curtis seemed happier too. Without the pressure of trying to make things work, life was suddenly easier.

She worked in a frenzy that week, as she had done for the entire previous year, hammering herself with work to fill the screaming void that was her mind when left to its own thoughts. She didn't want to be at home in the apartment with Curtis so she stayed later and later at work. That Friday, she stopped off on her way home from the office to look at a studio apartment. She hadn't told Curtis she was looking for a new place but she knew she would have to move out soon. For now, Curtis was sleeping on the couch and she was in the bedroom. The studio she had looked at had been good – bright and clean, with a nice energy. She was tempted to take it. She dawdled on her way home, walking east from the park. She checked her phone. Three missed calls from Curtis. She felt no obligation to call him back. In her head, he was already her ex-husband. She would talk to him soon enough.

She climbed the stairs to their apartment, a hopeful smile on her face. Maybe they would be one of those couples who remained friends after they divorced, maybe even introduce each other to their future partners. She imagined them all having dinners together from time to time, taking an interest in the big moments in each other's lives. She unlocked the door, pushed it open wide. The door handle hit the inside wall, where there was a smooth indent on the plaster from this repeated action. She cursed silently. She kept meaning to get a door stop.

She dropped her bag on the kitchen counter and saw a note from Curtis. He must have gone out, she thought with relief. A whole evening by herself in the apartment. She was already mentally deciding what she would eat and what she would watch on Netflix. She walked to the fridge and pulled out a bottle of wine to help her decide. It was only as she took her first sip from the glass that she picked up the note and read it.

I'm sorry for everything. I love you.

She felt the atmosphere shift, a contrail of something unknown streaking across the room.

She banged the glass down on the counter. Wine sloshed over the edge.

'Curtis!' She called his name with greater urgency as she walked through the apartment.

She found him in the bathroom.

After Curtis died, Adelaide recognised all of the cliches that she knew about suicides. Curtis seemed upbeat and happy for the first time in a long time. She was haunted by the missed calls that she had not returned. Was he ringing to say goodbye or to be talked out of it? And when had he decided to do it? After she suggested they break up or before? Was it her fault? She moved between despair and anger. She was so angry with him. How could he leave her alone with her grief for their son, the thing no one else could understand, the thing she could never talk to anyone about now?

She couldn't stay in their apartment. She called the broker who had shown her the studio and told her she would take it. It was tiny and anonymous, perfect for Adelaide.

Work at the newspaper was an escape and not an escape. Some people ignored what had happened to her completely, some wanted to ask her about it: 'Did you see it coming?' Or, 'Have you had a chance to process it?' And the worst, 'First the baby, and now this.' It was all too much. Even when people weren't actively sympathising, she could feel them scrutinising her. She knew people were just being kind, trying to do what they felt they *should* do but she couldn't go on like this. She had to start again, rewrite what were becoming defining parts of her story, consign the double tragedy of her life to the past, or at least to a private compartment. There was no other way she would survive. She couldn't live as *that* woman, the woman whose baby died, the woman whose husband had killed himself. She couldn't live with the constant pity. It was a wound that would not heal. She had to start again.

She made a call to a producer she knew at CNN and after a screen test and a meeting, Adelaide had an offer of a job. She told Max that she was leaving. He was surprised. People didn't leave the *New York Times*. But she decided to be honest with him, and told him why she needed a fresh start.

'Well, the door will always be open for you here, Adelaide, if you ever want to come back to us. You're one of the best journalists I've ever worked with.'

She hit the road with her new job covering national stories, on a beat that stretched from NY to LA and everywhere in between. The job demanded a nomadic existence. And she was just another nomad with no past, no history, no baggage. It was the perfect job for a fugitive from her own life.

'Don't take your coat off, Adelaide!'

Adelaide stopped mid-way through taking off her coat as she spotted her producer, Jimmy, hurrying towards her.

'You're going back to St. John's hospital.'

Please God, no.

'Dr Sue tried to kill herself last night.'

Her eyes went wide with fear. *I can't do this.* She took a deep breath. She felt her knees buckle. *Was this some kind of sick joke?*

'She's in the hospital now. Get over there and see what you can find out. Get the husband, get a nurse, anyone, just don't come back without something for the six o'clock.' He was practically ushering her back towards the elevator.

Adelaide was genuinely shocked that Susannah had tried to kill herself. *You never could tell.* Susannah certainly didn't look the type, so controlled and reserved, she looked as if she were made out of marble, a born survivor. Curtis wasn't the type either, Adelaide thought. She shook her head, she didn't want these old ghosts for company.

'Jimmy, please, I've been on this story for a month now.'

'Exactly, which is why you're the best person to keep covering it. You're up to speed. I'm not putting anyone else on it.'

'Jimmy, it's grotesque. Don't you think we should leave the poor woman alone now? Is this actually newsworthy, covering the suicide attempt of a grieving mother whose baby has just died? Is this the kind of journalism we're interested in now?'

It was the oldest defence in the book for a story you didn't want to cover, but she was desperate. She couldn't even think of a justification for asking Susannah the first question – *why?* – because she knew why. Curtis knew why. Because going on with life was so unimaginable.

'Oh, I'm sorry, Joan Didion, I didn't realise your sensibilities were so offended by *doing your job!*' His voice rang out around the office. People went quiet. They were pretending not to listen but every newsroom loved a good row.

'Don't you think there's an ethical problem with covering this? Is it even in the public interest? She's just an ordinary woman, Jimmy, who's clearly having a rough time.'

He sighed and hefted his waistband up, then hooked his thumbs on his hips. His elbows were out. *Power stance*. Adelaide crossed her arms.

'Adelaide, Susannah Rice is not an ordinary woman. Ordinary women do not have outfits that add up to $50,000. Ordinary women do not have personal trainers. Ordinary women are not known by their first names only. Think about it – you've got Beyoncé, Madonna, Oprah, Dr Sue.' He counted them out sarcastically on his fingers. 'Do you really need me to explain to you *why* this story is newsworthy? If they're famous, we cover it. Period. She's earned a lot of fame and a lot of fortune through telling ordinary people how to take care of their children, the very thing she doesn't seem capable of doing herself, so you could say she's a fraud, and now she clearly feels so guilty about it that she's tried to kill herself.' He turned and shouted across the floor to Luke, the cameraman.

'Luke! Get up to St John's with Adelaide now.'

Adelaide watched Jimmy's bullish back retreat towards his office.

'Fine,' she said after him, 'but if we end up before the press council on this don't say I didn't warn you.' She felt lame saying it. She knew the story was newsworthy, she just didn't want to cover it.

Most of the time Adelaide knew what her job was and why she was doing it. Her motivation wasn't as grand or noble as her socialist or investigative colleagues, who lived their lives in pursuit of truth, justice, positive change. Adelaide's goal was always simple – just tell the story. But on this job she had lost all perspective. On the way to the hospital in Luke's van, she checked her phone for updates. HOT CAR MOM SUICIDE BID was the *Post's* headline. There weren't many details yet but the story was out there. How on earth was Adelaide supposed to move this one along for Jimmy? Nobody was going to want to speak to a reporter about this – Susannah's colleagues, her boss, the hospital manager, the porter, the woman who worked in the cafeteria. Just do what you always do, Adelaide, she told herself. It didn't really matter who spoke as long as *somebody* spoke. TV news was all about moving pictures and talking heads. Even if the person you used said 'no comment', it was still footage.

When they got to the hospital, a group of reporters and cameras was already outside the main entrance. Adelaide hung back. If she had to cover this story, then she would try to do it well. She booked an interview with a grief counsellor who would run through the reasons a suicide attempt can happen in a bereaved person and the signs to watch for. A doctor came out and gave a statement in the hope that it would disperse the media. But Adelaide knew already that Jimmy wouldn't be happy with that. He'd call it a press release and send her back out to get something more. *It's this or look for a new job, Adelaide.*

'What now?' Luke asked. 'Back downtown?'

She didn't want to make Susannah's life harder but if a reporter was going to get to her it might as well be Adelaide . . . at least Adelaide could understand, empathise with what she was going through.

'No. We're going in.' She called the hospital switchboard. 'Oh hi, I'd like to send some flowers to my sister. She's a patient there, Susannah Rice is her name. Can you tell me where I should direct the flowers, please?'

'One second . . . St Monica's Ward, second floor.'

'Luke, let's go down to the basement car park,' she said.

Downstairs, she took off her blazer, pulled her T-shirt out of her trousers and wiped her lipstick off her mouth with the back of her hand. 'How do I look?'

'You've looked better,' Luke said.

'Great. Follow me and keep your distance when we get inside, okay?'

Luke knew the drill. Adelaide made her way to the service elevators. She checked it for security passcodes, but there wasn't one. She looked around, found a service cupboard, picked up a bucket and mop.

Luke watched her silently. He knew what she was doing, but he didn't have to approve. Adelaide knew what she was doing too, but she also knew her job was on the line and that she would be the most understanding journalist Susannah could encounter.

They got out on the second floor. Adelaide pushed the bucket out ahead of her. Nobody even looked at her. She scanned the walls for the ward names. St Monica's was ahead and to the left but just as she was turning the corner she ran straight into Susannah's husband, John. He was carrying their daughter, Emma, in a blanket.

Adelaide felt dread and adrenalin creep through her veins. She looked back at Luke but he already had his camera on his shoulder. They both knew their jobs even if they didn't want to do them.

'Mr Rice, I'm Adelaide Gold from CNN News. Can you tell us anything about your wife's condition?'

John was furious, appalled. 'How did you get in here?' he asked.

'Is it true she tried to kill herself?' Adelaide knew the best way to get any kind of comment was to barrage him with provocative questions.

'She did *not* try to kill herself. How ... how do you even know that?'

He looked angry enough to hit her. Adelaide felt sick to her stomach but she pushed on.

'There are many parents like you and your wife all over America who have lost children in tragic accidents, who are going through what you and your wife are going through, who will be familiar with the despair you are going through. *They* want to know how your wife is. They feel a great love and admiration for her, they feel that they know her from the television, they have raised their children on her parenting guides ... Can you tell us anything at all about how she's doing, for those people?'

Something about how she said it, or the tone in which she pitched it did something because Adelaide saw him relent.

'She is doing well. And she is going to be absolutely fine.' Something about her father's softened tone evidently gave Emma the green light to speak up.

'My mama is in the hospital,' Emma said.

'Is that so,' Adelaide replied.

John shifted the child from one arm to the other.

'Emma, shush.'

But Emma was having her moment in the spotlight.

'Yes, and she has a needle in her arm and it's ouchy

but she says she is going to be better and is not going to get deaded like Baba Loulou!'

'Well, I'm very pleased to hear that,' Adelaide said, with tears in her eyes.

'Excuse me but we have to go,' John said, brushing by them.

Adelaide looked at Luke, who gave her a thumbs up to indicate that he had gotten the footage, just as she saw John talking to a security guard and gesturing towards them.

'Time to go, Luke.'

Chapter 20

Susannah was discharged a couple of days later, complete with a twelve-week course of therapy with a new psychotherapist called Adam. She had her first appointment with him the next day and she wasn't looking forward to it. She had met him in the hospital, briefly, for an introduction and he seemed young, by which she meant irritatingly informal, soft-collared, sneakered.

As John unlocked the door and carried her bag inside, Emma came running towards her. 'Mommy!' Susannah let the warmth of Emma's hug suffuse her like a sun ray. It felt so good to be home.

Christina came out with her coat and bag. 'Welcome home, Dr Rice.' She picked up an envelope from the sideboard. 'A letter came for you today by certified mail. It looks important.'

'Thanks, Christina.'

'I'll put your bag away,' John said. 'I'll be down in a second.'

Susannah leaned her back against the door and exhaled. She shrugged off her coat and hung it on the rack and sat down on the bench beneath it. Life was a relentless series of nightmarish events. Would it ever stop? Her finger slid along the edge of the envelope and she pulled out a couple of creamy, official looking pages.

She wasn't sure what she was reading but the feeling in her stomach told her it was bad. She scanned over the reference numbers and legal language to get to the actual message.

You are commanded to appear in the United States district court at the time, date, and place set forth below to testify at a hearing in this civil or criminal action ...

Susannah scanned down again to find the date. '... Oh my God,' she said.

John was just arriving at the bottom of the stairs. 'What is it?'

She handed the letter to him.

'Susannah, this is next week,' he said. 'I'm calling Dana.'

Dana swooped in after dinner, removing her trench coat, silk scarf and briefcase in one fluid movement. 'Okay, so this is not something to worry about. This was to be expected. There's no need to panic. This is just a hearing where the police show the results of their investigation to a judge and he or she will decide if they think it should go to trial or not. It is part of the process. The charges will most likely be negligence or involuntary manslaughter or both and they have no evidence of neglect so I can't see how this can go to trial.'

Susannah was sitting quietly on the couch, John's arm around her.

'If there's no evidence, why are they having a hearing?'

'The cops have to investigate every child's death,' Dana said. 'In the meantime I'm going to work on getting this hearing rescheduled based on medical grounds.'

Despite Dana's assurances, Susannah's hearing was not postponed, the reasoning being if Susannah was well enough to be discharged from hospital, she was well enough to attend a one-hour hearing to decide whether her case would go to trial. The wheels of justice moved slowly enough as it was, apparently, and the judge said she didn't want to delay things unnecessarily.

'We'll get through this,' John said, squeezing Susannah's hand.

'It will be over soon,' he said, 'and, once it's over, it's over for good and you can work on getting your life back.'

Susannah disagreed. It would never be over. She was never getting her life back. She was never getting her baby back.

Chapter 21

The following week, Adelaide planned to keep her head down and stay out of Jimmy's sight. She needed a quiet day, an easy day, a day where nothing happened, no one died, and no one tired to kill themselves. She sipped her frappuccino at her desk. She was just going to try to decompress today by hiding behind her computer. Susannah had been discharged from the hospital last week and discharged from Jimmy's news list, too, Adelaide hoped. Today, she was just going to go through the motions of ticking off her checklists – ringing precincts, browsing the papers, scanning the court hearing diary for the day, hoping to stumble across a story. A nice, simple story, that didn't psychologically terrorise her or trigger her PTSD. It was dull work but at least she wasn't hiding in elevators, jumping out from behind stairwells, and mining people's grief for the six o'clock news.

She printed out the legal diaries for the district court for the week ahead and scanned the listings. Her heart skipped a beat as she stopped on one name. *Walsh, S., Dr.*

It might be nothing. It was a bit of a stretch but at the same time it was quite the coincidence. While most people knew Susannah Rice as simply Dr Sue, Adelaide remembered the name that was printed on her hospital name tag all those years ago. The name tag attached to the white coat that had told Adelaide that Zane was dead. The name tag that read *Dr S. Walsh*. Adelaide could never forget that name. It was Susannah's name before she became Susannah Rice, before she married John.

So there was going to be a hearing after all, Adelaide thought. She wondered what to do next.

I just want one day without Dr Sue in my life. Just one day.

She could ignore this information, pretend she had never seen it. Nobody had asked her to go through the listings for the court diaries. If she brought it to Jimmy's attention, he would most certainly put her on the story. If she didn't bring it to his attention she would get her ass kicked for missing it. And he would find out about it because there was going to be a hearing, and if there was a trial, she would be put on the story anyway.

What if you just tell him, just tell him about Zane, just tell him about Curtis.

But she would not risk becoming that woman, again, the one that everyone feels sorry for.

She printed off the court diary and decided she would go along, just to check it out. It might be another doctor called S. Walsh. She googled it. There were three doctors with that name registered in New York City and two of them were male. What were the chances? She would go along and see. She may as well get some brownie points if it did turn out to be Dr Sue. Then, and only then, would she tell Jimmy.

Better bring Luke along too, she thought, grabbing her coat ... just in case.

Chapter 22

Susannah had never been in a courthouse in her life. The building on Pearl Street was massive, looming into the sky in intimidating dark stone.

At least there are no journalists here, she thought. Dana's bright idea for Susannah to use her maiden name had worked.

They found Dana in the lobby and she guided them to the hearing room. Once they were inside the room, Susannah relaxed a little. It felt less like she was on trial and more like she was in a conference room, but as she made her way to her seat, her heart stopped as she noticed a familiar face sitting in the back of the room – the journalist. The one from the hospital entrance, and the funeral. She was everywhere but Susannah felt like she knew her from somewhere else too, not just from the TV. But *where?* She locked eyes with her and gave her a pleading look. Must every aspect of her torture be reported upon?

The DA presented a list of evidence from their investigation, including first-person testimony that 'would prove that Dr Rice had regularly prioritised her work over her children to the point of neglect'. Because she had received an emergency call on the morning of Louise's death, the prosecutors claimed this proved she consciously decided to leave her daughter in the car so that she could deal with the emergency rather than prioritise her child's care. Her plan was to then drop Louise to daycare, but she had been sidetracked and distracted once she was in the hospital and had forgotten about her baby until it was too late. Susannah tried to stay calm. Dana leaned in to her and whispered, 'Don't panic. Just because they say it, doesn't make it true.'

The DA listed off their interviewees, which included careworkers, co-workers, and employees who worked with Susannah. The DA claimed these parties' statements would prove Susannah took risks with her daughters' lives as a matter of course. Shock crept through Susannah's veins, solidifying in her body.

How? When had they spoken to them? Why had nobody mentioned it to Susannah?

'Your Honour, we feel these statements and the evidence we have gathered pass the required threshold for this case to go to trial.'

The DA looked at Susannah with disgust, and a hauteur that marked him apart from her, like an invisible velvet rope separated them. *I am a decent, upright citizen*, he seemed to say. *You are a degenerate who deigns to advise people on how to look after their children but can't even look after your own child. You should be in jail.*

Dana stood up.

'Your Honour, my client has already admitted full responsibility for what happened to her daughter. She has no history or record of negligence with either of her children. She is an upstanding member of this community and a dedicated healthcare worker. What the District Attorney has presented here is a list of hearsay, gossip and speculation motivated by envy, jealousy and God knows what else. Apart from the fact that the "evidence" list clearly does not meet any standards of required thresholds, even if it did, bringing a criminal case in this situation serves no one, not the child in question, not my client, not the District Attorney's office and not American justice. We therefore request that you dismiss.'

Chapter 23

Adelaide looked around the courtroom. She was unreasonably pleased to see that none of her peers were here. She loved getting the jump on a story, even if it was *this* story.

Adelaide watched Susannah and John and their lawyer as they arrived. Susannah looked thin, pale, but still impossibly glamorous. She didn't appear to be wearing make-up, yet her skin was perfectly even and clear. Her hair bounced as she walked in, moving as one seamless mass, resting on her shoulders when she sat down. How could she look so calm and well-put-together as she awaited her fate? Adelaide suspected she was just frozen with fear. What must she be thinking? What was she feeling? Adelaide's own grief was almost unbearable some days. She couldn't imagine how the stress of a trial hearing, and the accompanying publicity would exacerbate that grief. And she knew she was complicit in making things more difficult for Susannah but there wasn't much she could do about it. This was her job.

Adelaide had a bad feeling the minute she saw Judge Parker on the bench. She was impossible to read in Adelaide's experience but she had a sombre air as she announced her decision.

'I have perused the evidence submitted by the District Attorney and it is my opinion that it passes the necessary threshold for prosecution.'

Susannah looked at John and Dana, and Adelaide thought she looked like a little girl, waiting for her parents to tell her everything was going to be all right. But it wasn't going to be alright. John looked like he was about to cry and the lawyer's face was tight, her jaw clenched as she gathered her papers.

The judge went on.

'I am therefore passing this case with the charges of involuntary manslaughter and criminal negligence to trial by jury. Dr Rice, on the aforementioned charges, how do you plead?'

Dana stood up.

'My client pleads not guilty, Your Honour.'

'Very well. I am setting a date for trial for five months' time, Monday November 15th.'

The gavel came down.

*

Adelaide went back to the office and walked down the corridor to Jimmy. She stuck her head around his door.

'Hey, wanna hear something?

Jimmy looked up, his eyes were wide, his face unimpressed.

'Dr Sue is going to trial.' Adelaide felt like she had been failing ever since she had been put on this story. It was time to turn things around, or at least give the outward impression of turning things around.

Jimmy's face lit up. He jumped up, grabbed his remote control to turn up the volume on the muted TV.

'Why is this not on our breaking news ticker?' He looked at Adelaide. 'Why are we not covering this?'

'Well, that's the best bit ... because nobody knows yet. I was the only journalist at the trial hearing this morning.'

He looked at her. 'Don't tease me, Adelaide.'

'The hearing took place under her maiden name, Susannah Walsh. I knew it was her name from ... a long time ago, so I went along this morning to see if it *was* her. And ... jackpot.'

'Oh my God, this is great. But we need footage. What are we going to do for footage? You should have brought Luke with you ...'

Adelaide was nodding. ' I did bring him. He's in the editing suite now.'

Jimmy ran around his desk to her, grabbed her by

the shoulders and kissed her on the face. 'Did I tell you you're an incredible journalist? We're opening the one o'clock bulletin with this Adelaide, get down to hair and make-up.'

Chapter 24

After the shock of the trial announcement, Susannah felt a strange kind of relief at the judge's decision. Finally, there was a change to the limbo status she had been existing in while she waited for the police to make a decision as to whether or not they would proceed with their investigation. She was aware that there was one final uncertainty to come – would she be found guilty or not guilty – but even still, knowing there was a trial at which a conclusion would be reached, after which she would be left alone, for better or for worse, was preferable to the stasis. But then there was fear and panic too. What would become of Emma if she went to jail? She railed at John when they got home.

'I mean, it's ludicrous! How can they think that I did that, *deliberately,* just to clear a few patients? I'd give up everything to have Louise back.' She crumpled into the armchair in their living room, as much as someone as immaculately groomed as Susannah could crumple.

'And did you see the journalist sitting down the back?'

'Yep, she was the one who broke into the hospital and accosted me and Emma.'

'What?'

'I didn't tell you. I didn't want to upset you but the morning after ... after you took the pills, she was on her way to your room, as I was leaving with Emma. I put security on her. But yeah, she had some nerve showing up at the courthouse today. How did she even find out about it? I thought you were listed under your maiden name?'

'God knows how these people find out ... she probably has an informant in the courthouse.'

She and John had both taken the day off work. Neither had expected the hearing to be over so quickly and now they were at a loss as to what to do.

John sighed and leaned back. 'This is going to be really tough, Susannah, but I think we need to trust Dana ... trust what she says, that when the trial judge sees all the facts, they will see there is no case to answer. And it will be a different judge to the hearing judge, so you might get a judge who sees this case differently. Dana said she doesn't think the evidence met the threshold. Maybe whatever judge is put on your trial will agree with her.'

Susannah nodded. 'But did you hear what the DA said? All the things he said about me? They're not true. How can they get away with telling actual lies? It's slander.'

John took her hands in his, looked into her eyes. 'These lawyers are like performers. Their job is to make it sound as bad as possible. But the judge is used to that, they'll see through all that *showmanship*. Things are going to get better for us.' He squeezed her hand and she felt he really meant it. 'This will all pass.'

Maybe it would, she thought. They were so rarely physically affectionate these days, as if they were always too focused on keeping the functioning parts of life running smoothly to stop and actually enjoy the parts of life worth living, the warm moments like these. True, John stayed at work longer than he used to and when he was with her, sometimes he seemed to just be going through the motions, nodding and responding to her while a different soundtrack played in his head. But today, despite the morning's developments, they were at ease together for the first time in a long time. She took comfort in the warmth of his hand on hers. She squeezed his hand back.

'Why don't we do something together? Get out of the house, go somewhere, try to forget about things for the afternoon,' John said. Usually it was the kind of unrealistic suggestion she would dismiss immediately as being too busy for, but maybe some quality time together was just what they needed. Susannah sent Christina home early, and she and John took Emma to Union Square.

As Susannah pushed Emma on the swings in the playground, and watched her climb the climbing frame and go down the big slide, she thought, *When was the last time we did this together?*

At the giant cones that you could speak into, Emma stopped. Susannah hated her using these – all she could ever think of were the millions of children's mouths that had shouted their germs into these gramophone-shaped tubes – but Emma loved them so she resisted another lecture on hygiene. She and John watched as Emma put her whole face into the opening.

'Halllloo-oooo!' she shouted. 'Can you hear me, Baba Loulou?'

The words echoed out the other end of the pipe and Susannah covered her face. John pulled her to him.

'How are we ever going to get used to this, John?'

'Come on, let's get Emma an ice cream from the market,' he said. They walked home through the park, taking in the groups doing tai chi and the *plein air* painters who had gathered under the trees. It was strange to arrive home, just the three of them. Susannah switched on the TV for Emma and John made spaghetti bolognese.

'Is this what normal life is like, you know, for normal people?' Susannah asked him, sitting at the island, twirling her spaghetti on her fork.

He shrugged. 'Maybe. Would you like it, if this was your life, every day?'

Emma slurped a long string of spaghetti into her mouth. Her chin was now covered with tomato sauce and she giggled uncontrollably. The sound of her laughter was a balm and Susannah felt a thaw in herself for the first time since Louise had died. She smiled at John.

'If every day was like this afternoon, I think I would like it, yes,' she said.

After they had put Emma to bed, with extra stories – she was milking the fact that she had their undivided attention for once – they sat together on the couch, drank a glass of wine and talked late into the night, just like they used to do when they had first started dating. Since Louise was born, it had often felt like they didn't have much to talk about anymore, but tonight felt easy and Susannah felt good in John's company.

'We need to do this more,' she said. 'Just spend some time together, you and me. It's good for us.' John's phone buzzed, he checked the text, and swiped it quickly away.

'Who was that?' Susannah asked.

'Oh, just work. It'll wait.'

Later that night, Susannah found her way into John's arms and they made love, not on the clock, not because her ovulation sticks said they should, but because she wanted to.

Maybe things would get better, she thought. They couldn't possibly get worse.

Dana had advised Susannah not to go back to work again before the trial:

'It might look bad. They might use it against you, say you weren't even upset by the hearing, that you didn't care, that you always put work first, that the fact that you were going to stand trial for your daughter's death didn't take anything out of you.'

Susannah thought about the months between now and the trial, spending each day with Emma. The sudden possibility of it was all too much. She wouldn't cope without work, the endless days, with no escape from her own thoughts, no escape from thoughts of Louise.

She looked frostily at Dana. How much was she paying her again? 'Look, Dana, if me going back to work is going to be the thing that makes or breaks this case, you're not the lawyer I thought you were.'

She knew work was not quite a haven any more but even with the stares, the whispers, the moral objections from parents, she needed it. It eased something in her, part of her guilt about Louise, to spare parents the pain and grief that Susannah had to endure. And if she was buried in work, she had less time for her thoughts to go to those dark places, to go back to the car with Louise inside it. This was why she couldn't not work while she was waiting for the trial. She would go out of her mind. She would go back to work the next day, as normal, and keep working until the trial. It was the only thing that could offer her some normality, routine, a beginning and end to each everlasting day. And the idea that she could help children, make them better, was important to her. She felt like less of a monster if she was helping other people's children, even if it was too late to help her own child.

The next day, picking up coffee and papers in the canteen, she saw her picture again, this time it stung a little less, in fact, she was half expecting it. HOT CAR MOM BACK AT WORK DAY AFTER COURT DECIDES SHE WILL STAND TRIAL, read the headline. She looked at the pictures. She could see she looked all wrong. She looked like a hotshot lawyer or a celebrity turning up for a divorce hearing. She did not look like someone ravaged by grief. She looked cool, expensive and aloof.

Dana would be furious. The campaign had begun. She was officially on trial for being a Bad Mother, a Bad Woman.

Chapter 25

Summer dragged on. The dry heat of July intensified and gave way to the stifling humidity of August. Tempers flared, nerves frayed, car horns blared on every crosswalk. Adelaide's patience was almost used up, too. Jimmy had her doing weekly update reports on the Dr Sue story despite the fact that there was no change, no movement, no update.

She was sitting at her desk, wracking her brains for a new angle that would update the story. She thought about doing a 'the fashion of Dr Sue' report but she couldn't bring herself to. She cast her mind back to her own experience. What was she doing at this point after Zane had died, how was she feeling? She hated how this kind of spurious reporting made her feel, the grotesque gratuitousness of watching and chronicling Susannah's grief like a form of entertainment.

She picked up a copy of that day's *Post*. The trial hadn't even begun and this was already turning into a witch hunt. The news story was talking about how shocking it was that Susannah had gone back to work, the implication was that she had no feelings, no maternal instinct, no regret or sadness about what had happened to her baby. It seemed to say that there was one way to grieve, one way for this woman to behave. Adelaide remembered how work had got her through the worst part of her own grief, gave her occupation, preoccupation, something to do, the means through which to forget, if only momentarily.

Adelaide had no problem reporting court cases, facts, news that happened but until the court case actually started there was no real news to report on the Dr Sue story. Several months of nothing. It was a million miles away from the kind of reporting Adelaide had imagined she would end up doing. It felt so wrong, and yet all she could do was be as sensitive to Susannah as was possible. And so she resigned herself to a couple of months reporting on Susannah's mental health, her hair, her figure, her clothes, her face, her attitude, her personality, her friends, her family, her money, her ambition, her career trajectory, her fame, her love life, her age, whether she was too old to be a mother in the first place, and what kind of woman was she? It would boil down to whether Susannah was seen as a good woman or a bad woman. And perhaps Adelaide could help with that image.

If she's bad, so am I.

Chapter 26

Susannah was almost three months into life without Louise now. She was still seeing the psychotherapist she'd been assigned by the hospital. For the first two weeks after the overdose, she had been to Adam's mid-town clinic every day. They spoke as much about her relationship with John as they did about Louise's death. Things hadn't been great for a long time and they had made love only twice since Louise had died. The last time had been the day of the hearing. Most days she just didn't have the energy, but she knew it ran deeper than that. She also worried about her part in Louise's death and how it affected John's feelings for her. It was her fault Louise had died; John never blamed her directly but he must hate her for it on some level. She hated herself for it.

Adam had not given up suggesting she take some time off work. He and Dana were broken records playing the same tune. Only, she'd thought Adam might understand that she needed to be busy or she'd come face to face with the alternative – the things she didn't want to, couldn't bear to, think about.

'But perhaps the fact that you don't want to think about these things means that you really *ought* to think about them,' Adam said, sitting back in his vintage Eames chair. 'You're not addressing really important feelings. You're running away from them. And if you want to progress here, you're going to have to face the feelings at some point. You can't keep hiding from the feelings, denying them. They will be heard sooner or later, and if you don't listen to them now, they may start shouting later.'

She knew this to be true, academically speaking. But she also knew that hearing her feelings, letting them out, wasn't going to bring Louise back. It was just going to make Susannah sadder.

They had talked about almost everything over the past months but this week they had come back to her desire to have children.

'Why do you think you only realised you wanted children so late in life,' he asked.

She tried to shrug off the question. 'I was busy with work, building my career.'

'Did you ever feel pressure to have children,' he pushed her, 'that you would have failed in some way if you didn't have children?'

She thought about the question. She had definitely noticed that she was an exception amongst her peers, almost everyone seemed to have paired off and had children and she had not gotten the memo.

'I had started to notice as I got older that people had started to shift their view of me. I went from being an admirable go-getter to a woman who wasn't quite right. The older I got, the more I felt the lack of family had started to stack against me, like a black mark. I could be as successful as I wanted but *these* two personal achievements – *motherhood and marriage* – they still seemed to be the absolute metrics by which we measured *female* success.'

Adam made a sympathetic face. 'Did that have any influence over your decision to get married and have a baby?'

She paused. Normally she would deny this. It just felt too self-serving, amoral even, to admit to.

'I think I was tired of weathering that particular conversation.' Every time someone made a comment about her lack of husband or children, a little piece of her crumbled away. 'When I realised I wanted children, after Ralph and I had broken up, and then it turned out to be so difficult to conceive, it was just a really difficult time. Everyone I knew seemed to be getting pregnant, and I was struggling to do the same. Everyone seemed to be announcing their good news. I seemed to always be attending baby showers, and never having one of my own.' She smiled at a memory. 'The first baby shower I went to after I got pregnant with Emma was so different to the previous ones, I suddenly had a new perspective on the conversation and it was frightening.'

Caroline was a whole generation behind Susannah, a solid fifteen years younger than her, and everything was happening for her. Caroline was still in her twenties and she was already married a year and about to give birth to her first child.

After a few cocktails, mock-tails and canapés in a beautiful reception room at Caroline's parents' house, the party moved into the dining room, where conversation over lunch drifted towards maternity leave.

'What are you thinking, Caroline, six weeks?' asked Cordelia, a thirty-something mother of twins who Susannah knew for a fact had been IVF babies but who Cordelia insisted were a natural surprise and direct result of her feminine fecundity, the same way she claimed that sleep and lots of water were responsible for her line-free face.

Caroline laughed. 'Oh, I don't think I'll last that long,' she said. 'I was thinking more like two weeks. My PhD starts in two months so I need to be back in the swing of things before that.'

Susannah had been thinking of taking eight weeks off if her pregnancy went to plan. She had waited so long for this . . .

'I don't have a finish date,' Caroline was saying. 'Do you know Helen from Gastroenterology? She worked up until two hours before the birth of her second child. She was in labour for her entire last shift and nobody knew except her.'

There were disbelieving laughs from around the table. The women murmured with awe. Caroline leaned in.

'When her contractions began to get unbearable, she just clocked off, walked over to maternity and gave birth. Just like that. She was back at work five days later.'

A momentary silence fell over the table, like a blanket being put over a birdcage. It was broken by a hesitant admission by a woman called Naomi.

'I-I'm thinking of taking three months off,' she said.

Susannah remembered the expressions on the women's faces. They held their tongues.

'Bob makes enough money at Amazon for both of us so we're going to see where we are after the three months are up.'

The silence became uncomfortable.

'It's not that long anyway,' Naomi said, defensively. 'Jennifer took six months.'

'That's different, Naomi,' Caroline said coolly. 'Everyone knows Jennifer doesn't care about ... *progressing* in her career. I mean, we're always being told that pregnancy is not an illness. If we needed six months off after the birth of a child wouldn't we have state maternity leave? I mean for goodness' sake, this is not Scandinavia!'

'Honestly, Adam,' Susannah said now, remembering the comments with a shudder, 'they could not have been more horrified had Naomi said she was going to eat her own placenta. But the truth is the message we had all received from med school onwards was that if you want to be respected, if you want to progress in your career, don't talk about things like getting married or having children. And if you do have a family, don't lose pace, schedule the birth for a Friday evening and make sure you're back in work by Monday.'

'Is that what you and John did?' Adam asked.

'Yes,' she said, the slow realisation dawning that in the end she had bowed to peer pressure, and joined in a competition that was always going to backfire on her. 'Although it wasn't conscious.'

'How are things between you and John?' Adam asked. 'Have you started seeing anybody together yet?' Adam had given her a recommendation for a couples counsellor. It was still in the bottom of her handbag. It wasn't the kind of thing Susannah could see herself doing.

'Not yet,' she said, looking out at the buildings across the street instead of meeting his eye. 'Maybe when things are on a more even keel I might suggest it.' For now, they were each locked in their own private grief. 'I mean, things aren't *great*, but they're not terrible.'

Adam nodded. 'That's quite normal for couples who have lost a child. The point of a couples therapist is to help you keep communicating with each other, give you the tools to make things better, even if they're "not terrible".' She tried to ignore the voice inside her that pointed out that things hadn't been going great *before* Louise had died either.

'Sometimes I think our problems have nothing to do with Louise and more to do with the fact that we got married and had children so quickly, we didn't have the time that most couples have to get to know each other, to build a bond, before children come along. And we hardly ever see each other.' John was often missing in action. There were times she couldn't get hold of him, like the day Louise had died, the night Susannah had taken the overdose, and there were days where she didn't see him from first thing in the morning until bedtime. He was starting work early, staying late, and Susannah understood that. She was losing herself more and more in work too because she didn't know what else to do.

Adam nodded again.

'Sometimes a death can do that, highlight the problems that were already there.'

Susannah nodded.

'Yes, sometimes it feels like Louise dying just drove a deeper wedge into the cracks that already existed between us. We have had some very nice, intimate moments where I've felt really close to him but then things will feel distant again for weeks.'

'I did wonder, before Louise was born, and a few times since, whether he might be having an affair ...'

Adam's eyebrows lifted. 'Go on.'

'Well, I don't have any proof, but we don't make love very often. That might be more to do with the fact that we're not that close anymore, rather than any fundamental problem. We probably just need to reconnect emotionally.' But the idea of trying exhausted her, like it was more trouble than it was worth.

'Is there any reason you would think he is having an affair?'

'He's working more than ever. And sometimes he seems like he's *not there*, like he's just pretending to listen to me, saying all the right things, going through the motions, but in his head he is somewhere else. And I've seen him be quite ... *secretive* with his phone, putting it away when I am in the room, or dismissing messages quickly so I don't see them.'

'Do you talk about why you don't make love?'

Susannah sighed. 'No. We make excuses – we're tired, run down, burnt out, sad. We always told each other we'd get our love life back on track when Louise was a bit older and things were more relaxed, but that hasn't happened,' she said with watery eyes, 'for obvious reasons.'

She wondered now if life would ever get back on track, become the life she had always imagined she would live. A successful career, a decent work-life balance, a husband and children. How had that simple goal become so unattainable? She was forty-six. If it hadn't happened by now, when was it going to happen, when she retired? When she *died*? Was *this* her life? How had such a simple ideal become such an alien concept? She picked up a paperweight from Adam's coffee table and held it in her hands.

'When is the last time you were intimate?'

The question threw her a bit. 'I-I don't know … certainly a while ago. I just feel like my life, my marriage, what happened to Louise, it feels like I'm way off course and I don't know how to get back on course.'

He smiled. 'The trial is just over two months away now … Maybe we should discuss how you're feeling about that. Do you feel prepared?'

'I'm really worried about it. I can't sleep at the moment. One minute I'm sure they can't possibly convict me and the next minute, I'm certain I will be given a custodial sentence. I'm not saying I don't deserve to be punished but I just can't imagine having to leave Emma.'

Adam nodded soberly.

'That's understandable but I don't think any jury will be convinced that you were negligent. A baby died so the police have to be absolutely sure that they followed procedure and investigated thoroughly, even if it makes everything much more painful and prolonged for you and John. All you can do is sit tight until the trial and be as prepared as you can be.'

Adam brought his hands together in a silent clap.

'We're out of time Susannah. I'd like to pick that thought up on the point about regaining a sense of control of your life at our next meeting. I'd also like you to think about what intimacy with John means to you, what it looks like.'

Susannah always felt a little offended by these endings. As if she only mattered to Adam as long as he was on the clock. But she knew he had another patient waiting.

As she rode the elevator down through the building, she was bothered by Adam's ending with that comment about John. When *was* the last time she and John had made love? Months ago now surely, the day of the hearing? The end of June?

She picked up her pace as she hurried down the street away from Adam's office. She passed a Starbucks, a Strawberry clothing store, a Walgreens. In the window of the pharmacy, she caught sight of a poster of a baby, its perfect cheek gently touching a tastefully nipple-less mother's breast. Her heart caught in her mouth. When would this stop? When would she stop being ambushed by pictures of babies? When would she be able to look at a picture of a baby again without it feeling like a gut punch? She slowed her pace as her mind repeated the question she had been asking all along ... when had her last period been? Susannah's life had taken on a new rhythm in the run up to the trial. Work, Emma, John, therapy, lawyers, repeat. It was impossible to tell one day, one month, from the next. She counted back ... She couldn't remember. A month ago? Two? Time had lost all meaning since Louise had died. She stopped. Passersby knocked into her, laptop bags swinging – 'Watch it, lady!' – but she didn't feel them, didn't hear them. The last period she could remember having was the night she took the pills. She counted back ... Ten weeks ago. She walked back to the Walgreens. *Don't get excited. This is just menopause kicking in.*

Ten minutes later, she was in the Starbucks bathroom bathroom staring in disbelief at the pregnancy test. How had she not noticed? She had spent years monitoring her ovulation, pumping drugs into herself, bloating, pain, ovulation sticks, sex on demand, hormonal psychosis, gruelling disappointment. The news was simply too momentous to keep to herself. She had to tell John. She called him but his phone rang out. She left a breathless message. 'Call me as soon as you can. I have news! I'm on my way now. I'll see you when I get home.' But when she got home, John wasn't there.

*

By 11pm, he still wasn't home. He had texted to say he was at a business dinner and would be home as soon as he could get away. He clearly had just seen the missed call, hadn't bothered to listen to her excited voicemail. Susannah checked on Emma in bed and turned in herself. She lay awake in bed, too excited to fall asleep. She rested her hands on her stomach. She would have another baby. Emma would have a sibling after all. When John finally crawled into bed beside her he smelled of cheap generic soap. Had he showered?

'You smell nice,' she said, curiously, trying to keep the suspicion out of her voice.

'Oh, do I?'

Susannah spoke into the darkness.

'John?'

'Mm?' She could hear him rubbing his face in the darkness. He wanted to go to sleep.

'Did you get my message earlier?'

'Oh you left a voicemail. Sorry I didn't listen to it.'

'It's okay, I have something to tell you.' She heard him waking properly, turning over and propping himself on his elbow. He was listening.

'I realised today that I haven't had my period in a while, so I took a test ... and, well, I'm pregnant.'

What she heard from John's side of the bed, through the darkness, was silence. She felt the air change as clearly as if he had said, *Oh, no.* She realised suddenly that this was not welcome news for John.

His brain checked in a few seconds later.

'What – Susannah, how?' He switched on the bedside lamp.

'That night of the hearing, it has to have been then. Well, it was then, because we haven't made love since ... and I'm not sleeping with anyone else.'

'How do you feel about it? Are you okay about this?'

'Am I okay? John, we've just lost a child. This is a gift from God. I am more than okay about this. I am blessed. *We're* blessed.'

'I'm sorry,' he said. 'This is a lot to take in. It's just so soon. We're still grieving Louise. And with the trial coming up ... it's a lot. It just doesn't seem like the right time.'

'I don't have time to wait around.'

He hadn't touched her, didn't reach for her hand, didn't hug her. He lay still on his side of the bed, arms by his side. How could he be so cold?

On her side of the bed, Susannah was building her defences against him. Her mind went straight to that place of paranoia. If he was having an affair, he was being careful about it. *Be rational, Susannah.* Their relationship was in trouble and she knew it. She was already starting to think of herself, Emma and the new baby as a unit, just the three of them.

Chapter 27

Susannah woke early the next day. She looked over to John's side of the bed but the bed was perfectly made up. She must have been in a deep sleep when he got up. It was the first proper sleep she had had since Louise had died, the first proper sleep she had had in three months. She picked up her phone and tried calling John. No answer. She frowned at the phone. He must have had an early meeting with a client. She wanted to talk to him about the baby, wanted to know how he was processing the news.

She checked the time. Still too early to call his office. The receptionist didn't start until eight. She sent a message to John. Call me when you get a chance.

On the dot of eight, she called his office.

'Hello, JCM Building and Construction.'

'Oh, hi, Abbie?'

'No, this is Elena?'

'Oh, I'm sorry,' said Susannah. 'It's Susannah Rice here, I was hoping to speak to John, if he's there?'

'Hold for one second please ... '

Susannah listened to the cool French pop that was the company's hold music. The line clicked back and Elena said, 'I'm sorry, he hasn't been into the office yet. He could be on a site visit. Can I get him to call you back?'

'Oh, um,' Susannah tried to hide her surprise and her confusion. He was always in work by eight. 'No, no, that's fine. I'll get him on his cell. Thanks,' she said, but she had already been disconnected by the efficient Elena.

She tried his cell again but this time it went straight to voicemail. She thought about leaving a message but clicked off before the tone went and instead texted him again.

Hope everything is okay? x

Five minutes later, a response.

All fine, thanks. Just slammed. Haven't left my desk since 7.30am. Feels like I never left the office last night. Sorry I haven't managed to call. Call you at lunch. Hope you're feeling okay. 🙈X

Susannah stopped dead. Her body prickled. Her brain wrestled with her adrenal glands. Elena had specifically said he hadn't been in yet. She tried his direct line. It rang out. Maybe he had just gone to the bathroom when you called the office or maybe he just arrived as you hung up. She *said* he hadn't been in yet. Susannah tormented herself.

Her brain struggled to regain control: 'Okay, okay even if it is a lie, we don't know why he's lying. It doesn't necessarily mean the worst. Who has an affair at 7.30 a.m.?' she asked aloud.

But Susannah's adrenalin was pumping and it took the reins from her rational side and whipped the horse of her suspicion into a gallop.

At lunchtime, John called.

'Sorry I didn't have a chance to speak to you before.'

'It's fine,' she said. 'Let's have dinner this evening. I'm sorry I should have waited to tell you about the baby but I just couldn't keep it to myself.'

'No, you had to tell me. I'm glad you did.'

'Will you pick something up on your way home?'

Later that evening, when Susannah got home, John was standing in their kitchen, smiling at his phone.

'Hi,' she said, unwrapping her silk scarf and shucking off her blazer. 'Where's Emma?'

'Asleep since seven. She was wiped out.'

'You look nice,' she said, taking in his sports jacket and crisp shirt.

'Thanks.' He didn't return the compliment.

'Are we not having dinner?' she asked.

He shifted on his feet. 'There's a work dinner. Abbie has organised it for a few of us. We won the contract for that actress's house, remember I was telling you about it?'

She didn't remember. He looked at his watch then nodded towards a paper bag on the kitchen counter.

'I picked up some food for you at Dean & DeLuca. You should try to get an early night, you look tired.' He kissed her quickly, then said, 'I'll try not to wake you. Don't wait up.'

The door closed and she started to cry. She felt utterly alone.

She opened the bag of food. Sushi. 'But I'm pregnant,' she said, to the empty room. Of course it was something she couldn't eat. She put it in the fridge for John.

Unbidden, and with ominous timing, the memory of a conversation with John's ex-wife surfaced. She had met her at a hospital fundraiser. John's ex was a professional do-gooder, managing charity donations for corporate clients. When she saw Susannah there with John she went out of her way to get her alone.

'You're with John Rice?'

Susannah was taken aback.

'Ye-es, do I know you?'

'Sorry, I'm Marianne ... Marianne *Rice?* I was married to John for three years?'

'Oh, hi.' Susannah was intrigued. This woman was

tall and thin, jet-black hair, deep brown eyes. She looked French. Ultra-sophisticated. She saw Marianne looking at the diamond ring on Susannah's left hand.

'That's quite the rock. Things are serious between you two then?'

'Yes, we're getting married next month.' Susannah smiled but wasn't sure how to act.

'Congratulations ... and good luck.' She looked behind her, as if to check where John was. Susannah could see John engrossed in conversation with a young intern on the far side of the room. 'I want you to take what I'm going to say now in the spirit it is intended. I'm saying this because I really wish someone had taken me aside before *I* married John and told me what I'm going to tell you now. He cheats.' Susannah made to leave but Marianne put a bony hand on her wrist. 'Wait. He doesn't think it's cheating. It's not malicious. He can't help himself. He's an incurable romantic. He's a sucker for a sad woman who needs saving, cheering up. Let me guess, you were on a downturn when you met John? Possibly post-break-up, on the rebound? I bet you he told you he had given up on love?'

Susannah's silence spoke volumes.

'That's just what he does,' Marianne said. 'He's in love with being in love, he's in love with the the honeymoon period, everyday love can't really measure up. And when that happens he's on to the next one.'

Susannah peered across the room at John. He didn't

appear to be flirting with the intern. Everyone said he was so obviously in love with Susannah.

'I honestly wish you all the best but I'm just telling you what I wish someone would have told me,' Marianne said. '*Caveat emptor* and all that.' She smiled a sad sort of smile, before disappearing into the crowd.

When she had spoken to John about it later that night he had dismissed Marianne as 'crazy'. 'She's totally jealous. You're so successful, and beautiful and so much younger than her, Susannah. She was always going to take a swipe at you. Don't let her bother you. She's just a poisonous old woman.'

But Marianne had gotten under her skin and Susannah had never forgotten what she had told her, mainly because she had gotten some of the details right – Susannah *had* been on the rebound, in a rut, and John was so incredibly romantic. In the quiet of the kitchen now, those comments about everyday love felt amplified. Their relationship had changed when Emma came along, but when she got pregnant with Louise, it felt as if they were mere colleagues in the shared job of parenting. Their relationship both sexual and intellectual had suffered badly and it was just getting worse. Was he out cheating on her right now, saving some other lost woman?

And why would he not have an affair? They didn't spend any time together. She worked too late, they both left early in the mornings, and weekends were spent catching up on the staggering overflow of work that she hadn't gotten to during her eighty-hour week. Cold fingers of fear curled around her. How had she let *this* become her life?

As the weeks drew on Susannah was still not convinced that John wasn't seeing someone. He was attentive, but in a diligent way, like he felt it was his duty to make sure she was feeling okay but he didn't want to talk about the baby, didn't want to plan for it.

'Working early again today?' Susannah asked as John swept by her. It was 7 a.m. She was sipping coffee and cajoling Emma into eating her porridge.

'Oh yeah, it's all hands on deck now with the actress. It'll settle down soon. It's probably going to be another late one tonight, though.' He kissed her and she bristled. Was he kissing someone else?

At 8 a.m. she was at her desk. She rang John's office.

'Oh, hi, Elena, it's John's wife, Susannah. Is he at the office yet? He's left his cell phone at home . . . Oh, he's not? Oh no, don't worry, I'll drop it to him. And, Elena? Don't mention I called. He thinks it's embarrassing when I fuss on him. Thanks, you too.'

Next, she texted John. How's it going honey? Hope you're not too busy. To which he replied, Been stuck in the boardroom since I got here but getting through it. Talk later. x

Where was he? What was he doing? Abbie would

know. Abbie was John's office manager and she had everybody's schedules.

She called Elena back and asked for Abbie.

'I just need to check a date from John's diary with her.'

'Uhm, Abbie called to say she won't be in until nine thirty this morning,' Elena said.

'No problem, I'll get her on her cell.' She was typing a text to Abbie when a penny dropped, slow and cold. Abbie? She was missing from the office last time she couldn't get hold of John too. She continued typing the text.

> Hi Abbie, it's Susannah Rice here. I can't get through to John on his cell. I'm just wondering, could you send on his work schedule for the month please? I'm trying to sort childcare and work to fit around preparations for the upcoming trial. Thank you.

Abbie texted back. Hi Susannah, and here she did one of those stupid smiley faces. What was she, fourteen? We are just in a conference at the office right now but we are due to break at 9.30 and I'll mail it right over to you. Have a great day. Another smiley face. Susannah was tempted to send her the aubergine emoji but she just sent back Thanks, no rush.

She wondered if Abbie was showing John the text,

were they laughing about it in their conference of two?

It wasn't proof but it was a hell of a coincidence.

She called John on his cell phone around 11 a.m.

'How was the morning? Do they even get coffees and pastries in for the boardroom? ... Well, that's something at least. Is everyone in so early? *Really*, even Elena and Abbie? Wow, they must be paying a tonne in overtime. Is it worth it? Are you at least getting a lot of extra work done? Oh, well that makes it all worthwhile doesn't it? Anyway, what should we eat for dinner tonight?' Susannah was furious at how easily John lied. She wanted to confront him but she didn't want to do it without absolute proof. She didn't to be *that* woman. *I don't trust him any more. When did I stop trusting him?*

How could he do this to her? After everything they had been through with Louise. Surely the loss of Louise should have brought them closer together. Did he just want to throw it all away? And now she was pregnant again. And he didn't seem at all happy about the pregnancy. In fact, Adam, her therapist, had had a more enthusiastic response, hugging Susannah when she told him as she had bumped into him at the entrance to his building on her way to a session with him.

But did she really want to be this woman? The one who sets traps for her husband just so he can walk into them? No, but she couldn't keep going without knowing.

Chapter 28

The month before the trial was a blur. The nights began to draw in as the trees turned from green to burnt orange to red. Adelaide was preparing for the trial by cramming on Susannah. She needed to know Dr Sue's life, and her work, inside out. She already knew what she must be feeling.

She had read all of Susannah's books, she had memorised her resumé, her professional timeline, her personal biography. She had the facts about her relationships, the bullet points about her areas of expertise. She had pulled clips from the archives department of Susannah in various iterations of doing her job, paying particular attention to her comments on childcare and child protection. Adelaide ran through the details in her mind. The information was there at her fingertips, ready to recall at a moment's notice for her live reports. Prepping to report on a case like this was like studying for an exam. When the jury was out for judgement or on days where not a lot was happening in the courtroom, Adelaide needed enough background information to talk off the cuff about Dr Sue.

She wondered how Susannah must feel now. Adelaide had no idea how she herself would have coped with being put on trial, judged by a jury, judged by the media. She wondered how she would feel if she had been the subject of media scrutiny in the way that Susannah had been.

As it happened, Zane's death didn't even make the national papers, just a three-paragraph story in a community newspaper.

Chapter 29

Susannah spent the last weeks of October in a daze, while her lawyers put her through a high-intensity legal boot camp. They walked her through every possible question that might come up, along with the impossible ones too.

Why did you have children if you knew you were too busy for them?

Why did you continue to work at the same pace as before you had children?

Why did you think it was a good idea to have children at your age?

They coached her on what to wear, and what *not* to wear. *Nothing sexy. No exuberant colours. Nothing too sumptuous. No cashmere. Plain cotton or silk only.*

They told her when to cry – *when they mention Louise*; when not to cry – *Don't cry when they upset you, when they make you angry. You'll look guilty.*

They told her when to smile – *if possible, only smile when recollecting happy memories of Louise*. When not to smile – always. They coached her on how not to get provoked, baited, angry, outraged.

Her lawyers had prepared her for every possible outcome, but which outcome would win? Worst-case scenario was a guilty verdict and a mandatory custodial sentence of at least two years and everything that entailed. Only seeing Emma on visits, having Emma see her mother in prison, as a prisoner, missing her growing up, missing her conversation, missing her development . . . and worst of all, having to give birth in custody. Would Emma even remember who Susannah was, by the time she got out of prison?

The day before the trial she was sick with nerves. She and John were supposed to be meeting with Dana for some last-minute briefing but John had said he needed to go to the office, unexpectedly and now he wasn't answering his phone. She went for the meeting with Dana alone. She was filled with trepidation about what lay ahead, but she knew she had to go forward, had to go through it in order for it all the end. What they were relying on, as her lawyers had ominously informed her, was whether she could convince the jury, and whether the jury liked her, whether they connected with her, sympathised with her.

She had some advantages in that she was a public figure who had positive connotations – she was seen as benevolent, in that her work related to helping children and parents. But she was also seen as controversial, alienating, because of her career success, her achievements, her perfect appearance, her wealth, her privileged lifestyle. The illusion of a smooth surface of perfection grated with the very people she was trying to connect with – tired, stressed parents. They might enjoy seeing her fall all the more.

'That's just the reality of jury cases, Susannah,' Dana had said matter-of-factly. 'Our society thinks almost exclusively in terms of entertainment now. You have reality TV to thank for this. So, if you think of it as a reality show it might help – you're a contestant and you *don't* want to get voted off.'

Chapter 30

On the morning of the trial media vans lined the street outside the courthouse, doing their best to fill the 24-hour news cycle until there was any real news to report.

Adelaide and Julie stopped passers-by to get their opinions on the trial. Yes, they said, it was a terrible tragedy. Of course, it could happen to anyone. There but for the grace of God ...

Some people said other things, too, like Susannah had sacrificed her children at the altar of her career. Or that this was where the ship called 'equality' ran aground. If women wanted to have children, they should realise something has to give. Some said it was unnatural for a woman of her age to have such young children anyway. She should never have been allowed to play God and meddle with her own fertility. People with so much money thought they could buy anything.

Adelaide couldn't help noticing that Susannah's gender, wealth, success and good looks seemed to form the core of the criticism levelled against her. It didn't bode well for Susannah.

After finishing their vox pops, Adelaide and Julie walked into the courthouse together. They needed to be seated before the judge arrived. Luke would capture Susannah's arrival on camera.

They walked into the main lobby and switched to single file to walk through the security check. Julie went through first, then Adelaide.

The security guard, a young man – he looked more like a boy actually – smiled at her kindly and said, 'Defendants processing is straight ahead on your left, ma'am.'

Adelaide smiled back, bemused.

'I'm sorry, what?'

Julie had walked on ahead but idled now, waiting for Adelaide.

He seemed confused now too.

'The entrance for ... defendants is just up ahead ... on the left.'

Adelaide almost laughed before a flush of rage engulfed her from her feet to her face.

'And what makes you think I'm a defendant?'

The security guard recognised his mistake instantly and went a paler shade of white man as Adelaide's voice dropped to a tone far more threatening than any shout.

'I'm a TV reporter. Here to cover the Dr Sue trial.

I presume it's okay to bring my notebook and pen in with me or are you worried I might use them to attack someone?'

'I'm sorry, it's your friend . . . she looks like a lawyer. I thought, I just thought . . . '

Julie had sidled up by now and got the full drift of proceedings.

'You just thought . . . You really shouldn't do that. This *defendant* is only the chief reporter with one of the biggest, most powerful news corporations in the country, the kind that cover systemic racism, and racial profiling in state systems. If I were you I'd shelve the thinking for the rest of the day.'

The guard stood back and made way for Adelaide. She joined Julie and they took their places in the press gallery.

'That was really not okay,' Julie said. 'You should report him.'

Adelaide was burning with anger, but she was also exhausted.

'There's no point,' Adelaide said. Julie retracted her head. 'What? Why not?'

'Because it won't change anything.'

Adelaide looked at her watch, impatient for Susannah to arrive. Still half an hour to go. The courtroom was packed. The media section was full, and the public gallery was too. Everyone was looking forward to this case: a high-flying, wealthy and beautiful woman, gilded by fame, brought crashing down to earth.

Chapter 31

Susannah ran over all the do's and don'ts that Dana had drilled into her over the last few months as she dressed herself slowly. It felt like getting dressed for Louise's funeral all over again. She removed all of her jewellery apart from her wedding ring, just as Dana had advised. The Cartier watch went back in her jewellery drawer. She put on flat loafers. She went for the Tods over the Gucci ones in the hope that the brand would be less recognisable, even though they had actually cost more. The truth was she didn't own a pair of shoes that cost less than $400. It was ridiculous that the clothes she wore might make a difference to how a jury might judge her. It was ridiculous that the jewellery she wore might be the difference in whether a newspaper article was sympathetic or not. But it was the way it was. The media reports from the funeral, the hearing and the past few months waiting for the trial to begin had taught her a harsh lesson. Now wasn't the time to try to change the system. She knew now she had to work within its parameters, unfair as they were, play by their rules. She opted for the black Louis Vuitton bag because the logo was almost invisible, but she was sure the press would have a detailed rundown of how much it had cost anyway. Everything she owned was designer so she opted for the least showy outfit she could find, a plain black dress that flared flatteringly from the bust and grazed over her bump.

There was no denying she was pregnant. She was five months along now and she was showing much more obviously this time. Maybe it's a boy, she thought. Maybe that's why my bump is so much bigger this time. She hadn't found out the gender yet. She still wasn't sure how she would feel if it wasn't a girl.

John walked into the room. He looked like he hadn't slept at all. So it was all real then, she thought.

'How are you getting on, honey?'

'Fine, just about ready. I'll just brush my teeth and be down in a second.'

It was a painful echo of the last morning Louise was alive, when they had had almost the same conversation. She brushed her hair until it flicked obediently at her shoulders.

She and John drove to Dana's office together, where they had a coffee and a final briefing.

'Keep your answers directly related to the questions,' Dana told her.

Susannah nodded tersely. 'Right.'

'Remember, yes and no answers are fine.'

'Mm-hmm, okay.' Susannah nodded again.

'Keep your answers short.'

'Right.'

'Do not elaborate.'

'Got it, don't elaborate.' Susannah tried to memorise everything Dana was saying but her mind was reeling.

'Do not give them anything they can use against you,' Dana was still rolling out her list.

'Yes, okay,' Susannah said. She put her hand on her bump.

'Try to do that on the stand if you can remember to ... remind the jury that they'll be condemning a pregnant woman to give birth incarcerated.'

Susannah hadn't been aware that she was holding her bump and she certainly hadn't considered *using* it as a prop to win favour. But Dana was right, she needed all the help she could get to stay out of prison for Emma's sake, and for the sake of this baby.

'Okay, good idea. I'll try to remember,' Susannah said.

'And above all do not let them provoke you.'

'No, I won't.'

Dana paused for breath. Susannah already felt dazed and blurred. If this was how she felt when her own lawyer was trying to prime her, how was she going to feel when the prosecution had their turn with her?

Chapter 32

The atmosphere rippled with excitement as Susannah and John entered the courtroom. Susannah looked polished and self-possessed, a glossy celebrity amidst the mortals. Adelaide could see the jury take it all in, wondering how someone could manage to look so put together, especially after losing a child. Susannah turned sideways and took off her light trench coat. Adelaide found herself beadily looking for signs of a label, signifiers of a design house. She saw the Burberry check lining and made a quick note. When she looked back up at Susannah, she thought she was seeing things but the murmur that went around the room, like a Mexican wave of outrage, told her she wasn't imagining it. *Susannah was pregnant.* How had she not noticed this before? She had only seen Susannah entering and leaving the hospital for the last couple of months and her coats and briefcases must have hidden her growing bump.

Adelaide could hear the stage whispers from the public gallery, which meant Susannah could hear them too.

'Oh my GOD! Do they think they can just replace a baby?'

'She shouldn't be allowed to have another baby after what she did to the last one.'

'All rise.' The judge entered the room and a hush fell. The judge was Ruth Donnelly, not as tough as the hearing judge but not known for going easy on women either. This one would be hard to call.

The courtroom stood as one, like a murder of crows rising, feathers ruffling and resettling as the judge made her way to the dais. The judge took her seat and called for order. Adelaide thought she looked weary already and the trial was just beginning.

Adelaide searched Susannah's face for points of recognition, searching for her own grief's reflection. But Susannah was wearing the mask, the one that sees nothing, feels nothing, shows nothing. The one that deals with raw grief by deporting all emotions to another country. Adelaide still wore the mask herself most days.

Adelaide's eyes moved to Susannah's husband. He wore his grief on the outside. He was smartly dressed too in a chic suit in a superfine wool, and his silver hair had the same television neatness as Susannah's, but you could see the loss on his face, his mouth set in a grim line, his eyes bloodshot, shoulders slumped.

The judge interrupted Adelaide's thoughts.

'We are not here today to decide whether what happened to Louise Annabel Rice was a tragedy or not. That is not in question here. We are here to discover only if there was deliberate negligence. Was this a tragic accident or must someone be held responsible? No matter that her death might have been an unintended consequence of neglect, was that neglect calculated, deliberate? And if so, how do we punish it?'

The jurors shifted in their seats. It was day one, they were giving the judge their full attention, showing her just how committed, earnest and attentive they were. Adelaide had seen how quickly this changed, how quickly jurors became inured to the process, how quickly they took sides. The judge lifted a sheet of paper, placed it aside and moved on to her next point.

'Over the course of this trial, we will hear evidence from both sides. I must make a difficult but essential request upon you, the jurors. I must ask you to put all emotion and preconceptions aside, please try to forget everything you have seen in the news up until this point and ignore everything you see reported after this point. You must consider and listen only to the testimony presented *in this courtroom*.' She swivelled her head on her neck, eyeballing each juror individually to make sure they got the message. 'Follow the evidence, *not* what might be in your hearts. Prosecutor Rogney . . .'

Julie leaned over to Adelaide.

'Yeah, right. Like anyone could forget those pictures from the car park.'

Adelaide raised her eyebrows and nodded. She didn't want to think about them.

The prosecutor stood. Rogney had an unseemly pink face, almost childlike in its plumpness. His wedding ring sank into the flesh of his finger.

'Thank you, Your Honour.' He stood squarely facing the jury, a gold, bracelet watch hung loosely under his shirt cuff, his trousers sat double cuffed on his shoes. He waited until every eye was on him before he began, as if he was on a stage.

'What kind of woman leaves her baby in a car on one of the hottest days of the year?'

Julie elbowed Adelaide and raised her eyebrows as if to say, 'See?' Adelaide grimaced.

The jury looked a little confused, as if they weren't sure whether his question was rhetorical or not. He had the air of a teacher, the kind of teacher who might pick on you for an answer at any moment so you had better be paying attention.

'A *bad* mother? Sure. What about the kind of woman who sees children as an achievement?' He swung around to take in the expanse of the courtroom, letting them know he was speaking to everyone here, not just the jury. *Clever. He's getting the whole courtroom onside. He's treating them like an audience.* 'The kind of woman who has spent her life achieving, and sees children as just another item to tick off her long list? Absolutely. Maybe the kind of woman who is *obsessed* with her career, yes, that too. The kind of woman who can't – who *won't* – give an inch in her crazed climb up the career ladder, not even for her own children.'

The public gallery grumbled their disapproval and Rogney shook his head sadly.

'Yes, believe it or not, it happens.' He went on. 'The kind of woman who is so busy working and progressing her career that she nearly leaves it too late to have children.' He looked around with a 'Can you believe that?' look on his face. 'So that when she does realise that she wants children, she needs prohibitively *expensive* medical intervention to do so.'

Adelaide inhaled deeply through her nose. This was going to be rough. She looked over at Susannah. Her head was down. She appeared to be staring at her hands. Her husband sat behind her, his arm stretched forward, to squeeze her shoulder. *What must she be going through?*

Rogney was taking his time.

'Ladies and gentlemen of the jury, we will prove to you beyond all reasonable doubt that Dr Susannah Rice was wilfully and frequently neglectful of her children and that her baby daughter, Louise Annabel Rice, died as a direct result of that *habitual* behaviour. This was a woman,' he said, flinging his fleshy pink hand towards Susannah, as if the jury didn't know who was on trial, 'who put her child at risk for the sake of her career and that child paid the ultimate price.' He dropped his hand and walked towards the jury's bench, his pointed black shoes clipping expensively on the floor.

'This baby's death was the senseless result of a woman who felt she was entitled to have *everything*, a woman who felt she did not need to change her life to accommodate anything or anyone, not least her own helpless children. This is the price of having it all, and the sooner that women like Dr Susannah Rice realise having it all means losing something, the better.'

'Objection, Your Honour!' Dana was on her feet.

The judge rolled her eyes.

'Mr Rogney, I will ask you to dial down the histrionics in my courtroom and stay within the confines of the law, your evidence and rational thought,' the judge said. 'Please leave your moralising and opinions on fourth-wave feminism at the door.'

'My apologies, Your Honour ...' Rogney turned back to the jury. Adelaide noticed he rolled his eyes, as if to say what a stickler the judge was. She watched the faces of the jurors. She saw at least three of them smile back at him. They liked him. 'Parenthood seems to be an inconvenience these days but if we parents don't look after our own children, who should? If Dr Rice is not responsible for her child's *death*, then who is? Jesus said, "Suffer little children" ...'

'Oh Christ,' muttered Adelaide, and now it was her

turn to elbow Julie. She whispered through gritted teeth, 'Can you believe what we are witnessing here?'

'Yep,' said Julie with a sigh, 'a good, old-fashioned witch hunt.'

Rogney wrapped up.

'It is our assertion that on June first of this year Dr Susannah Rice unlawfully caused the death of her then six-month-old baby girl through negligence, neglect and I will add selfishness and self-interest to that list.'

Dana was on her feet again.

'Your Honour, objection!'

Susannah looked like a bewildered child as she looked from Dana to the judge and back again.

The judge addressed the jury.

'You will disregard that last statement. And Mr Rogney, you *will* respect this courtroom or find yourself in contempt.'

Rogney half-bowed and took his seat.

Now it was Dana's turn.

'Your Honour,' she addressed the judge directly, 'the fact that my client is in this courtroom today is a gross violation. It shows the lack of compassion that this society extends to parents. What happened to my client could have happened to anyone,' she said turning towards the jury. 'Indeed, it does happen to approximately forty sets of parents every year in the United States of America.' The jury expressed surprise. Some were impassive, some shocked. Adelaide thought she could tell which ones were parents from their reactions. Would they be kinder or harder on Susannah if they were parents, she wondered? They could often be the harshest of judges.

'Over the course of the next few days we, will prove to you the jury, beyond any reasonable doubt, that Louise Rice's death was not a deliberate act of negligence punishable by law but a tragic accident, caused by the unreasonable and inhumane demands that society puts on our working parents. My client will punish herself for the rest of her life for her baby's death. As for my esteemed colleague Mr Rogney's accusations that my client is selfish and career-obsessed, I ask you to dismiss these as the rantings of a misogynist.'

'Objection!' From Rogney's table but the judge overruled him, warning Dana to, 'Keep it clean, please.'

With that, it was time for Rogney to call the prosecution's first witness.

'Your Honour, we call the defendant. Dr Susannah Rice.'

Chapter 33

Susannah dry-swallowed. She placed her hand gently on her stomach. Dana had warned her that this would be the approach but she was still reeling, panic battering at her ribcage. She looked at Dana, who gave her a sympathetic nod that attempted to reassure. Susannah didn't move, couldn't move. Every comment the prosecutor made had landed like a tiny feathered barb, piercing her self-belief. Death by a thousand cuts. She tried to catch her breath. She was in shock. She recognised the symptoms even as her mind was shutting down. She seemed to have forgotten everything her lawyers had coached her on, including Dana's pep talk from that morning. Dana walked over to Susannah and gripped her elbow. Susannah could hear the speculation. *What's she doing? What's taking so long?*

'Susannah, it's time to take the stand,' Dana whispered. She pulled Susannah up to standing and accompanied her across the floor as the spectators hummed with ghoulish anticipation.

Susannah took her oath, parroting the words. She might have said anything. Her spirit had reduced to a tiny kernel, retreating deep inside her body to wait out the storm.

The jury's eyes were on her, watching her every move, noting every detail of her composure. She felt her anger rise. Who were they to sit in judgement of her? What could *they* know about her grief, and how she should display it? What did they know about what she had been through?

Chapter 34

Rogney's clear loud voice rang through the courtroom.

'Dr Rice, is it not true that you had an extraordinary number of patients to see on the morning your baby died?'

Susannah opened her mouth to speak but Rogney didn't wait for her answer.

'Is it not the case that you thought you could leave your baby sleeping in your car for an hour and then drop her to daycare after you had cleared the most urgent cases on your list?

'Is it not true that you put your duty as a doctor above your sacred primary duty as a mother?' The triplet of questions made Susannah feel like she had been batted about the head.

'No, that is not true.' Susannah wanted to laugh at the hammy approach that the prosecution seemed to be taking but the jury were enthralled by the court-room drama. They bought into the performance. She turned white with rage, barely able to contain her fury at this *man*, hyping up allegations that she had neglected her child, just so he could get the jury worked up.

'Do you often take calls whilst driving with your children in the car, Dr Rice?'

'Um, I have a hands-free device, Bluetooth connec-tion, it's perfectly safe, so yes, yes I do take calls when driving alone, and with my children.'

'It's perfectly safe,' said Rogney, 'you think that, despite the fact you've admitted in police interviews that taking a phone call was a determining factor in forgetting your child was in the car with you.'

'Objection, Your Honour!'

'Sustained. Mr Rogney, Please stick to the facts.'

Rogney didn't waste time shifting gear.

He brought up a picture on the TV screen. It was taken from CCTV footage of a gas station forecourt.

'Dr Rice, can you identify the person in this image, please?'

'It appears to be me.'

'Appears to be?'

'Yes.'

'Can you read the car license plate?'

'XYB 2370.'

'Is that your car?'

'Yes, it seems to be.'

'Can we agree, for the record then, that this *is* you and your car, rather than just *appears* to be?'

She gave him a withering stare. 'We can.'

'And what are you doing here?'

This time, an 'are you serious?' stare. 'Filling my car with gas.'

'And are you alone here?'

'I appear to be.'

'Can you see the time signature?'

'7.03 a.m.'

'I'll repeat the question: are you alone here?'

'I must have been on my way to work ... Oh, I can see my daughters in the back of the car.'

Using the present tense about Louise made her feel sick, like a basic law of physics had been warped. She could make out the girls in the back of the car but she couldn't see Louise's face.

Rogney picked up a remote control and pressed play. Susannah thought she was going to faint. She hadn't looked at videos of Louise since she had died, hadn't been able to. She couldn't predict what would happen. She listened to them though. She liked to remember how Louise sounded when she thought she couldn't remember her baby's voice but she could not look at them, could not see that child so full of life and know what had happened to her, after. To watch the videos felt like bringing her back could be as easy as pressing rewind. If only she could do that. She forced herself to watch the video now playing in the courtroom. She saw herself wind down the windows a couple of inches and could just make out a tiny hand waving about inside, Louise's hand. Alive. Vital. Pulsing with life. She put her hand to her mouth and covered a sob. She couldn't watch. Rogney skipped the video forward until Susannah was inside the gas station paying for the gas. She looked ridiculous sped up like that.

'What are you doing here?' he asked.

Susannah forced back the tears, forced herself to stay composed. She looked back at the screen.

'Paying for gas.'

'Dr Rice, have you left your children unattended in your car?'

She gawped at him. It was obvious that she could see the children in the car through the large glass windows of the garage. She was ten feet away from them. She had clearly locked the car as you could see the hazard lights flashing when she walked away and she had clearly cracked the windows too.

'No! I can see them from where I'm standing. It's completely safe.'

'Do you know it's illegal to leave your children unattended in a car?'

'They're *not unattended.*'

'Let me read this quote for you: "I have never left

my children unattended in my car." Want to know who said that? You, Dr Rice. You told police, in your interview with them dated,' he looked down at his note, 'June 9 of this year, that you never left your children unattended in your car before. And yet it's clear here that you lied to police and that you lied to us – under oath – as you clearly did leave your children unattended in your car.'

There was an unsettled muttering throughout the court, as if this ordinary act, that parents did every day, had somehow revealed Susannah as a child killer. As if none of them had ever left their children in their cars while they paid for gas.

Susannah looked panicked turned to the judge, as if to ask, Is he for real? Can't you do something?

The judge just watched and waited.

Susannah made a disbelieving noise.

'I think you can agree that this is not the same as leaving them unattended in a car. I could *see* them! We did this every Monday on the way to daycare!' Rogney raised his eyebrows at the jury as if to say, Wow, this wasn't even a one-off. He ignored Susannah and moved on with his next question.

'Dr Rice, is it true that you recently attempted to take your own life?'

Susannah heard the hum of anticipation in the courtroom. *This is just entertainment to them*, she thought, again. She trembled and declared clearly, 'No.'

'No?' Rogney feigned surprise. 'I'm sorry, my mistake. Let me rephrase. Did you end up in hospital following an overdose of sleeping pills?'

'I did, but it was an accident—'

He cut her off.

'What kind of a mother would overdose when she is pregnant?'

'I wasn't pregnant back then . . . '

Another gasp went around the room. Susannah realised her mistake immediately. She had tacitly admitted to attempting suicide. He had walked her into it and she had stupidly followed.

'Objection, Your Honour, leading the witness.'

'Sustained. Mr Rogney, please try not to speculate as to what the defendant's inner thoughts may have been in any given circumstance. Stick to the facts and your evidence.'

Rogney simpered, 'Thank you, Your Honour.' He smiled to the jury as well. 'Okay, so,' he said, turning back to Susannah, and playing confused. 'You say you weren't pregnant . . . but I think you can't claim ignorance of your status as a mother to your other daughter, Emma. You were *still* a mother to her. How could you contemplate leaving her, after she had already been through the trauma of losing her baby sister?'

Susannah was ashen-faced. She stared down at her hands again, too ashamed to meet Rogney's eye, his sneering expression.

'The overdose was accidental. I wasn't trying to kill myself. I just wanted to get some sleep. I haven't been able to sleep very well since Louise died.'

'Well, that's understandable,' Rogney said moving towards the jury's bench. 'Simple mistake. Could happen to the best of us, really. Remind me again, just how many pills did you *accidentally* take that night, Dr Rice?'

Susannah knew she was beaten. She refused to look up at him. She didn't want to see the jury either.

'I don't know, I can't remember,' she said.

'Twenty. Four,' Rogney said. The cry that went up from the jury and the rest of the courtroom was one of high drama. Did people have no decorum? This wasn't a TV show. This was her life.

'I wonder if anyone here, any members of the jury maybe, has accidentally taken twenty-four pills. Has anyone here even accidentally taken three pills instead of two?' He rapped his knuckles on the bench. 'It takes quite some doing, doesn't it? A handful of pills I can imagine, but twenty-four? Who accidentally does that? It certainly makes your overdose look a little deliberate. Maybe it wasn't sleep you were in search of that night. Maybe it was an escape from living with the guilt of knowing what you had done. You felt guilty because you *are* guilty.'

'It's 11 a.m.,' the judge interrupted. 'We will take our recess and reconvene at 11.15.' Susannah wanted to scream, wanted to explain that she had just wanted it all to stop, but she knew every attempt to explain, to justify, to qualify seemed only to incriminate her further.

Chapter 35

Susannah was grateful for the time out. She was not grateful for the way that Dana was drilling her in the conference room assigned to them by the courthouse. It smelled arid and hot; like the inside of the car that day she found Louise. She tried to swallow but her throat was dry. She didn't want to be in this room but it felt like the only safe place to be right now. The news channels were running reports and updates on the trial every fifteen minutes. Her lawyers and John sat at the conference table and discussed tactics, lines of defence, lines of attack, how they were doing with the jury, which jury members were sympathetic. They ran through cases just like hers, precedents, best-case and worst-case scenarios. But they didn't make Susannah feel any better. Dana, meanwhile, was running over Susannah's performance, as she called it.

'Susannah, please don't take what I am going to say

the wrong way.' She flicked her eyes up from the lid of her coffee then returned them to the table. 'How you're doing on the stand, I think maybe it would be worth loosening your grip on yourself a little more. The times you got upset on the stand this morning, you could see the jury were really on your side. Some were crying with you. Rogney saw that too so now he is trying to make you seem angry instead of sad. That's less sympathetic, less appealing to the jury. You are incredibly strong and composed but – can I be frank?'

Susannah nodded coldly.

'The times he has succeeded in making you angry, cold, furious, I think that's working against us right now. While it is taking all of your strength to hold yourself together, what the jury might be seeing is this perfectly groomed, composed woman who they might interpret as, well, uncaring. I know it goes against the grain but instead of playing into Rogney's hands, letting him provoke you, make you hard and angry, try instead to show the jury just how much he is upsetting you.

John was leaning against the wall by the door.

'It's grotesque, Susannah, but Dana is right.'

Dana pulled out a chair and sat down at the conference table beside Susannah. She spoke gently now.

'I know this feels like a gross invasion of your privacy, your most personal grief, but you can't appear to be too cold or angry on the stand, even if your coldness and anger are directed at Rogney, the jury might not see that.' Susannah gave her a look. 'Let's just do everything we can to help ourselves here.'

It was obvious that Dana was starting to regret putting Susannah on the stand.

She blew the steaming mouth hole on the lid of her takeaway coffee.

'The law is a funny thing and sometimes, particularly in an emotional case like this, it comes down to who believes whom as opposed to who is telling the truth. This is not an open-and-shut case of facts. This is essentially a popularity contest. This case will be won on opinion, on whether the jury believe you were negligent, on whether they believe you are sorry, on whether they *like* you, Susannah. You have to be the image of the grieving mother that they have in their minds, not the reality of the grieving mother you are, violated, grieving in private. There is no room for nuance here.'

Susannah pushed back her chair sharply and stood up in one fluid movement. 'We'd better get back in.'

Chapter 36

As the courtroom resettled into silence, Rogney stood up, pulled his cuffs sharply from under his suit jacket and walked into the centre of the room.

'Dr Rice, do you see a therapist?'

'I do. Adam O'Shea. I started seeing him after ... after my time in hospital,' Susannah answered.

'Your overdose,' Rogney asked.

Susannah gave the most imperceptible nod.

'Oh, no, I'm talking about your *other* therapist.' Adelaide watched Susannah from the press gallery. Her eyes widened. *If looks could kill.*

Rogney smirked. Adelaide could tell he was enjoying wrong-footing Susannah.

'Why and when did you first engage that therapist?'

'When I was a young doctor, just out of college. I employed a therapist to help me with skills for balancing work demands, a busy schedule, juggling life and work commitments and also the difficulties of seeing patients die. I struggled a lot with that as a young doctor. I still do. It's hard when your patients are children.'

'Hmm,' Rogney said, this was not the direction he wanted the story to go.

'Is it not true, Dr Rice, that you employed this therapist after you suffered,' here he lifted a piece of paper as if he was quoting from a medical document, 'a complete nervous breakdown requiring hospitalisation when you were a young doctor?'

Adelaide thought Susannah looked like she was going to explode. Her voice trembled as she answered.

'No.'

'Were you not a patient of the Huft Clinic for the duration of three weeks in July of 1996?'

'I was.'

'So, let me see if I have this correct, you have seen one therapist for over twenty years, and you now see another therapist as well ... That's quite a lot of assistance just for juggling a busy schedule, even for someone as busy as you, Dr Rice.'

Bastard, Adelaide thought shaking her head at Rogney. Dana used different language.

'Objection, Your Honour!'

'Sustained, get to the point, Mr Rogney.'

'You are an accomplished woman, Dr Rice. Your academic career is littered with achievements. Medals for this, awards for that, appointments to international boards and societies, memberships of associations, not to mention your book and TV career. You're famous. You collect accolades wherever you go. If I were to draw your career on a graph, it would be one smooth, upward-curving line.

'However, there has been a personal price to pay for this. You did not attend your senior prom. You didn't have a boyfriend in school or in college. While your friends were adding the status of married and mothers to their lists of achievements, your achievements remained resolutely professional. How come you didn't marry in your twenties, like everyone else? Was it because you were recovering from a nervous breakdown?'

Dana was on her feet. 'Objection your honour. Relevance?'

'Overruled. Please answer the question, Dr Rice.'

'I guess I just didn't meet the right person,' she said.

But Rogney wasn't having that.

'Is it true you had an affair with a man called Ralph Lyons, a cardiologist who works at the same hospital where you work?'

'An affair? No. We had a relationship for three years. I was single and he was too, to the best of my knowledge.'

'I'm not sure that's how his girlfriends saw it,' he said to the jury, some of whom laughed. They liked

Rogney, Adelaide realized with a sinking feeling. 'They said you were always around, always coming between them, their relationships never stood a chance with you around. Was it the case that you were jealous of friends and colleagues who were settling down and having children while you were left alone with your glittering career?'

'Objection, Your Honour!'

Dana was starting to look hysterical but the judge coolly said, 'I'll allow it. Proceed, Mr Rogney, and do so quickly.'

'Your Honour! What is the purpose of allowing . . . '

'Take your seat, please, Ms Miller.'

Dana slowly sank back down into her seat. Susannah answered.

'I was not jealous. I just realised late in life that I had not paid attention to my personal life and that at the age of thirty-nine I wanted to start a family. Mr Lyons didn't feel the same so we parted ways. Amicably. It happens.'

'And you met your husband, John, when?'

'As luck would have it, I met him very soon afterwards. We clicked. It was a case of good timing. Synchronicity. Serendipity.'

'But by the time you and he got around to having children, it was too late, right?'

'Well, no. Obviously. We had two children.'

The jury smirked.

'What I mean is. you needed help, you didn't conceive naturally?'

'That's correct,' Susannah said.

'But that didn't matter, because you've always overcome any obstacle that stood in your way, that's how life has always been for you, hasn't it? Achievement after achievement after achievement.'

'Objection, Your Honour,' Dana said. 'My client is not on trial for over-achievement.'

'Sustained. Get to the point, Mr Rogney.'

'Once you became a mother,' he said, 'is it fair to say that nothing really changed for you?'

'In my job? No, nothing changed. And nobody let me off the hook either. Work stayed the same and I had to figure out a way to make my family work around that . . .'

There was more muttering from the court. It sounded like judgement. Adelaide could see the point she was making, but she could also hear how it sounded – *I sacrificed my family, not my career. I made a choice.* The jury could hear that too. And if they didn't, Rogney slam dunked it for them.

'As opposed to finding a way to make work adapt to your family?' he asked.

'Would you say you bonded well with Emma during those first few weeks . . . sorry, days?'

Susannah glared at him.

'Yes. We were very close, I felt very connected to her. It was very difficult to leave her.'

'And when Louise came along four years later, how did that change things?'

'It was a lot of work, but again, I was lucky enough to have a lot of help.'

'It seems to me that you liked the *idea* of having children, of calling yourself a mother, more than the reality of it.'

Susannah scoffed, and looked around her as if to say, Can you believe this guy?

She laid a protective hand on her stomach.

'Is it not true, that in a conversation with your employers about returning to work early you said, "I don't think I'm cut out to be a stay-at-home mom"?'

She rolled her eyes.

Careful, Adelaide thought.

'I do remember saying that but I remember saying it lightheartedly. I don't think *any* of my colleagues are actually cut out to be stay-at-home parents. We are all very invested in what we do and I don't see any incompatibility between maintaining a career, setting an example for your children, particularly daughters, and being a loving parent. All I'm doing is what men have done for aeons.'

One woman on the jury nodded knowingly at this, the rest remained stony faced.

Encouraged, if only a little, Susannah carried on.

'But the other reason I might have said that is because seventy per cent of my colleagues are men, at directorate level it's more like eighty-five per cent, so it's possible I felt that I had to say that to reassure them that I wasn't going to "go soft" now that I had children, that I was still as serious as ever about my career. I have observed how my female colleagues have been treated after they have had children. I've seen them overlooked for promotion, sidelined because they weren't available for late-night work or early-morning calls. I didn't want that to happen to me and as a feminist I didn't want to make things harder for my female colleagues.'

Adelaide saw Dana drop her pen on her yellow pad. The jury frowned at Susannah. Rogney suppressed a tiny smile.

'No further questions, Your Honour.'

Dana stood up and approached Susannah. 'Please describe to us, Dr Rice, in your own words and your own time, what happened on the day your daughter died.'

Susannah had tunnel vision. She went inside her mind and settled into the memory as if she was there again. In truth, she rarely left this day.

'The day started just like any other day . . .' she began, haltingly. 'Well, there were a few things that were different.' She went over the what-ifs. What if John's car had started? What if the house hadn't collapsed? What if she hadn't got that phone call from the hospital? What if she hadn't put Louise in daycare at all? What if she had been a stay-at-home-mom?

'Were you stressed by the phone call from work?

'A little. I knew it had to be one of two things, and I knew both were time-sensitive and one of those things was potentially fatal if not dealt with in a timely manner.'

Some of the jurors pursed their lips at this. A couple of them made notes in their notepads. Susannah saw this and stopped talking. *What did I say? Did that sound incriminating? Shit.*

Dana spoke quietly.

'At what point did you realise you had left Louise in the car?'

'It was when my childminder, Christina, rang. She was at the daycare to collect Louise like she always did but ... Louise wasn't there. I don't remember a lot about things after that. How I got to the car park, I don't really remember what happened there. I remember doing CPR. And I remember the paramedics arriving. I think I must have known that Louise was already gone, that I was too late, but I didn't want to believe it. Her hair ...' Susannah's eyes filled with tears. She opened them wide to stop the tears brimming over. 'It was so *soft*.'

She was in a different place, back in the bedroom that morning, nuzzling Louise's hair. A single tear rolled down her cheek. A few members of the jury started to cry. Dana passed a tissue to Susannah, waited for her to compose herself. She walked across the room and placed a box of Kleenex on the edge of the jury's bench.

'I know this is difficult to remember. Please take all the time you need.'

Susannah dabbed her eyes.

'Sorry,' she whispered into the microphone.

'Did you have any idea, up until the moment you received the phone call, that you had left your baby in the car?'

Susannah looked down at the tissue in her hands, which she was shredding finely.

'No. I thought she was in daycare.' She covered her face with her hands.

Dana changed tack.

'Dr Rice, what is the average time off taken by your colleagues when they have babies?'

Susannah was confused at the change in subject, but was relieved to be able to answer the question unemotionally.

'Most take anything between two days and two weeks,' Susannah said, sniffing and dabbing her eyes. Dana had told her to use her tissue as much as possible.

'What is the average time off taken by your male colleagues after their wives have children?'

'They don't take any time off in my experience.'

'How much time did you take off work after the birth of your first daughter, Emma?'

'Officially, I had planned to take six weeks.'

'You went back to work sooner than planned though? Why was that?'

'I had just been made Professor of Paediatrics so there was an added pressure to familiarise myself with that role and I could either do it gradually by going back to work earlier than planned, or I could put myself under a lot of pressure when I got back after the originally planned six weeks' leave. I decided it would be best for me and the family if I had a more gradual introduction so I went back less than two weeks after Emma was born.'

'You went straight back to work, just two days after having your second daughter, Louise. Why did you go back so quickly the second time around?'

Now that they were talking about work, Susannah felt silly for having cried. She felt like she had lost control: predictable, clichéd woman. She balled the tissue up in her fist and squeezed it tightly. She straightened her posture, cleared her throat. She wanted to show the courtroom that the momentary lapse in self-control was now over.

'Well, there were lots of reasons,' she said, clearing the tremble from her voice with a sharp cough. 'Excuse me ... First, there is an expectation that you return to work quickly, particularly after a second child. Like I said, most of my colleagues in St John's returned within a couple of days of having their second or subsequent children. And there was pressure. I had received a negative response to taking so much time off with Emma, my eldest daughter.' She stopped; she still hadn't figured out how to talk about herself as a mother of one, how to stop talking about Emma as her elder daughter and start talking about her as her only daughter. 'It had inconvenienced colleagues, put a kink in the hospital's rota. Even though it was only a couple of weeks. Honestly, I was surprised by how my colleagues reacted.'

Dana interupted.

'How so?'

'I was told I was going soft, taking my foot off the pedal, one younger colleague told me I was making it harder for female colleagues to have children because it would be viewed as disruptive to the hospital. Frankly, it was openly frowned upon. I ended up feeling really bad about it. From what I can gather, it's the same for most women in most jobs, it's not just medicine.' She dared to flicker a glance at the jury. She saw two women nod.

'So when you had Louise, you felt you had no option but to go back to work as soon as possible. Did anybody come to you and suggest that you should take some time off, bond with your baby, recover from the birth? Did you have a conversation with the HR department about it?'

Susannah shook her head.

'No, it wasn't seen in that way, like it was something to recover from. It was something to get on with,' she said, a note of bitterness creeping into her voice. 'I spoke directly with my boss, Brian Gore, the clinical director of the hospital. He told me that they needed me back as soon as I was able, so there was no pressure but nor was there any suggestion that I should take longer than I needed. He mentioned a colleague who had recently returned the day after she gave birth and how helpful that had been. I'm sure he didn't mean to add pressure but it certainly felt like he was saying if my colleague could come back twenty-four hours after giving birth, why couldn't everybody?'

She looked at the jury again. The women were shaking their heads in disbelief. She felt for the first time that they might be on her side.

'And so you returned to work, two days after giving birth to Louise? Did you never consider bucking the trend, taking a few months to recover, to be with your newborn baby?'

Susannah sighed and visibly slumped in the chair.

'It is my single greatest regret.' She paused, unsure of how to go on. If she had known that she'd only have Louise for six months, she'd have taken the time, all the time, the full six months. 'At the time, it just wasn't realistic. It was fantasy stuff. The message in my job is, if you want to have a family, do it on your own time. Of course, I was tired, I'm not a young mother, but I had a responsibility to the hospital, and a duty to the children who were my patients.'

Did she detect a brief intake of breath? Had she said something she shouldn't have? She felt the need to defend herself.

'And for the first month, I made sure that I wasn't gone from home for more than four hours at a time, so as not to stress Louise, and I always left expressed breast milk so Christina wouldn't have to feed her formula while I was gone. I didn't want her to miss out. If there had been any other option, I would have taken it.' She sounded desperate now, and was close to tears again.

Dana stepped in.

'Tell us about your patients.'

'Well, my speciality is paediatrics so a lot of the time my job is like being a detective, you're racing against the clock, trying to figure out what's wrong with these tiny babies and children who can't tell you what they're feeling. I'm experienced and specialised in the field, I'm in a position of authority in the hospital. If I don't go to work, children will suffer, something will be missed. I've always had that understanding of my work, and that's why I'm so committed to it, not out of some misguided sense of career progression or achievement.'

'Did you feel you were doing the right thing by your babies, going back to work when you did?'

Susannah took a long pause.

'I don't think I ever felt I was doing the right thing by Louise, or Emma or my job or my husband ... I always felt like everything was a compromise.' She'd never said that out loud before, never realized that was how she felt. 'I was just doing the best that I could in a complicated situation. I felt guilty about everything.'

The jury were nodding again. They get it, Susannah thought. Don't they?

Dana changed tack again.

'Why didn't you get your childminder to look after Louise at home all day, instead of putting her into day-care? I'm assuming you could afford it.'

There was a murmur of interest. Susannah was momentarily wrong-footed by the financial question, she hadn't expected it to come up here. Wasn't Dana supposed to be on her side?

'Uh, yes. I think it would have worked out cheaper actually, if I had kept them at home with Christina.'

'So why didn't you?' Dana asked.

Susannah hesitated. Was this a trick question? 'W-well, obviously Emma is in Montessori, that's important for her education and development but with Louise, I thought it would be a good idea to have her in a daycare close to the hospital, particularly while she was so young, so that if I got a spare thirty minutes at work, I could go visit her. And I wanted to be involved with them, in a meaningful way, at some point during the day. By doing the morning routine, getting them dressed, washed, fed and bringing them to daycare, I felt as if we had some quality time together every day. I wanted to feel like I was taking care of them, at least a little bit, because I was rarely home in time for bedtime. I guess it made me feel like I was more of a hands-on mother.'

A communal murmur came from those gathered in the courtroom. Susannah couldn't tell if it was sympathy or judgement. She was uncertain now, as to how to continue. She looked directly at a juror who had caught her eye. She didn't look away.

'I just didn't want to be one of those mothers, one of those people who has children and then never sees them. I wanted to be involved but I realise now it was a futile and selfish thing to do. They would have been safer at home with Christina.' Susannah didn't recognise her voice as it broke on the last word and turned into a high-pitched wail. She buried her face in the shredded tissue.

'So here you are, this working mom, doing her best in demanding circumstances. You're juggling high-level work, literally life-or-death work, children's lives are in your hands every single day. While you were dealing with this, you were also trying to play a part in your own daughters' lives and keep up with demands from your bosses, your husband, friends, family . . . ' Dana turned to the jury. 'Is any of this sounding familiar?'

The jurors smiled, nodding sheepishly.

Dana walked closer to Susannah.

'I have to ask, Dr Rice, has anything like this ever happened to you before? Did you ever forget to collect one of your children, did you ever miss an appointment, or leave one of the girls behind anywhere?'

Even though she knew this question was coming, Susannah was affronted. Her voice came out in a high pitch.

'No.'

All twelve jurors looked at her with surprise.

'No,' she repeated, in an attempt to sound more measured. She was furious with herself for letting her emotions overpower her. She didn't want to show her grief to these strangers, these strangers who didn't know Louise, didn't love her, didn't care about her, these strangers who saw Susannah as a TV celebrity rather than a person.

'Did you ever leave your child sleeping in the car outside the house when you got home for example? Lots of parents do it.'

'No. I would never do that.'

'Have you ever left your children unattended?'

Susannah looked at her like she was a simpleton but she knew she had to answer calmly and sensibly.

'No.'

'Not even in the house, to take a shower, say?'

Susannah almost laughed. If only they knew what her shower situation was. A playpen and a bouncy chair set up in the bathroom so she could watch them as she showered, but she wasn't about to tell the courtroom about that. Remember, don't elaborate, just answer the question.

'No,' she answered.

Dana moved on.

'What did it mean to you to have children, Dr Rice, to become a mother?'

They had discussed this question too. Susannah had been primed and she tried to recall all the things Dana had advised. *Be humble. Let the jury know that you know how lucky and privileged you are.*

'It meant everything to me,' she whispered. 'I met my husband late in life. We were very lucky to have children at all, never mind two children.'

Dana smiled at Susannah, and then gave an identical smile to the jury.

'How difficult was it for you and your husband to conceive?'

Susannah bristled as she laid out the most intimate details of her faulty fertility to these strangers.

'We did some tests and discovered we would be very unlikely to conceive naturally. Because of our age – I was already in my forties and my husband is older – we decided to take the most aggressive course of IVF available to us.'

'No further questions, Your Honour.'

'The defence calls Professor Michael Thomas, Professor of Neurology with Columbia University, and director of the Thomas Neuroscience Research Centre, Yonkers, New York, New York State.'

Adelaide took the professor in. He was wearing corduroy, cotton, wool and tweed, a heady melange of medicine and academia in terms of sartorial taste. But despite this, he looked handsome. Dark, thick hair, swept back from his temples in a somewhat old-fashioned style, gentle eyes and a curious expression.

Dana approached the witness stand.

'Professor Thomas, let me start by asking you about the question that is on most people's minds today, the question that gets to the heart of this case – is it possible for a parent to accidentally *forget* that their baby is in their car, for them to think that their baby is actually safe at daycare?'

'Yes. It is more than just possible. It is scientifically proven. Most people are familiar with the term autopilot.' He shifted in his seat to face the jury. 'Have any one of you ever set out from home, on a familiar route to go somewhere, and realised at a certain point that you had missed your turn, taken your usual route to work or the children's school, instead of your planned destination?'

There were rueful smiles of acknowledgement from the jury, the gallery, and a slow single half-nod from the judge.

'That's autopilot. And the more ingrained a daily action becomes, like our commute to work – or to daycare, for example – the more readily autopilot takes over.'

'Okay, but usually we realise at some point – we *remember* – that we've taken the wrong route and we correct it. How does this autopilot idea apply to Dr Rice's case? Why did she not remember that her baby was in the back seat?' Dana asked.

'Because in her brain there was nothing *to remember*. In Dr Rice's brain, her baby *was in daycare*.'

The jury smiled at him. Adelaide could see why. He had no airs. He used simple language but didn't patronise.

'The point is, human beings are fallible and when we are in a situation like Dr Rice's – busy mom, full-time career, multiple responsibilities, unexpected additions to the daily routine, a phonecall from work – mistakes are made, even by the very best of us, but we can't be held responsible for them because we did not know – consciously – that we were making them.'

'No further questions, Your Honour.'

Rogney was on his feet before Dana had sat back down.

'How common are these kind of deaths?' Rogney asked.

'They range between around thirty and fifty every year in the United States. They are on the increase. My research can scientifically ascribe a lot of these deaths to our increasingly frantic way of living. But there are other reasons too. Changes in car safety regulations, rear-facing car seats, blacked-out windows ... all of these things, while they keep babies safe in transit, they make it much easier for babies to be forgotten.'

'With all due respect, Professor Thomas, are we expected to believe this?'

'You don't have to believe me but the evidence proves it. My peers and I, both in the United States and internationally, have carried out scientific research over years of studying memory and brain function. I have seen hundreds of cases like Dr Rice's all over the world and the pattern is almost identical. As humans, we are simply not equipped to cope with this level of functioning, this level of neurological stimulation.'

'If this really is the case, why does it not happen more often, then?'

'Luck. And it happens often enough that we have a scientific term for it. We call it Forgotten Baby Syndrome. It's not a fanciful theory. Unfortunately it is borne out by the evidence, year after year after year. I have examined Dr Rice's psychiatric assessments. I have read every statement and I understand how much trouble she and her husband went to in order to conceive. It's obvious that their children were much-wanted, well-cared for and loved. Dr Rice made two drop-offs and the diaper bag that would usually have been in the front footwell was in the trunk. Her morning was disrupted and she lost her usual cues. I am satisfied that what happened to Dr Rice was another tragic case of Forgotten Baby Syndrome.'

Rogney cut his losses. 'No further questions, Your Honour.'

'This court will break for lunch,' said the judge. 'We will reconvene in ninety minutes at 2 p.m.'

Chapter 37

'What did you make of the professor's evidence?' Adelaide asked Julie in the diner across the street.

'Sounds made up to me,' she shrugged, not lifting her eyes from the menu.

Adelaide was disturbed by the professor's evidence. Haunted by it, in fact. Could our brains turn on us so easily? Convince us so simply that our babies were safe? Did we really have so little control over our own actions, so little control over our children's safety? She shuddered.

'I think it's terrifying, Julie. It made me think of a story I worked on years ago, when I was still working with the paper. It was just a kicker with a happy ending and it was treated as kind of comic, which makes my blood run cold now. There was this mother who got on a plane but forgot her baby. They had to turn the flight around when she remembered. She had just left him in the stroller in the airport, boarded the flight and then halfway through started screaming, "My baby, my baby!" We ran it as a "flaky moms do the darnedest things" kind of story but now I think it was probably the same thing as what happens with all those babies left in cars. That baby survived because he was lucky enough to be forgotten in a boarding hall full of people.'

Julie deigned to raise her eyes above the menu and stare at Adelaide like she was a gullible fool.

'Come on, do you believe that?'

'I don't know but I think something's going on with *moms*. Like, I remember interviewing another woman for a business article. She was in finance, quite high up, and I was talking to her about market predictions or something mind-numbing like that but after the interview she started talking to me about being a mom and she told me she was only working so as not to lose face with her female friends, who mocked stay-at-home moms. But she really wanted to be a stay-at-home mom herself.'

'So why didn't she just be a stay-at-home mom?'

'Don't you get it? She didn't do it because then she would be *just* a mom. And that is clearly the worst thing you can be in this country. She wanted to stay home with her kid but she was afraid her friends would dump her because they would think she was boring, or wasn't like them anymore. So she put her baby in daycare and went back to work. I mean, when did even the women *with choices* become choice-*less*?'

'But she did have a choice,' Julie said, still browsing her menu. 'She was just too weak to stand up to what people thought about her to make a decision for her own happiness, so, well . . . that's on her. I don't really have any sympathy for her.'

Sometimes Julie really could be so harsh. It seemed stunted, Adelaide thought, to not be able to empathise with this state of mind. Adelaide had experienced something similar herself when she had found herself divided, her loyalties split and her free time curtailed after having Zane.

'But is nobody allowed to *just* raise their kids any more?'

'Maybe the Amish?' Julie said.

'I'm serious,' Adelaide said. Why did Julie always have to make a joke of things? 'Is raising kids not a noble enough occupation without having to achieve professionally as well?'

Julie snapped her menu shut. She took control of the conversation.

'Jesus, Adelaide, would *you* want to give up work, stay home with your baby all day?'

Adelaide went quiet. That was exactly what she had wanted, at least for a temporary period. The waitress came by and took their orders.

'You'd go out of your mind. And as far as I can tell any women I know who have decided to stay at home are living out a waking nightmare, a twenty-first century version of *The Feminine Mystique*, women with degrees and intellects and rich interior lives spending all day washing and cooking and cleaning. Would you really want that?'

'I just think that there should be a choice. Why has being a mother become so difficult for so many women? Why are they so pressurised that they're forgetting their babies in cars, in airports? Something is all wrong with the picture. I think they need help.'

Julie looked at her as if to say, *and how are you gonna help all the moms?*

'I guess what I'm trying to say is men have never tried to do it all and aren't expected to do it all so why are women breaking themselves and putting their children in danger by trying to do everything? Why is there no support, no maternity benefit? Why are we *expected* to do it all?'

Julie sighed.

'Maybe because we *do* it all ... we're our own worst enemies I think.'

Evidently bored of the topic, Julie switched to one she was happier with.

'So,' she said, 'the professor. He's nice looking, isn't he?'

Adelaide rolled her eyes. 'I can't say I noticed.'

'No wedding ring either. I love the buttoned-up ones,' Julie said, making a slightly crushed face. 'They're always so passionate underneath it all, you know? Like you end up feeling like you've done some really good civic duty after sleeping with them,' she said happily. 'Speaking of which, I have to show you this guy I'm messaging on Tinder.' She took out her phone and started clicking.

Adelaide knew that Julie loved life as a roving reporter, loved the chase, whether it was a story or a man. She had a low boredom threshold and the thing that kept her curiosity sated was meeting new people. Part of the enjoyment of her one-night stands was finding out all of the details of a new person's life, how they functioned, what they did every day. Adelaide had watched Julie do it a million times. She put the data through her brain and came up with a fully fleshed-out imaginary life for that person, like a high-speed novelist.

The romances only ever lasted as long as Julie's work posting. Adelaide thought a big part of why Julie was a correspondent was it enabled her addiction to romance and her phobia of commitment.

While Adelaide's mind was still mired in the morning's evidence, Julie seemed to have the ability to simply switch it off. Perhaps that was why she had lasted so long in the job. She watched Julie, swiping and texting. Adelaide was only thirty-eight, and looked younger still. She still liked company, and conversation, and plenty of men showed an interest but she didn't like the fluttering feeling of attraction any more. It made her feel guilty to hear herself laugh or flirt, to catch herself being happy, however briefly. What about Curtis and Zane? Were they happy? Why did she think she deserved to be?

Her ability to have a relationship was like a phantom limb now. She felt an echo of that part of herself, but if she tried to touch it, to feel it, to use it – there was nothing there. Nothing scared her more than the idea of getting involved in the messy uncontrollable world of love again. She had been atomised by her losses so she shut it all down, powered it down piece by piece, like a computer system shutting off servers until it was running on a skeleton system, just enough power to keep the essential operations going. She never wanted to engage so much that she could experience loss on that cellular level ever again.

At night, she still dreamed about Zane, his cheek flattened against her breast, the way his top lip curled back on itself when he latched on to nurse. She could still smell him, he was still inside her somewhere and whenever she woke up after one of these dreams she was filled with a desperate rage, sobbing and searching for the child she scented in the sheets and screaming into the pillows with the realisation that it was all just a dream, again. So many nights she had decided that if she had the dream about Zane one more time she would kill herself. It was too desolate to wake up to his smell in her mind and yet find her empty bed, her empty reality.

As their food arrived, Julie shoved her phone across to Adelaide.

'What do you think of this guy? He's in LA but I'm back and forth enough to set up a date.'

Adelaide murmured her assent.

'He looks nice. Is he on top of a mountain here?' she asked, turning the phone sideways.

'He's a day trader but he's big into free climbing.' Julie put a french fry in her mouth and said, 'But this is a long game. I'm going to ask the professor to meet us tonight, ask him to explain his scientific theory to us.' She smiled wickedly.

'Will you come with me?'

Adelaide laughed as she bit into her sandwich. Because Adelaide was phobic of both romance and relationships, she was the perfect wingwoman for Julie. She was never going to run off with Julie's guy.

'How could I say no?'

Chapter 38

After lunch, the prosecutions' witness list brought blow after blow for Susannah. They called people from her private life, her professional life and her social life, interrogating them about what kind of person Susannah was, what kind of boss she was, what kind of mother she was. Classified information Susannah would have termed it. By the time Susannah's fertility specialist and OBGYN took the stand she no longer felt surprised, just utterly betrayed.

'Dr Sharad, when you first met with Dr Rice, what were her chances of conceiving?'

'Low – she was forty-plus and perimenopausal.'

'Do you often treat menopausal women in your clinic?' Rogney asked, his tone all innocence.

'We do, but we don't as a rule treat women whose chances fall below a certain threshold. The treatment is so expensive and the return is so low, below that threshold, we usually advise against it. But Dr Rice is a colleague, so I made an exception.'

'So under normal circumstances, she would not have been eligible for treatment at your clinic?'

'I would have advised her against it.'

'What were her chances statistically of conceiving and carrying a child to term?'

'I put it at less than five per cent. We would never normally advise anyone with a statistical probability under five per cent to pursue treatment.'

'But she was still determined?'

'I could see that she was. She had worked out a plan for surrogacy if the IVF treatment didn't work.'

'Did you discuss why she hadn't had children sooner?'

'She said the time hadn't been right. She hadn't been married long when she came to us but I think it was the closing of the window, the looming threat of menopause, that had focused her mind. We see it a lot, people think they have forever to make a decision and it's only when the choice is almost taken away from them that they realise they really want children.'

'So would it be fair to say she only really wanted children when she realised she might not be able to have them?'

'Objection! Leading the witness.'

'Sustained.' The judge shot Rogney another of her withering looks. If Susannah wasn't mistaken, the judge seemed to despise him and his style as much as she did.

'Let me rephrase ... Did her determination to have children seem reasonable within the context of the facts? Did you ever consider telling her it was just too late for her?'

'Dr Rice has the kind of personality that must be very valuable to her patients – she doesn't give up easily. And she's not the type of person you say no to, either,' he said smiling. The jury did not smile back. 'What I mean is nothing is impossible for her. I felt comfortable going ahead with the treatment because, like I said already, as a physician herself I felt that she understood the true meaning of the statistics in a way that very few of my patients understand. She knew what a less than five per cent chance meant.'

'Did it seem to you that she really wanted a baby?'

Susannah's hand went to her bump.

'Nobody goes through IVF unless they really want a baby. It's a gruelling process. I would say that there are two types of IVF patient. There are those who have reasonable expectations, a budget and a time frame after which they agree they will stop trying. Most patients don't have a limitless budget, most patients will have to stop at some point. And then there is the other type of patient, the type who will not rest until they have a baby. I've seen women burn through marriages, destroy relationships, destroy friendships, take on unmanageable financial debt and drive themselves to the edge of sanity to get a baby.'

'What type of patient was Dr Rice?'

'I would say she was the second type of patient. It seemed to me that she wanted a baby at *any* cost.'

'How much on average did each round of Dr Rice's IVF treatment cost?'

The money, always with the money, Susannah thought.

'It's not cheap. In total, I would say somewhere in the region of $150,000.'

There was a sharp intake of breath in the courtroom, low whistles. The judge called for order.

Rogney bared his teeth at the judge. 'No further questions, Your Honour.'

Dana stood up.

'Dr Sharad, what is the average age of the patients who come to you for fertility treatment?'

'We help people of all ages, from twenty-somethings with certain fertility-limiting conditions to older women with issues conceiving, but the average age of the women we treat would be forties.'

'How common is it for women to have IVF treatment these days?'

'It's very common now. More and more people seem to be having trouble conceiving. Even anecdotally, ask yourself do you know anyone who has had IVF treatment, or some assistance with conceiving? The answer is probably yes. Also, women are putting off having children until much later in life because of their careers.'

'Would you say that Susannah Rice was unusual in her employment of your facility to help her get pregnant? Was she "playing God" with her reduced fertility, using her money to buy a baby?'

'It's perfectly normal now to have IVF treatment and very few people see a woman in her forties having IVF treatment as "playing God".'

'I'd like to address the cost, Dr Sharad, to put the cost in context. What is the average cost to the average family? Am I right in thinking that even the most inexpensive treatment is not cheap?'

Dr Sharad smiled. 'You are correct. Considering parents who conceive naturally and have straightforward natural births can expect to pay around $50,000 for the medical treatment involved, those seeking the most basic programme of IVF treatment would be looking at something like $70,000.'

'That's for an average treatment, that a lot of people on average salaries pay for ... I think it's safe to say Dr Rice did not see children as an expensive accessory, another achievement for her trophy cabinet.' She turned to the jury. 'Do you know anyone who would pay $150,000 for something they didn't really want? Me neither. Thank you, Dr Sharad. No further questions.'

The judge adjourned proceedings. 'We will resume tomorrow at 10 a.m.'

Chapter 39

When Susannah and John arrived home that evening the house was quiet. Christina took her coat and scarf and bag as they came into the living room.

'Hi, Christina, how's everything? Is Emma okay?'

'She's fine, fast asleep. She had a bath and a story and fell straight asleep tonight,' Christina said smiling. 'How did today go?'

'Oh, okay, thanks.'

Susannah didn't want to get into it. She had been leaning on Christina for childcare. Susannah had kept Emma out of Montessori for the week – she didn't want the press bothering her or Christina – but she realised they were asking a lot of her.

'Thanks for staying so late. Are you still okay to come tomorrow morning?'

'Of course, I'll see you then,' she said.

When the door clicked quietly behind Christina, all of the frustrations of the day spilled out.

'They're trying to say Louise died because I love my work more than I loved her.' The wild cry she had been suppressing all day erupted from her.

'This is what they do, Susannah,' John said. 'They're trying to get a reaction from you and make you seem uncaring, unstable.'

John stroked the back of her hair, softly. The house creaked and settled in the silence.

'I'm being punished, John,' she whimpered leaning into his chest. 'Not because my baby died but because I dared to have a career as well as a family and I dared to have it on my own terms! Did you not hear those questions, where they were leading? It's all so absurd.'

'This isn't doing you any good,' John said. 'It's not good for you or the baby to get upset like this. I'm going to make something light for us to eat and then I think we should have an early night. We're both exhausted. Tomorrow's not going to be any easier.'

Susannah opened the fridge and pulled out a half-bottle of Chablis.

'Susannah,' John said. 'You're pregnant. You really shouldn't . . .'

'I'm aware of that, thank you! It hasn't stopped you doing what you shouldn't do, has it?'

He tilted his head, looked at her quizzically. 'What's that supposed to mean?'

She poured a huge glug of wine into a head-sized glass and took a sip that seemed to give her no pleasure.

She slammed the glass down on the counter and left the room, tears now in full flow, furious with herself.

John found her in Emma's room, sitting on the floor by her bed, stroking the sleeping child's hair. He reached for her shoulder.

She couldn't have the conversation with him now. 'Please, just leave me alone.'

After she had calmed down, she left Emma and got ready for bed. John was asleep. His phone vibrated on the bedside table. She looked at him but he didn't stir. She looked at her own phone. 10 p.m. Who the hell was texting him this late? The phone buzzed again and she saw him stir, and roll over. She wanted to check his phone but she didn't want to risk being caught snooping. She crept downstairs. The house smelled warm and a little stagnant, dust motes floating in the still night. She knew she shouldn't but she was now a woman on a mission. She found his iPad in his briefcase in the study. She flipped open the soft cover, opened the messages app. Two messages. From Abbie.

> It was so good to see you yesterday. I hope
> today went okay. I was thinking of you.

Still innocent enough, she thought. Still explainable. But it was the second message that did it.

XXX.

Her hand instinctively went to her stomach. She nearly jumped out of her skin when the messages disappeared before her eyes. Had she imagined it all? Had she even seen them? But she had. She really had. John must have deleted them from his phone upstairs. He was covering his tracks. She bundled the iPad back into his bag.

She couldn't go back to bed to lie beside him. What did Abbie mean by 'good to see you yesterday'? Was that why John had had to go into work, instead of meeting Dana with Susannah? She was certain now that he was having an affair with Abbie. She made some tea and curled up on the couch with a blanket. As she sat there sipping her steaming tea, Rogney's words from that day came back to her. Had she been selfish? Had she wanted too much? Had she sacrificed her children and her marriage for her career?

Chapter 40

Adelaide spotted the professor immediately. Julie, on the other hand, was nowhere to be seen. *I'll kill her*, Adelaide grumbled to herself. She thought about pretending she hadn't seen him, sitting at the end of the bar and having a drink alone until Julie made her appearance, but at that same moment the professor caught her eye, smiled and waved her over.

Great, thought Adelaide.

He had changed. He looked less ... *tweedy*. He was wearing a relaxed shirt, open at the neck, sleeves rolled up to reveal strong, olive-skinned forearms. She looked down at her own outfit – black skinny jeans, flat studded ankle boots and a silk shirt. It was an easy uniform, comfortable after a day in heels and suits or dresses, but still chic, presentable.

She smiled and waved back, made her way over to his booth. He stood up as she approached.

'Hi, Adelaide ... Can I get you a drink, a glass of white wine, perhaps?'

'Sure, thanks,' said Adelaide, and as he put his hand on her arm as she slid into the booth, she felt a charge. She was so rarely touched by anyone, it always came as a shock, a surprise. He looked at her, just a second, as if to ask, did you feel that too, then went to the bar. She pulled out her phone to check for messages from Julie. Nothing. Where *was* she? She tapped out a furious message – I'm here WITH THE PROFESSOR! Where are you? – and tucked her phone back in her bag as the professor came back with two glasses of wine, a bowl of nuts balanced in the crook of his elbow.

'Oh thank you, I'm starving,' Adelaide said, as he pushed the nuts between them. He slid back into his seat, brushing her knees with his as he did. 'I'm *so* sorry.' She laughed. And he did too.

'So,' he said, 'you're a reporter. Do you always report on court cases?'

The professor took a sip of his wine and sat back. Dammit, she thought, I wanted to ask the questions, drink *my* wine and casually zone out while he droned on about himself and his research.

'Oh no, I'm not a court reporter,' she said, noticing how the soft lights of the bar turned his thick hair a glimmering shade of burnt caramel. 'I report on lots of different stories, but unfortunately they tend to fall into the categories of murders, disasters and tragedies.'

She laughed. 'What about you, do you do a lot of court work?' There, she thought, taking a sip of her wine and sitting back herself.

'All the cheerful stuff, huh?' he asked, ignoring her question.

Jesus! she thought, *infuriating.* She leaned forward to take a nut, just as his hand was reaching into the bowl. Their fingers touched and she pulled her hand back softly. There it was again, like an electrical charge. 'Sorry,' she said.

'No, please,' he said, pushing the bowl towards her. 'It sounds like a tough job, covering that kind of material.'

'Well, if it's going to make national TV it tends to be either extremely frivolous or extremely dark,' she said. 'Which makes for a strange mix. One week you'll be covering a story about a newborn panda, the next something like this.' She felt his gaze on her like a spotlight. 'What about you, Professor, are you one of those experts for hire?'

'No,' he said, looking down at his glass. 'And please, call me Michael, for God's sake.' He laughed, seemingly embarrassed by the title. 'I try to limit my involvement in court cases as much as I can but there are not that many experts in this particular area of neurology and unfortunately it is increasingly in demand.' He picked at the card coaster under his glass. He seemed unsure whether to continue or not. 'In a case like this, where the parent is so obviously not at fault, I see it as a duty to defend them with my research.'

'Do you really think she is not at fault?'

'Do you think she *is*?' he asked, surprised.

She held up her hands.

'I'm unbiased, remember?'

'Okay, well, she doesn't fit the profile – IVF babies, mature, middle-class, high-income, high-performing. She *does* however fit the profile of people that Forgotten Baby Syndrome happens to.'

He was looking at her, waiting for a contribution. She held his gaze. He had a rare kind of empathy, the kind she had been looking for in Julie earlier on that day. She felt if she spoke now, she would tell him everything about her whole life, about Zane, about Curtis ... he had that kind of face, the kind of eyes that made you want to keep talking, just so he would keep looking at you, just so you could keep looking at him. She stuck her nose into her wine, inhaled deeply.

'What is this wine?' she said. 'It's delicious.' She lit up the screen of her phone inside her handbag. Still no response from Julie.

The professor looked at her like he had just snapped out of a spell.

'It's a sauvignon blanc. It had a screw top ... Look, your colleague is here.'

Julie swept in, a cloud of perfume, her hair and make-up perfectly done. She was wearing what looked like a cocktail dress. No wonder she was late, Adelaide thought. She had clearly spent the last hour doing her hair and make-up. It seemed a little conspicuous in the small bar but Julie was nothing if not confident. She shrugged her coat off to give Michael the full effect of her cleavage and then squeezed in beside him on the bench with a swish of her hip.

'So, what did I miss?' Julie asked, eyeing Adelaide, and taking in the charged atmosphere between them.

'Oh, nothing, we were just talking about Dr Sue. Here,' Adelaide said, pushing the menu card across the table at Julie and Michael. 'Let's order, I'm starving.'

An hour later, Adelaide was on her third glass of wine, an unprecedented move for her. Adelaide usually made her excuses after the second glass and left Julie alone with her mark but she was enjoying the conversation and, after the last six months working on the Dr Sue story, she was particularly grateful not to go home for another early night with her demons and ghosts. Julie was pouty and exasperated. She had used all of her usual tactics on Michael, to no avail. She was baffled.

'So, Michael, are you married? Got kids? Any significant others?' Julie firmly believed that if she wasn't connecting with a man there was a simple reason for it.

'Ah, no, no. I am not married. Divorced. I don't think my ex-wife liked sharing me so much with my mistress . . .'

Adelaide and Julie both sat back, eyes wide. Adelaide was surprised at the depth of the disappointment that shot through her. *He did not seem like that kind of guy*, she thought. She had clearly read him all wrong. Here she had been thinking what a nice guy he was.

He saw their faces, started to laugh ...

'I mean, my work. My *work* was my mistress,' he said. 'Don't believe everything you hear about men. We got married young, straight out of college, it was all over within a couple of years. Never had kids so it was a good clean break-up. We're still friends.' He said all of this directly to Adelaide.

'Oh, well that's something,' Adelaide said, slightly embarrassed by the intensity of his stare. She felt Julie's eyes boring into her. She saw realisation dawn on her friend's face.

'What about you two,' he asked, 'ever married?'

Adelaide blanched, while Julie smiled. 'Not yet ... excuse me, I'm just going to powder my nose. Be right back.'

'And you Adelaide, have you ever been married?'

Adelaide found herself nodding. Something told her not to lie to this one. 'A long time ago. It didn't work out.'

'I'm sorry to hear that,' he said, and reached across and squeezed her hand briefly before letting go. 'I'll get us some more drinks.'

Twenty minutes later it was clear that Julie was not

coming back, but Adelaide and Michael were so deep in conversation that it took them a while to realise.

'Do you think you should go check on your friend?' Michael asked. 'She's actually been gone a while.'

Adelaide looked around, then laughed lightly and said, 'She's fine.' She nodded over her shoulder and he stretched to see what was so funny. Julie was sitting at the bar, her legs neatly slotted between a good-looking guy's man-spread.

'I think I may have disappointed her,' Michael said.

'Oh no,' said Adelaide. 'Julie is never disappointed.'

'What about you? I don't imagine you are often disappointed either?'

Adelaide felt the boldness of his question gust through her. Was he flirting with *her*? It knocked her off balance.

'Ahmmm, well, ahaha, I, uhhh, I . . . I don't date,' she blurted out.

'Me neither,' he said, holding her gaze thoughtfully.

There was a very long pause, heavy with meaning.

This was all getting too intense for Adelaide.

'I think I might call it a night. Early start tomorrow and all that.'

'You're right. I'll walk with you,' Michael said, grabbing his coat.

He paid, for everyone, Adelaide noticed, and she went to tell Julie they were leaving.

Adelaide looked down at her feet shyly as she and

Michael made their way out of the bar onto the street. This was uncharted territory for her.

'So, do you have to give more evidence tomorrow?'

'No, thankfully. I go back to Yonkers first thing in the morning.'

'Oh, that's a shame.' She was surprised at herself, but she realised it was how she felt. He smiled at her.

The evening breeze moved around them. They walked closely, side by side, but not touching.

'So where are you based Adelaide? When this case is over, where do you go next?'

'Oh, I'm not actually based anywhere. Sorry, what I mean is, I live here, in New York, I have a small apartment at East 79th and 1st, but I travel so much I don't really feel like I live anywhere. I usually don't find out where my next assignment will be until it's happening so it's all very short notice. It's a strange way to live but I've gotten used to it. It suits me. I don't have anybody to answer to. What about you? Is Yonkers not a little quiet for a doctor like you? I know it's only thirty minutes from Manhattan but it's still . . . ' She paused, assessing whether he could take a joke or not, then decided he could. ' . . . *rural*.' She loaded the word with mock horror.

He laughed, and pushed her a little. She wanted him to keep his hand there but he dropped it casually.

'I grew up there. I like it there. I travel a lot too, so being based there makes things feel less transient.

Besides you can do so much remotely now, you don't need to be in the centre of things to be central to things.'

She laughed, 'Oh, I have no doubt that you are integral to neurology.'

'I'm in the city a lot, though,' he said, suddenly serious. 'I have my professorship at the university and I come to a lot of society meetings and conferences here.'

They arrived at the subway station. It was getting colder but it was still mild enough that she didn't need her hat. The air was crisp though, a harbinger of the cold snaps that would arrive in the coming months.

'Well, this is me,' she said.

'I really enjoyed tonight,' he said, shoving his hands into his pockets, 'and I didn't expect to,' he added with a laugh.

Adelaide laughed too. She looked around her.

'Well, that makes two of us.'

'Could I call you sometime?' he said, suddenly. 'Maybe we can do this again?'

She was ready to say no. It was her standard response. But something stopped her. What if she just gave him her number, what if she just said yes? What was the harm in having a drink, some food with someone interesting, someone nice. It was just dinner, a date, it didn't have to be a big deal. She saw him waiting for her to answer. *You're turning it into a big deal by taking so long to answer.*

'Sure,' she said, smiling, and scribbled her number on

a page from her reporter's pad, which came everywhere with her, even to the bar in her handbag. When she looked back up, Michael leaned in swiftly, and kissed her firmly, the French way, on both cheeks.

'Goodnight, Adelaide.'

She was surprised to feel herself flush, the outward expression of something blooming inside. Something she hadn't felt in a very long time. Something she thought had died.

'Good night, Michael,' she said, and as she stepped down into the subway, she smiled to herself.

Chapter 41

Susannah woke to John's voice in the kitchen. She must have fallen asleep on the couch. Again. He was on the phone. He was laughing. When he hung up, he said, 'Good morning. Are you feeling any better?'

She ignored him.

'Who was that on the phone?'

'Oh, just work.'

'Elena?'

John paused.

'No, it was Abbie. She said to say hi. She was ringing about—'

'Let me guess,' Susannah said bitterly, 'an emergency at work? With the actress? You're not going to make it to court today?'

'No, Susannah, please. I am going to make it to court, of course I will, I'll just be a little late. I just have to go in for an hour, two hours max. You're not even on the stand today. I wouldn't go if I didn't have to.'

'Don't worry about it, John. I'll see you in court.'

She couldn't believe he was doing this but she just didn't have the emotional bandwidth to get into it with him right now. It would have to wait.

Chapter 42

'Well, here she comes now,' said Julie, smiling. 'The man trap.'

Adelaide rolled her eyes.

'Will you stop! How was *your* night Julie?'

'Satisfactory, even if the man I went home with wasn't the man I intended to go home with. What happened with you and the professor?'

'Nothing!' Adelaide said, craning her neck and waving her hands in a motion she hoped the waitress would interpret as 'please bring coffee'.

'Nothing happened,' she hissed. 'He walked me to the subway and I said goodbye.'

'That's *it*?' Julie said, horrified.

'That's it – oh, thank you,' Adelaide said to the waitress. 'Could I get scrambled eggs and some sour-dough toasted, please? Thank you. Okay, he asked for my number.'

'I knew it!' said Julie, triumphant. 'I threw everything at him and he barely looked at me. I thought I was losing my touch, getting old, until I realised it was *you* he liked. Not a lot a girl can do about chemistry.'

'I'm sorry. I really didn't do anything to encourage him. I knew you were interested.'

'Don't worry, Adelaide. You couldn't have encouraged him less. But the heart wants what it wants I'm afraid and the doctor looks like he has set his sights on you, *despite* your flirting skills.'

'Well thank you very much but I am not in the market for a relationship. He's very nice but nothing's happening there.'

'All right,' Julie said sipping her coffee and flicking her eyebrows.

'What about the guy you were with at the bar, who is he? And will you be seeing him again tonight?'

'We've arranged to meet for dinner . . . Actually, he is quite sweet. He's a bit young and a bit enthusiastic but I'll set him straight. I don't want to break any hearts. And then I'll be on my way again, the littlest hobo of romance.'

'*Ho*-bo is right,' said Adelaide laughing.

'Hey!' Julie protested, but she was smiling too. Adelaide picked over her eggs. She was thinking about seeing the professor again. Nothing had happened and yet it felt as if something had.

Chapter 43

Susannah sat beside Dana, John's seat empty behind her. By 11 a.m., he still hadn't shown up.

'Where is he?' Dana whispered, as she stood to question the next witness. 'It looks bad that he's not here supporting you.'

Susannah's secretary, Roberta Melfini, who had alerted her to her car alarm going off on the morning Louise died, took the stand.

'How long have you worked for Dr Rice, Mrs Melfini?' Dana asked.

'Ten years this year.'

'What sort of boss is she?'

'She's fair. She expects high standards but she is very kind and decent, particularly if I ever need time off for my kids or my mother. Dr Rice is always very understanding around that. She is generous too. She always gives me a personal gift at Christmas and flowers on my birthday and I get an annual bonus that I know my administrative colleagues don't get from their bosses.'

'How would you describe your relationship?'

'Professional, supportive, with very clear boundaries. I like her and respect her and I think she feels the same way about me but we don't socialise ever, and we are not friends. We are ... friendly, though.'

'On the morning in question, did Dr Rice seem worried about anything, or hurried, as if she were trying to get through her patients more quickly than usual? Did she seem different to you in any way? Did she seem particularly distracted, or upset to you?'

'No, she seemed her normal self.'

'And how would you describe that?'

'Efficient, unhurried. She never got panicked or stressed that I could tell.'

'No further questions.'

Rogney stepped up.

'What kind of a mother would you describe Dr Rice as?'

'I don't have a lot of insight into that. I have rarely seen her with her children.'

'Oh? Doesn't that strike you as strange?'

'No, none of the doctors at the hospital bring their children to work. She has a framed picture of her husband and daughters on her desk if that's the kind of thing you're talking about?'

The jury sniggered. Susannah felt a rush of love for her secretary.

'On the morning in question, when baby Louise died, did anything strike you as different that day, anything out of the ordinary?'

'We were busier than usual that day. I had texted her the previous night to tell her we had a very tight morning ahead of us. We were overbooked, as we usually were, but we were down a doctor too so things were a bit more pressurised than usual. But nothing she couldn't handle.'

'At what time did you notice Dr Rice's car alarm was going off.'

'The first time was early enough, maybe 8.30 a.m.? I told Dr Rice. She seemed irritated about it. Asked me to book the car into the garage. It was a new car.'

'Yes, a top of the range Mercedes, I believe,' Rogney said, with a side-eye to the jury. 'Did she at any point look concerned, worried, upset? Did she look as if she might be doing something wrong, as if she needed to go check on the car?'

'No.'

'At what point did you realise something was wrong?'

For the first time Roberta's feisty demeanour abandoned her. She started to talk quietly.

'I was just packing up for lunch and I saw her run by me, like *really run*. She was gone so quickly but I could hear her. She was sort of whispering and shouting at the same time. I knew something was really, really wrong so I followed her.'

'And what did you discover, when you found her in the car park?'

'I'll never forget it.' She started to cry. Susannah gave her a tight smile and a nod from her table as the tears rolled down her face too. They were both back in the moment, back on that awful day. The courtroom door banged open and John finally made his entrance.

'Excuse me, your honour.'

Rogney looked irritated by the interruption but found his way back to the question he wanted to ask.

'And can you tell us did she say anything, at any point?'

'She just kept saying, "My baby, my baby, I've killed my baby."' Roberta let out a sob. Rogney put her out of her misery.

'No further questions, Your Honour.'

John took his place behind Susannah. He leaned forward and squeezed her shoulder. There was that scent again. The unfamiliar soap, becoming more familiar. The prosecution called Joy Leung, Managing Director of Baby Einsteins Montessori.

'Ms Leung, how long have you been running Baby Einsteins?' Rogney asked.

'Seventeen years.'

'Have you always provided a weekend service?'

'No, but I noticed about eleven years ago that there was a gap in the market. A lot of parents don't work nine to five, Monday to Friday, so I thought a weekend service would be a good way to increase revenue without expanding our premises. Turns out we were right and our weekend service was at capacity as soon as we introduced it.'

'Did Dr Rice avail of this service?'

'Yes, maybe one weekend in four, two in four if she was on call.'

Rogney pounced again.

'What do you mean, "if she was on call"? Did she use the weekend service when she wasn't on call?'

Ms Leung squirmed.

'Ye-es, a lot of our parents will use the weekend service so they can catch up on unfinished work, do grocery shopping in peace, things that they don't have time to do during the working week. Some parents use it just to rest, have a little quiet time or a little quality time together as a couple. Dr Rice left Emma with us every day and we took both girls once a month on the weekend so she and her husband could have a brunch together on Saturdays. She said it was their date night but they had to do it in the morning because they were too tired to do it at night.'

Susannah lifted her hand to her forehead in mortification. She was horrified. So many things that had been laid out as evidence in this court case had been things she had said in jest, or out of discomfort, or out of social awkwardness, trying to fill uncomfortable silences in conversation. Most of the times she used the weekend service she had actually been working. She said the date night thing because she didn't want to be judged for working at the weekend instead of seeing her kids.

Rogney walked slowly around the court room.

'Ms Leung,' he began. 'How would you describe Dr Rice?'

'Very nice, very polite, always on time with drop-offs and collection. Emma and Louise were always well-looked after, very clean, always beautifully dressed.'

Rogney laughed in a patronising way.

'Oh no, I'm sure that's all true, but what I meant was what kind of mother was she? Was just like all the other parents or was she different?'

'Objection, Your Honour. Relevance?'

'I'll allow it.'

'Not particularly. Well, maybe only that Dr Rice was always very quick. She was never rushing but you could see she had somewhere to be. She never hung around to chat. But we knew she had a very important job.'

'Did you ever get to see Louise on these drop-offs?'

'Only from a distance. She always stayed in the car.'

'Right,' said Rogney. 'So she left baby Louise *unattended* in the car, with the engine running while she dropped Emma in to you?'

Susannah's heart sank. Everyone left their engines running. The daycare encouraged it. They wanted to create a drop-and-go system like the ones that operated at the nearby schools. They actively discouraged parents from coming in, from hanging around. It was starting to look like Louise spent half her life waiting in Susannah's idling car. She tried not to panic but the word 'Guilty' was ringing in her ears.

'Well, the car was right beside—'

Rogney cut her dead.

'What about Christmas shows, end-of-term performances, that kind of thing,' he said. 'Did she attend those?'

'Not every parent can go to these events during work-time. We always send a DVD recording to all the parents.'

'Just answer the question, please, Ms Leung.' Rogney could turn so nasty so quickly, thought Susannah. Joy made an apologetic face at Susannah. She looked so humiliated.

'No.'

Rogney was quiet. He looked at the jury, with raised eyebrows.

'My wife and I have six children – yes, God has been good to us. When the kids were small, and life was very, very busy, my wife and I, we split the school concerts up between us,' he said casting a conspiratorial look at the members of the jury who smiled back at him. 'Just so we wouldn't have to both attend all of the performances but so that our children would still know that we cared, that we were there for them. It was tough getting out of work, finding the time, but somehow we found a way. No further questions, Your Honour.'

The judge gave him a weary look before announcing a recess for lunch. 'We'll hear from the final witnesses after lunch.'

Chapter 44

When the court broke for lunch, Adelaide and Julie went to the local diner to go over the morning's testimony.

'The thing I can't stop thinking about is how does she manage to look so composed, so *normal?*' Julie asked. 'How do you go on after something like this?'

Adelaide looked down at the menu and pretended to be preoccupied choosing between the chicken salad and the Caesar salad, even though she always had the same thing.

'Mmm,' she said. The truth was she knew too much about it.

'Could you ever be happy again? Especially if it was *your fault*, as opposed to, say, they got cancer or had a crib death or something?'

'Thanks for those hypothetical examples of blame-free child deaths, Julie,' Adelaide said. 'Jesus, can we talk about something else?' She ordered the Caesar salad and folded her hands. She closed the menu.

'But seriously,' Julie went on, 'how would you go on if something like that happened to you?' Adelaide accepted, as usual with Julie, that she would just have to engage. Her palms were sweating, her heart beating as the memories swarmed her head. She knew her emotions were getting the better of her but she felt she couldn't *not* say something.

'Have you read the stats about parents whose kids die? Do you know how they go on? They kill themselves, Julie. Or they become alcoholics. Or their lives are ruined. They get fired from their jobs. Their marriages end. They can't function. Even in cases like crib death, the parent will often blame themselves: "Was the room too warm?" Or, "Should I have put them down on their back instead of their side or their front or upside down?" and it's all a way of trying to imagine they could have done something but for the most part these things are tragedies not because the parents did something wrong but because they just had utter, awful bad luck. Usually parents with other children manage to keep going for them. I was surprised to learn about the doctor's suicide attempt because of that. Usually the parents can keep going for the other kid.'

'Jesus,' said Julie. 'How do you *know* all this?'

Adelaide felt like she had been caught out, she had

said too much but she fumbled an answer. 'I read it somewhere in my research for the trial.'

'Did you never want to have a kid?' Julie asked. It came like a lightning bolt. Adelaide would never, ever get used to being asked this question.

Every time Adelaide thought about telling Julie about Zane and Curtis it was like a bubble inflated in her throat, the words stoppered securely underneath. It was physically impossible for her to do it, whether she wanted to or not. Sometimes she felt that if she didn't tell anyone, it couldn't be real and she could keep pretending that it had happened to someone else.

'I think that ship has sailed for me,' said Adelaide. 'But you're still young – would you?'

It was an inelegant sidestep, a gentle slice shot that put the ball back in Julie's court.

Julie scoffed. 'First of all, I am two years older than you. If the ship hasn't sailed for me, it's certainly still in the dock for you. But whether it is biologically possible or not is beside the point for me, I decided a long time ago that I just don't want to have kids.'

'Really? Why not?'

'When I was twenty-two,' Julie said, 'I was in a really serious relationship with a guy. We met at college, we dated for a while, graduated, got jobs here in New York and got serious. When he asked me to marry him I was one hundred per cent invested. I had our lives all planned out. We would live in our little one-bed apartment until we had our first child and then we would move to a big family house in the suburbs. I was so keen on us having a big family, at least four children, and I couldn't wait to marry him.'

'So what happened?' Adelaide asked, cramming a cos lettuce leaf into her mouth.

'He was a TV cameraman and used to tour around the states a lot. It turned out I was his at-home-girlfriend and he had found an on-the-road-girlfriend too, who just happened to be the reporter on his news crew.'

Adelaide whistled.

'How did you find out?'

'Banal. She called him and I answered his phone. I was devastated, beyond shocked. It turns out she was too. From that moment on I became a little bit cynical, like, I lost that belief that things always turn out for the best.'

'But did he ever explain himself?' Adelaide asked.

'He told me he loved us both, that it wasn't as simple as choosing one of us. And then it turned out, it *was* actually that simple because he chose her.'

'Wow, Julie ... so you never wanted kids after that?'

'Well, I think it was always going to be the whole package or nothing. I certainly never wanted to get married after that and the two kind of went together for me so I went off the whole idea. It did teach me one good early lesson, though. I gave up a lot for him and his career. I shelved my plans and I worked in casual jobs because it allowed me to be the anchor for his peripatetic life and career. I had slowed down my own progress for him. After he left, I quit freelancing and got a job in *Fox*. Men come and go, but I love this job. And can you imagine what would happen if I met someone now, or had a kid? All this would go away.'

Adelaide found she couldn't disagree with her because she knew work was never quite the same.

'Has there really never been anyone serious since, though?'

'There have been some really nice guys who have been sincere, you know, who wanted to have relationships and I've been tempted, but when it came down to choosing, I always chose me. It's strange, I didn't think this at the time of the break-up but looking back now, I think that something broke in me at that point. I have always thought that I'd get back to the person I was before then but now I think we don't ever really get to go back to being the people we were before bad things happened to us.'

Adelaide found she had no answer for Julie on this one. She agreed and she realised she too had been living her life in expectation of getting back to the person she was when she first became a mother, the person she was before she had lost Zane and Curtis. But she was never getting back to that person.

'And besides,' Julie went on, 'media is not a career that cares about any kind of relationship, whether you're a parent or a wife or a lover, it comes first, *it* is the baby that needs constant feeding. So why complicate all that *and* give someone the chance to screw me over ... *again*?'

'You are such an incurable romantic,' Adelaide said. 'Maybe men can feel your icy winds blowing.'

'Look who's talking. They call you the Ice Queen in the press pool. Beware the frozen heart.'

Suddenly Adelaide wasn't laughing any more.

'Do they?'

'Not everyone,' Julie said, realising the fun had gone out of the conversation. 'It's more that they feel they don't know you, you're closed with the guys. Most of us have had a few drunken slip-ups on the circuit but you've never shit on your own doorstep.'

Adelaide felt wounded. She had never considered that her efforts at self-protection and self-preservation could come across as aloofness. 'What can I say,' she stammered, a little tetchy. 'I don't sleep around, which saves me the whole, "It's not you, it's me" conversation or the, "I'm really sorry, but I'm just too busy for a relationship" one. When really what I mean is, "I don't like the way you chew your food, and I didn't like the way you were unexpectedly wearing briefs and not boxers underneath your trousers, and I also didn't like the way you made yourself at home in my kitchen the next day and wouldn't just *leave* when all I wanted to do was get on with my day." It's just easier this way. So no, I don't think I'll be having children any time soon either.' Adelaide was trying to laugh it off as a joke and really hoped Julie was buying it, even though her heart was pounding so loudly she thought Julie must be able to hear it.

'I'll drink to that,' said Julie, clinking her can of Coke against Adelaide's. 'Still though, I can't imagine what it must be like to lose a child like Dr Sue. It must be the worst feeling on earth.'

Adelaide nodded, 'I'm sure it is.'

Chapter 45

Susannah sat in their courthouse meeting room. John sat across from her in silence. Dana had suggested she use the time over lunch to rest, gather her energy, take her mind off things but that was impossible in this room. Impossible, really, at any time for Susannah.

She didn't know how to switch off. It was something she read about on *Goop*. It wasn't a real concept, a thing that people actually achieved. It was terminally aspirational.

If you wanted a clean house, a high-flying career, date nights and sex with your husband, 21st-century friendship groups, *and* children, something had to be thrown onto the sacrificial bonfire.

Susannah had discussed the issue with John before. His answer had made her blood pressure skyrocket. He had said, 'You feminists started it all anyway.'

'Excuse me?' Susannah said, whipping around to

face him so fast that a strand of blonde hair got caught in her mouth.

He laughed nervously.

'I just mean when women started working full-time, it skewed the norm. It inflated the basic family income to double what it was before, well, *not quite* double ...'

'No,' she said sourly.

John ignored her petulance. '... But that increase in income as standard inflated the housing market so that pretty quickly *only* two-income families could afford a home, even an entry-level starter home, and once that became embedded it meant both parents *needing* to work was also a standard and they would have to work two jobs for ever to keep up with the inflated mortgage payments, not to mention the vast cost of childcare.'

'John, if you're trying to piss me off, it's working. Are you honestly suggesting that women becoming financially independent is the reason we are where we are? Jesus, you don't even *see* your misogyny.'

John recoiled.

'It's not misogynistic for me to present the economic facts, Susannah. I think you're taking this too personally,' he laughed. 'The facts are, if you want to live in a house, drive a car, buy health insurance and have a baby, it is simply impossible to do it on one wage. That is the legacy of feminism. The fact that families used to do it on one wage is as irretrievable a dream as the fact that dodos used to exist. Unless, of course, you're on a wage like yours but that basically applies to about one per cent of the population.'

Susannah had been furious with him at the time but she knew one of the reasons it had made her so angry was because there was some truth in it.

'Susannah? Susannah?' She looked up. Dana was staring at her. 'Are you okay, honey? You're miles away.'

'I need to get out of here,' she said. 'I'll be back in a bit.'

Chapter 46

Julie and Adelaide finished their food. It always amazed Adelaide how quickly they fell into a routine, eating lunch in the same diner, at the same table, every day. Getting to know the waitresses by name, in whatever location they were working before disappearing again, on to the next story. At least they were in New York for this one. Adelaide had to admit, it was nice to stay put, on home soil for a change.

Adelaide's phone buzzed. A text. She sneaked a look at it under the table. Her heart skipped a beat. It was Michael.

I am in the city tomorrow for work. Would you
have dinner with me? M

Adelaide smiled what she thought was a secret smile but Julie sniffed it out. She took a slug of her Coke.

'Was that the professor?'

'Oh Jesus, Julie, for God's sake,' said Adelaide.

'What? I can tell when people like each other. It's my Spidey Sense. Why are you blushing?'

'Please stop.'

'What!? You just look ... happy.'

Christ, she missed nothing. Adelaide tried to shut her mouth but found she wanted to talk about him, which was also unusual for her.

'He wants me to go for dinner but I don't think I can.'

'What, why not?'

'Because ... he'll probably wear briefs instead of boxer shorts and then I'll just have to hurry him out at breakfast and I'll never have a decent neurologist to call for a quote again because it will be too embarrassing.' She tilted her nose at the clock. 'It's nearly two. Come on.'

'Spoilsport,' said Julie and they paid for lunch and started to head back to the courthouse.

'I'll catch up with you,' Adelaide said, 'I just need to use the ladies.'

She took her phone out while she peed. She followed her usual routine – Twitter updates, quick look at Instagram, and then another look at Michael's text. She couldn't suppress the smile that seemed to start inside of her.

She read and re-read the text:

I am in the city tomorrow for work. Would you
have dinner with me? M

She typed quickly, not giving herself time to think or change her mind.

That would be lovely. You choose where. Her finger hovered before she added an 'x' and pressed send. She felt dizzy. She hadn't put an 'x' after anything that wasn't a multiple-choice box in a long time. She watched the message turn blue and felt her heart beat like a butterfly.

The sound of a flush in the neighboring toilet stall snapped her out of her reverie. She left the cubicle and washed her hands. She smiled stupidly at the sink, not feeling the water run over her hands, lost in her thoughts as she mechanically rubbed soap between her fingers. She was startled out of her trance by a woman emerging from the other stall. Adelaide saw her in the mirror, recognised her immediately, knew her face nearly as well as her own by now. She cast her own eyes down, grabbed a paper towel and hastily left the bathroom, narrowly avoiding having to speak to Dr Sue.

Chapter 47

Back in the courtroom, Susannah felt like layer after layer of skin was being stripped away from her. With each witness, she became more exposed, more raw.

Her boss was on the stand. Brian Gore was chief clinical director of the hospital. Dana opened the questioning.

'What is Dr Rice's position at the hospital?'

'She is clinical lead in Paediatrics and also runs the medical assessment unit. She sits on several boards, teaches at the university attached to our hospital and is lead researcher on clinical trials that we run with patients. She publishes her findings regularly in inter-national journals, and she sits on the European and American representative societies for paediatrics.'

'What would you say her average week looks like?'

'Well, I can tell you she is contracted to work sixty hours a week, which she does and then with the external commitments, societies, research papers, any other extracurricular work like TV or media appearances, I would estimate she works at least an eighty-hour week. She's very organised.'

'How reliable is she?'

'Rock solid. She's one of our best doctors, probably our best. A quick-response mind, rapid and accurate diagnoses, superb expertise and knowledge. I have called her on Christmas Day, on personal days, on Thanksgiving, and she has always picked up the phone. She even came in to work on her daughter's first birthday.'

Dana practically cut him off.

'Thank you, Mr Gore, no further questions.'

Something cold and dreadful seeped into Susannah's blood. Rogney stood up.

'Listening to you describe Dr Rice's schedule, I found myself wondering when she gets time to see her patients, never mind her children.'

'Objection, Your Honour!'

'Withdrawn.'

Susannah was being punished for being all of the things she was supposed to be: responsible, reliable, dedicated.

Rogney looked down at his notes.

'You mentioned that Dr Rice came in to work on her daughter's first birthday? Well, that really is dedi-cation,' he said, making eye contact with several jury members, his voice dripping with sarcasm. 'Was she rostered to work that day?'

'No, she had booked the day off for the birthday party. But we got an acute patient, a kid with sepsis and they were going downhill fast. We just didn't have anyone with the expertise that Dr Rice has. So we called her and asked could she take over the kid, which she did. We apologised naturally but she said it was okay, her husband was at their little girl's party and she was only gone for an hour or two, max. She saved the little boy's life.'

Rogney ignored the last sentence.

'But missed her daughter's first birthday party. Mr Gore, forgive the personal question, but do you have children?'

'Yes, I have two boys, twins,' he said with a proud smile.

'How did you celebrate their first birthday parties? Big deal?'

'Oh yes, well, they're twins so it was a landmark. My wife organised a party, caterers, magicians, the whole shebang. I don't think our wedding was as big an affair,' he laughed, but it died on the air.

'Let me ask you, if someone had called from work on your sons' first birthday party and asked you to come in to work, would you have left the party?'

'Are you kidding? My wife would have killed me . . . ' The realisation finally dawned on him. He had hung

Susannah out to dry without intending to. ' ... I, but I mean, if the requirement was there, if it was necessary, well then yes, yes, any of us would, we *all* would. That's the deal, that's the job.'

'But would you perhaps had tried to solve it over the phone instead of rushing in?'

'That's our protocol. The same protocol Dr Rice would have followed that day.'

'Let me ask a different question. In terms of how important Dr Rice's job was to her, where do you think it ranked on her personal scale?'

'Objection, Your Honour. The witness is not in a position to know this.'

'I'll allow it. Please answer the question, Mr Gore.'

He paused. He didn't want to answer the question.

'Number one,' he said miserably.

'No further questions, Your Honour.'

Chapter 48

The last witness of the day was Adam. Susannah was flooded with relief. She knew Adam was steady, scientific, and most importantly on her side. She knew the legal team were relying on Michael and Adam's testimony in particular to clear Susannah of any guilt. Michael was there to show that it was possible to accidentally forget a baby and Adam was there to show that Susannah was not the kind of person who neglected a baby.

Dana stood up.

'You've been treating Dr Rice for five months now. What was your first impression of her?'

'Actually, my initial feeling was one of respect, awe: that she was still functioning under the incredible stresses and strains that she was facing. Admiration at how well she seemed to be coping.'

Calm washed over Susannah. Yes, this was what

the jury needed to hear. After two days of warped and twisted testimony, speculation about Susannah's mental health, Adam would clear the water.

'As you have gotten to know her over the past few months, have you come to any conclusions about what happened to Louise that day, how it could have happened?'

Rogney rose.

'Objection, Your Honour, the witness is not qualified to comment.'

'Sustained.'

'I'll rephrase. Is Dr Rice the type of person who neglects her duty of care?''

'Absolutely not. Everything about her refutes that. Her *raison d'être* is her responsibility, the duty she feels to her patients. Dr Rice is a classic overachiever, but when we see this personality type in women often it is combined with an identity issue. There is no separation between their personal selves and their professional achievements. You usually end up with someone who puts enormous pressure on themselves to succeed, in every area of their lives. They go above and beyond to deliver and they care *deeply* about doing the best job they can, because it is not just a professional reflection but a personal reflection. For someone like Dr Rice, this would apply to motherhood too.'

'Do you believe she is capable of consciously, intentionally having left her baby in her car that morning, putting her baby in harm's way? Was it possible in your informed professional, medical opinion that she could be deliberately negligent?'

'No.'

Susannah let her head fall back a little with relief. Adam turned to the jury.

'Dr Rice is simply not wired to break the rules. She is simply too invested in doing the right thing. She would never have done that deliberately. She would never have left Louise out of her sight for even a minute. It would never have even crossed her mind. I believe it would be so far out of character as to be impossible.'

'No further questions, Your Honour.'

Rogney stood up. Susannah instantly felt on edge. He smiled a little at Adam.

'You say that any kind of neglect would be completely out of character for Dr Rice. But she has already shown that she can have moments where she behaves – in her own words – "out of character". She behaved "out of character" when she tried to kill herself—'

'Objection, Your Honour!'

'Withdrawn,' said Rogney, throwing a smirk to the jury. They had heard what he needed them to hear.

'You said you "admired" Dr Rice. How so?'

Rogney could regroup and change tack at the drop of a hat. If Susannah wasn't on the opposite team, she might have been impressed.

'Well, as I said, she was coping admirably in the face

of unbearable tragedy, functioning way past the point where most normal people would have collapsed.'

'What do you mean by normal people?'

'Well, the average person, people like me, or you, people who don't reach the highest points in their careers and industries.'

'Dr Susannah Rice is not normal, though, is she?'

'I'm not sure what you mean?'

'Her drive, her ambition, her desire to succeed at all costs ... it's not normal.'

Dana was on her feet.

'Objection, Your Honour!'

'Withdrawn.' Rogney held up a hand in lukewarm apology to the judge without breaking stride. 'You have been treating Dr Rice for more than five months now. What is your opinion of the kind of person she is?'

'She is kind, a loving mother and a good wife, very generous towards other people, completely dedicated and committed to her job and the children she treats, at the cost of any kind of social life or downtime.

'Would you describe yourself as friends?'

'Our relationship is professional but I am interested and invested in her personal welfare.'

'What about your former patient,' he glanced down at his notes, 'a twenty-four-year-old girl called Elaine Baldwin? Were you invested in her personal welfare?'

Rogney held up a picture of what was clearly Adam kissing a very young-looking woman. There were cries and gasps. Someone clapped. Susannah squeezed her eyes shut. *This is not happening. This is not happening.*

Adam paled, visibly.

'I, uh, I don't see—'

'Were you invested in her personal welfare,' Rogney carried on, 'when you began a sexual relationship with her when she was still under your professional care?'

The courtroom erupted again into gasps and cries and the judge snapped her gavel angrily.

'Order! Order!'

'Objection, Your Honour!'

'I'll allow it. Please answer the question, Dr O'Shea.'

'That was a long time ago. And I had stopped treating her when we began having a relationship. It's not illegal.'

Susannah looked at Dana. *Why didn't we know this?* Dana was as wrong-footed as Susannah.

'No, it's not illegal,' Rogney said, 'but it is frowned upon and advised against by the national governing body, the Association of Psychiatrists of America, under whose codes of practice you are bound.' Rogney turned to the jury. 'Are we to trust testimony from a man who can't maintain a professional distance from his patients?'

'Objection!'

'Sustained.'

'Dr O'Shea, I'll ask you again, is your relationship with Dr Rice purely professional?'

Susannah put her hands over her mouth. Rogney was holding another photo in his hand. She couldn't see it yet.

He held it up for the jury to see before swinging around to face Adam. The picture showed them hugging. It was the day she had told him that she was pregnant. He had hugged her to congratulate her. The hug had lasted all of two seconds. Susannah looked behind her at John. He had questions written all over his face. How could he even consider it?

'Are you having an affair with Dr Rice?'

'I am not.'

'No further questions, Your Honour.'

Adam stepped down from the stand. He looked at Susannah and mouthed the words *I'm so sorry* as he passed her. What was he doing? That just made it look like he was guilty of something, like they *were* having an affair. Christ, what a mess!

The judge looked mad as hell. She spoke tightly.

'That concludes the witness testimony. As we are ahead of schedule we will break for fifteen minutes and I'll hear closing arguments when we reconvene.'

Susannah looked at Dana. This couldn't be happening. The trial felt imbalanced, even to her inexperienced legal mind. Rogney was winning. She had been hopeful, right up until Adam's bombshell, that it might be alright, that things might come good for her, but now she knew it was all stacked against her. She panicked.

Her heart started to race, darkness edged in from her peripheral vision, a prickle crept up her neck. Could that really be the sum of her *defence*?

Everyone around her stood, stretched and shook out their legs as if they had just seen a particularly long and harrowing movie, before walking outside into the sunshine. Susannah couldn't move. She was certain of one thing only. She was going to jail.

Chapter 49

Adelaide didn't drink much any more but she really wanted a drink now. Instead, she lit a cigarette with trembling hands and inhaled deeply. *Get it together, Adelaide. You just need to make it through the next hour or two of closing arguments and then this whole nightmare will be over.* She sat back down beside Julie, who was swiping left, hard and fast on Tinder. How could she do that, just switch off the part of her brain that dealt with the court case?

'Any luck?' Adelaide asked, in an effort to distract herself.

'It's not a great app for the female thirty-four to forty bracket,' Julie said clicking her screen off. 'I'm not old enough to be a cougar and I'm not young enough for the septuagenarian billionaires. It's a sugar baby's market, Adelaide. Got a spare one of those?' She nodded at Adelaide's cigarette.

Adelaide passed her the box of cigarettes and the lighter.

'Well, things have taken a turn for the grim, no doubt about it. Did you see the doctor during that testimony? She was on another planet.'

'I can't say I blame her,' Adelaide said. 'We've covered a lot of tough stories but that was difficult to listen to.'

Julie twirled the filter of the cigarette between her finger and thumb. They were unusually quiet; Adelaide kept trying and failing to think of something light-hearted to say to shift the bleak tone back to their usual jocular footing. Instead they sat and smoked in silence. Julie stood up to return to court but Adelaide felt physically incapable of going back inside. Her mind was with Louise, with Zane. Did he suffer? Was he in pain before the childcare workers found him? The thoughts were unbearable. She felt so sorry for Susannah too. She was clearly paralysed by her grief but it looked like she was frozen. Adelaide knew she was just unreachable. Adelaide knew it because she was a frozen splinter herself. But she was worried now. She knew in her heart that Susannah was innocent but she had sat through enough court cases to know when a trial could go either way and this one was as unpredictable as they came.

Chapter 50

'Whatever way you look at it, this woman,' Rogney said, pointing towards Susannah, 'is responsible for the death of a *precious baby*. Louise Annabel Rice. I say her name lest we forget her.'

Susannah felt sick at the sound of her baby's name in Rogney's mouth. It disgusted her, she felt it sullied Louise to have him speak about her.

'Ask yourself, if Susannah Rice is not to blame, then *who is*? If someone else was minding Louise that day – a childminder, a daycare worker, a stranger – would she still be alive? Most likely. Or if this had happened to Louise while she was in the care of such a person, would Dr Rice be suing them right now for the unlawful death of her child? You can be sure of it!

'The facts of this case are undeniable. An innocent baby is dead because her mother refused to change her way of life to accommodate her tiny baby's needs. Her mother thought she could leave her sleeping child in her car while she sorted out what she considered to be more important problems. She even turned off her car alarm, which was set off by her baby desperately struggling for help, for her *life*. Susannah Rice could have saved her baby. If she just walked out to her car, checked why the alarm was going off, she would have found her baby alive. But no. She was too busy. Too important.'

Susannah felt like she had been punched. She knew he was right. She looked over her shoulder at John. She had wondered all along how he had felt about this, the fact that, if it wasn't for her, their daughter would still be alive. But John was staring straight at Rogney.

'Then, after the perfectly avoidable death of her baby, we saw that she was willing to take her own life and leave her one remaining daughter orphaned without a mother. We all know how difficult minding children can be, most of us accept it. But not Dr Susannah Rice. Her intellect could not lower itself to such menial work. Her numerous degrees from Ivy League colleges were not hard-earned just to be wasted pureeing vegetables. She made her choice, between her first love and her baby, and let me be clear, her first love, her career, won out.'

Rogney played the avenging angel of helpless children and perfect self-sacrificing mothers. He beat his breast at the jury's bench, he beat his table and wrung his hands to hammer home his points.

'I beg of you, ladies and gentlemen of the jury, do not let this happen again. Do not let this happen to one more child. Let Susannah Rice be a warning to all those parents who take risks with their children. Let her be an example to those who put their babies somewhere down the line in their order of priorities. Your car is not childcare. Your phone is not a babysitter. Your TV is not a school. It's time we woke up to our responsibilities and started looking after our most precious resource – our children. Ladies and gentlemen of the jury, I thank you for your service to this court, and the children of this nation.'

Susannah was slack in her seat. Rogney had appealed to the jury to use Susannah as an example, a deterrent. How could anyone refuse that?

Susannah was glad that Dana got to speak last. At least the final impression, and her final memory of evidence, would be positive.

Dana spoke calmly, reasonably. She spoke about herself as a mother, spoke about seeing Susannah with her children. She reminded the jury of their most powerful defence, the testimony of Professor Michael Thomas's *scientific* evidence – she stressed the scientific part.

'I put it to you ladies and gentlemen of the jury, that my client, Dr Rice, is also a victim here, a victim of the society we live in. A society that expects mothers to work as if they don't have children, and to mother as if they don't have careers, and to maintain the veneer of perfection all the while. A society that doesn't offer them any maternity leave or benefit, a society that suggests they are a worthless underclass if they quit their careers to look after their children, a society that suggests they are unnatural, unfeeling, incomplete women if they don't have children. Susannah Rice's dedication to her career as well as her children is clear for everyone to see. But if you can't see all of this from looking at Dr Rice, I ask you to look only at the evidence. And I'm talking about the real, scientific evidence, not the opinions, not the gossip and hearsay that has been dressed-up and passed off in this courtroom as evidence. I'm talking about facts, hard, indisputable facts.

'And the fact is, the prosecution has not presented a single shred of evidence to support its idea that my client is a bad mother, that she made a deliberate decision to leave her baby unattended in her car. And by doing so, in damning Dr Susannah Rice in this way, they are condemning every ordinary mother and father in this courtroom today. Every mother and father who has filled up their car on a gas station forecourt and left their child in the back seat as they paid for gas. Every parent who has made a mistake or forgotten something or taken the wrong route to work or taken their eye off their child in a mall or the soft-play centre. We live in a society at breaking point – stress, speed, traffic, smart phones, work, family, partners, financial burdens, guilt, pressure to be fit, pressure to be thin. Our human brains were simply not built to cope with this.'

Dana paused to mark a shift in tone to the conspiratorial one that Rogney had been using with the jury all along, the tone that said, *We're just the same, you and I.*

'Let me make a confession. I have forgotten to put my child's seatbelt on, more than once, and not realised until I've gotten home. I have been so distracted that, more than once, I have accidentally driven off with my latte on the roof of my car.' This got a few smiles of recognition from the jury. 'I've accidentally locked my kids in the car and had to call a mechanic to get them out.' This one got a couple of solemn nods. 'When my youngest child was just an infant, I put her in her car seat, got in the driver's seat and drove off leaving her stroller on the sidewalk.'

There was an appreciative murmur of laughter from the room. Dana turned to take in the whole courtroom now.

'You're laughing because these are familiar scenarios. You recognise the situation. They have happened to most of us because in the world we all live in, we are *all* running on empty, we are *all* under pressure, we are *all* trying to be in three places at once, and in the worst case scenario, we are *all* Dr Susannah Rice.'

She looked at the faces of the jury.

'We're all living in the same world. The only

difference between you and me and my client here is that we got lucky.'

The judge spoke. 'This court is now in recess until Monday morning at 10 a.m. when we will hear a verdict, if the jury has reached one.' She banged her gavel.

Dana stood and started packing her files away into her little wheelie case but Susannah sat frozen in her seat. She couldn't move.

'Do you think the jury will have a verdict by Monday?' John asked Dana.

'It's hard to say,' said Dana.

'How do you think we did? Do you think the jury is on our side?'

'You can never really tell,' Dana said, 'but I think we held our own.'

'Are we going to meet up to run through things over the weekend?'

'There's nothing left to go through now,' Dana said, a weary quality to her voice. 'I suggest, if you can, you should try to relax, take your mind off things. I know it's difficult to do but Monday will come around very quickly. Try to make this weekend a special one for you two and Emma.'

The inference was, it might be their last together for a while.

Chapter 51

When Susannah and John got home, the house was quiet. Oppressively so. Susannah felt like she had been both reprieved and condemned. She was relieved that it was all over, though she knew it wasn't really. At least she didn't have to take the stand, be questioned, hear other people say terrible things about what a terrible mother she was anymore. That part was over.

'I'm so scared, John. I'm so scared of losing everything. I've already lost Louise, and you. I don't want to lose Emma too.'

'What do you mean you've already lost me? You haven't lost me. You have me. I'm yours.'

As she put Emma to bed that night, she wondered would it be one of the last times she did so. She lingered over stories, read five where normally three was the limit. She sat by Emma's bed, holding her little hand, pudgy in hers, until she drifted off. She kissed her velvety cheek, inhaled her head and went downstairs. Every trivial action felt different now, imbued with the weight of the knowledge that it might be the last time she did these things for a long time.

John was standing at the stove, smiling at his phone, while steam enveloped him. She knew from his face he was texting Abbie, even before he hurriedly put his phone down when he saw her.

'I'm making a stir fry. You need to eat, Susannah.' He took a sip of wine. Something felt different between them too.

'Thanks.' She sat up at the island, opposite him. Every time she tried to think of something to say to him the silence wrestled her thoughts into non-existence. John tried a few times himself but each attempt came out as a false start. After a while, the only thing Susannah could think of saying was, 'I know you've been sleeping with Abbie.'

John looked up.

'Susannah . . .'

He looked terrified. What was he going to say? 'It's not what you think'? Or, 'It meant nothing'? But she found she didn't want to hear. Nor did she want to fight. She was too tired.

'It just happened, a couple of times before Louise

was born ... and a few times since. You and I barely saw each other Susannah and most of the time it felt like you didn't want me here. When I tried to talk to you about Louise, you didn't want to hear. And I know it's harder for you but she was my daughter too. I just wanted someone to talk to ...'

She stopped him. 'John, I'm not angry. I realised what was going on a while ago now ... I realise now that things were pretty bad between us before Louise died. And I know I've been wrapped up in my own grief since then and I haven't been fair to you, to the fact that you are grieving too. And I am sorry I couldn't comfort you, couldn't be there for you the way a wife should be. I can't even comfort myself. But John, I think the truth of the fact is I'm not angry because things weren't ever really right between us.' She said this miserably and he nodded his head sadly too. He was breathing oddly and it took a moment for her to see he was crying.

'I've been a bad husband. This is my second marriage and I keep making the same mistake.' He pulled the wok off the hob and came around the counter to her. He stood between her legs, and hugged her tightly, burying his wet face into her neck.

She put her hand on his head.

'It's okay, John. I think we have to try to put this behind us, just put everything behind us and start over again. I think it is best for everyone – we need to think about what's best for this baby, too,' she said, pushing him back to arm's length so she could put her hand on her bump.

'You're right,' he said, smiling. 'We do.'

Chapter 52

The next night, Adelaide was nervous. She walked the seven blocks to the beautiful Spanish restaurant that Michael had chosen. Her lingerie was chafing. She wasn't used to wearing anything fancy but she had run out and made a rash purchase of some black lace underwear that afternoon because she had spent the last ten years wearing utterly utilitarian underwear, designed for function only and she suddenly realised she couldn't possibly wear any of her beige or grey-white memory foam bras and large seamless knickers on a date. That's what this was, wasn't it? A date. Was she really going on a date, after all this time? Her stomach lurched.

She was nervous, she realised, because she cared. She cared about Michael. She wanted him to like her. She wanted to see him. She got a thrill when she thought of him.

The food was tapas. He ordered for them both, but only after checking with her. He ate there a lot and knew what was really good.

The food was spectacular. They managed not to talk about Susannah. They spoke about work, books, films, life, family and friends. Adelaide managed to keep the conversation away from her past and Michael was polite enough not to press her too hard for details.

The chemistry was spectacular too. She hadn't imagined it that first night in the bar. Every time he looked at her a different part of her lit up, she felt as if energy was surging around her body on a constant loop so that every time his fingers accidentally brushed hers it set off a charge.

After a near-perfect dinner, she did what she hadn't done once since she had been made a widow – she invited someone back to her place. After she and Michael had made love, so much of the stress and fear Adelaide had felt about moving on, betraying Curtis, betraying Zane came to the surface and she was embarrassed to find herself in tears. But instead of asking her what was wrong, like most people would have, Michael simply wrapped his arms around her and spooned her tightly, gently kissing her shoulder until she fell into a deep sleep.

When she awoke, she could hear Michael at the kitchen counter. She could smell fresh coffee too. She sat up in bed, sheepish, a little awkward.

'Good morning,' she said.

'Adelaide,' he said, bringing her a cup of coffee. He took her fingers gently with his hand, and sat down on the bed. 'How are you feeling?'

'Ugh, I'm fine. A bit embarrassed,' she said smiling awkwardly.

'Do you want to talk about it?'

Adelaide gave the question some time, and found that, no, she did not want to talk about any of the things that had happened to her. How could she have thought that she could ever do this again? The fear was overwhelming. She bit down on the emotion she felt rising.

'This is why ... why I don't date.' And then, just in case he hadn't got it, she said, 'This is why I don't think I can do this again.'

There was the sense of something fragile shattering. Michael winced as if he was having a splinter extracted.

'*This* is why *I* don't date,' he said, sounding hurt. 'Adelaide, last night was something I don't do lightly.'

'Me neither, I just ... look, you saw what happened. I am an emotional wreck. I am just not capable of anything serious.'

'Adelaide, we can go at your pace.'

'I'm sorry. I just, I can't. I think you should go, Michael.'

He gathered his things quickly and left. The slam of the door behind him echoed in Adelaide's mind.

Chapter 53

The weekend passed slowly for Susannah. Time seemed to be standing still and then racing forward. She was torn by questions of how best to spend what could be her last weekend with Emma. She felt like a prisoner already. But in the end, instead of doing something seismic, she decided to do small things. They went to the funfair as a family, where Susannah bought Emma cotton candy on a stick, and John paid dollar after dollar to win her a giant teddy bear. They went to her favourite pizza restaurant for dinner and ate dough balls with garlic butter until they were ready to burst. It was normal life but it seemed so acutely perfect to Susannah now that it was about to be taken away from her.

She couldn't quite bring herself to think about how things might go against her on Monday. *How* could they? It was an accident. Nobody could prove that she was reckless, negligent, malicious if she hadn't been. But they could certainly try to prove that she cared about her job more than they thought she should and link her refusal to sacrifice her career to her baby's death. And that seemed to be what every thread under every article written about her emphasised; the comments all asked, 'Could a mom really forget her baby?' People commented about fault. It was always her fault. Most added a kicker like, 'I hope she gets sent away for a long time' or, 'I hope she suffers ... just like her baby did.' She didn't recognise the demonised figure she read about in these comments but she could see how that might be how others saw her, how the jury might see her.

On Sunday evening, after Emma was in bed, she sat quietly with John. He tried to talk to her, apologise to her about Abbie, but it all seemed so mundane, so unimportant in the face of what might happen. She couldn't talk to him about all that now; those small concerns were for life after the verdict.

Chapter 54

On Monday morning, Adelaide was sitting in her broadcast van, pre-writing her scripts – one for a 'Guilty' verdict, one for a 'Not Guilty' verdict. She always did this to be prepared for the result on big trials, especially ones that were as hard to call as this one. News moved fast and she needed to have something ready to go when the verdict came in. She could add in whatever incidentals happened but usually it was a predictable sequence of events. She was trying not to think about Michael.

Adelaide could usually predict what defendants would say before they said it, and she was never far off the mark. For example, she knew that after the verdict was announced, Susannah and John would stand side by side, either a little behind their lawyer's right shoulder or else flanking her. Then the lawyer would read a prepared statement about how they wanted to prevent something like this from happening again so they were setting up a foundation called, oh, let's say, Baby Louise's Foundation. Sometimes Adelaide didn't have to change a thing in her pre-prepared script, which always gave her a chill. She worried she was becoming a different person since she had taken on this job. Maybe it was the kind of stories she worked on – always negative, always sad, always tragic. Her role was to watch the suffering of others at a remove, instead of empathising with them. She had become an observer, untouchable and untouched.

She felt like a wreck. Michael crept back into her thoughts. She had been unfair to him. She had slept with him, then asked him to leave. If the shoe was on the other foot here, she would be saying he had used her for sex. She was emotionally exhausted by the encounter, and she felt guilty. She needed a coffee to kick-start her brain.

Chapter 55

Susannah refused to spend what might be her last remaining hour of freedom in the courthouse. She took the risk of going for a coffee. The media didn't tend to move far from the entrance of the courthouse. John dropped her a block away.

'Want me to come with you?' he asked.

She smiled, shook her head.

'I just need twenty minutes by myself,' she said. 'I'll follow you in.'

She made her way down the block towards the diner across the street from the courthouse and she sat at the bar. She wanted to postpone her fate for just a few precious minutes, remember what it felt like to be just an ordinary person in the world again.

She kept her gaze low so as to remain unnoticed.

A woman sat at the bar, a few stools down the way. Susannah looked up. It was the journalist. The one who was at the funeral, the hospital, the hearing, the one who sat quietly in the court room, watching her, always watching. She was wearing a simple black suit today, her striking features enhanced by her short hair-cut. She was lost, staring at her phone. More and more, Susannah felt sure she recognised her from somewhere other than the TV, the courtroom . . . but where?

Chapter 56

Adelaide was thinking about Michael, while she waited for her coffee. She had received a text from him the previous night apologising for getting angry, telling her he respected her decision and that he hoped they could be friends, but she hadn't got back to him. What was she supposed to say? She was paralysed by fear, confusion. Her thumbs hovered over her screen as she tried to figure out how to reply, when a cool voice broke through her thoughts.

'Hi.'

Adelaide nearly jumped out of her skin. She looked up. It was Susannah. Adelaide's heart started racing. Was she going to pull her up on her reporting? Adelaide was as familiar with Susannah's face as with her own by now but it still felt strange to be this close to her, to see the pores on her perfect skin, smell her sophisticated perfume, see the whites of her eyes.

'Hi,' Adelaide said, but couldn't think of anything more to say.

The waitress put a mug of coffee on the bar in front of Adelaide.

'Your coffee, hon.'

'Thanks.' Adelaide said. She picked up the mug and her phone and stood up. 'I'll leave you to your coffee. I'm sure it's a very difficult morning for you, Dr Rice. Good luck with the verdict today.'

Adelaide walked nervously to a booth at the very back of the diner. She could feel Susannah watching her. She sat down, unlocked her phone again and went back to brooding over Michael's message. A minute later she looked up. It was Susannah again.

'Do you mind if I join you for a minute?' Susannah asked.

'Of course not. Please,' Adelaide said, gesturing at the seat opposite her. Adelaide swallowed. This was it. This was the moment when Susannah would tell her exactly what she thought of her and her whole profession.

Susannah slid into the booth. Adelaide clicked off her phone's screen.

Susannah smiled as she squeezed her bump past the edge of the table.

'When are you due?' Adelaide asked.

'I'm five months along now,' Susannah said. 'Do you have children?'

Adelaide froze. There was that question again. It

was the second time in as many days that she had been asked about Zane. But this time, for the first time, she felt able to talk. She cleared her throat.

'I did, once, Zane was his name, but ... he died.' Adelaide felt like the lid of her skull had been peeled back. Recognition dawned on Susannah's face.

'I knew I recognised you. I thought it was just from the TV. But that was you, that day, in the hospital.'

Adelaide remembered Susannah standing in the hospital corridor, entirely focussed on the gurney coming towards her.

Adelaide nodded.

'And your husband, he was there that day too ...'

'Yes. I really admire how you and your husband are so supportive of each other in this.' She didn't want to talk about Curtis. 'I couldn't even look at my husband after Zane died. I blamed him completely even though it wasn't his fault, it wasn't anybody's fault,' Adelaide said sadly.

'Did you break up?' Susannah asked.

Another pause as Adelaide weighed up whether or not to tell Susannah.

'A year after Zane died, Curtis took his own life. I still can't believe that's nine years ago now. It feels like it only happened last year.'

'I'm so sorry, that is so *awful*,' Susannah said.

Adelaide kept talking. Now that she had started, she found she couldn't stop.

'That's why I started working as a TV reporter. I had to change jobs, I just couldn't stand people knowing what had happened to me, all that sympathy, people always asking how I was, my bosses assessing each story they assigned in case it was triggering ... it was so suffocating. I couldn't just do my job, everything was filtered through my tragedy.'

Susannah nodded intensely in agreement.

'And so useless.'

'Exactly,' said Adelaide. 'It didn't change anything, it wasn't going to bring anyone back. In fact, all it served to do was to continue to remind me of my loss, to cut off those areas that might have been an oasis or a haven for me. People were constantly treating me differently, handling me with kid gloves ... I couldn't breathe in that environment. In this job, I move around a lot, and nobody knows anything about me. I haven't really spoken to anyone about it before,' Adelaide said, swiping away a tear.

Susannah's hand glided protectively back and forth over her stomach and she chose her next words carefully.

'Did you ever think about having another baby?'

'You know,' Adelaide said, 'there's nothing I wanted more and yet I found the idea too terrifying. I just couldn't risk it. To go through it all again, to love a baby again, so overwhelmingly, was just too scary for me. I felt I would drown in my own fears. I could never relax again if I had another child. I could never be free from the fear and the worry that something might happen to them.'

Susannah nodded.

'For me, it was the opposite. I felt if I didn't have another baby I wouldn't survive,' said Susannah. 'I *need* to have another one, so I can protect her like I didn't protect Louise.'

Adelaide had a brief vision. It slipped in and left again as smoothly as a knife, but like a knife it left damage. She saw herself nursing Zane in her old bedroom. She could still smell his head, feel the heat of his body, all these years later. She started to cry.

Susannah stood and moved across to Adelaide's side of the table, gently squeezing in beside her. She put her hand on Adelaide's arm and said, 'The idea that you are protecting yourself from pain by sealing yourself off from love is a fallacy.'

Adelaide recognised some of these words from the hours of footage she had watched of Dr Sue giving advice to parents.

'I know, I know . . . but it's just the safest way for me to go about my life. Aren't you scared now, of something awful happening again?'

Susannah was looking out the window at the rain shower that seemed to be passing. 'I blame myself every day for what happened to Louise but I'm trying to accept that it wasn't entirely my fault. I'm not going to be that person ever again, so busy that I forget what's most important.'

Adelaide was getting more and more uncomfortable. She put a few dollars down for her coffee and started putting her notebook and phone in her bag. She felt a sudden urge to get away. She wished now that she hadn't told Susannah about Curtis and Zane. She felt trapped. Susannah didn't stand up to let her out of the booth.

Instead she said, 'You weren't responsible for what happened to Zane. I know it's nearly impossible to think that if we just did something differently, we could have saved them . . . but I don't think that's how it works. I don't think I'll ever be able to forgive myself for what happened to Louise but I understand that I have to try, if I want to have any sort of life. If I can try to forgive myself, surely you can too.'

Adelaide couldn't say what she was thinking, that she just didn't feel anything anymore. Instead, she smiled and said, 'I know you understand better than most people.'

Susannah squeezed her hand and stood up.

'I'd better get to court.'

Adelaide smiled.

'Me too. I hope the verdict goes your way,' she said. 'I really mean that.'

'Thank you,' Susannah said.

With that she was gone. Adelaide watched her cross

the street to the courthouse. She took out her phone, opened Michael's message and started to text.

Hi … she typed. I'm so sorry for acting the way I did. Can we meet up? I'd like to explain.

She stared at the blue messages. Inanimate. Static. The ellipses that meant he was typing appeared and she felt her heart light up too.

Adelaide watched the dots as Michael typed. She didn't expect much. She knew she had wounded him. But she dared to hope.

The dots disappeared.

Adelaide stared at the phone, at her messages, sitting there in space. What had he typed? Had he changed his mind? Deleted her message? Then his message appeared. It was hard to tell whether it was good or bad.

I can meet tonight. How about Vicolo's at 9pm?

Vicolo's was the Italian restaurant two blocks from her apartment.

She texted a hurried Perfect. I'll see you there. X and ran back across the street and into the courthouse for the verdict.

Chapter 57

'Ladies and gentlemen of the jury, have you reached a unanimous verdict?'

The courtroom was deathly silent. The air was gone out of the room. Everything was happening in slow motion. Susannah blinked and saw black around the periphery of her vision. She felt every motion of her eyelids as if they too were opening and closing in slow motion. She looked at the jury members' faces, one by one, then studied their body language for any kind of hint as to what was coming. She noticed a fleck of something on juror number three's cheek. A piece of toast from that morning, perhaps. Had he had a cheerful breakfast, unbothered by the day ahead, or had he been stressed as he left home, carrying the weight of this monumental decision? Juror number seven had freshly applied lipstick, slicked over with a gloopy lip gloss. She must have reapplied just before she came into court. Did she have a boyfriend or a husband, or both, Susannah wondered. She knew that each and every one of these twelve people would soon return to their ordinary lives and that they would, in time, gradually forget about Dr Susannah Rice. She would fossilise in their minds, a cipher of a person, not a *real* person. Was she ever real to them, she wondered? One thing she knew with certainty looking at juror eleven, who shifted impatiently in his too-small chair, was that she would not be returning to her normal life that evening. Whatever way the verdict went, Susannah's life was about to change and she felt a hot pang of jealousy for the lives of these people sat in front of her. They just wanted to get back to their old lives, sweating the small stuff.

But what life was waiting for her after this?

Susannah looked across the room at the press gallery. The journalists' eyes were fixed on the jury, all except Adelaide Gold, who looked at Susannah. Adelaide gave a firm smile and Susannah felt something deep from this woman she hardly knew. For this journalist at least, Susannah was a real person.

The forewoman of the jury stood. She wore a colourful wrap dress that showcased her classical figure, bosoms and haunches that spoke to Susannah, at this time above all, of fertility. Her make-up was perfect, her hair freshly blowdried. Susannah imagined she smelled expensive.

'We have reached a unanimous verdict, Your Honour.'

Dana looked grim-faced. She must know something. Susannah looked at the beautiful face of the fore-woman, searching her expression. She looked slightly ashamed, as if she couldn't bring herself to look at Susannah. John reached over the bench from the seat behind Susannah. He put his hand on her shoulder and squeezed. She was surprised by the warmth of his fingers. She put her hand on top of his and squeezed back. She was glad he was here, regardless of everything.

The stenographer's fingers paused on the tiny keypad before beginning to type.

'On the charges of involuntary manslaughter and criminal negligence, how do you find the defendant?'

There was a collective intake of breath. 'We find the defendant ...'

The world stopped. Susannah squeezed her eyes shut as the room began to spin.

'... guilty.'

Nobody moved. Then suddenly the spell was broken by the sound of shrieks, cries, protests. Noise flooded the room from all sides. It was so loud. Susannah tried to stand but she was rooted to her chair. Her mind swam in the sea of voices. She heard John's voice loud amidst the clamour.

'My wife is not guilty of anything. This is an outrage!'

She could hear Dana saying calmly, 'It's okay,

Susannah, we'll appeal. There's no way this verdict will stand. You're being scapegoated.'

There were what sounded like hundreds of voices talking animatedly and, above it all, Susannah could hear the judge's gavel battering for order. She dared to look at John. He looked terrified.

'It's all right, don't worry. I'm fine.' She tried to lift herself up to standing but still found she was too weak. She was overcome with a wave of nausea. The baby. She put her hand on her stomach.

The judge snapped her gavel.

'Ladies and gentlemen. I will remind you that this court has not been adjourned.'

When there was complete silence, the judge began to speak.

'Ladies and gentlemen of the jury, I thank you for your service to this court and your attention to what has been one of the most difficult cases I have worked on in my twenty-seven years as a judge. Every year, anything up to fifty children die of vehicular hyperthermia or FBS – Forgotten Baby Syndrome.'

Susannah tried to follow the judge's speech but John was whispering gently in her ear.

'We'll fight this, darling. We will get you cleared. Don't worry. We can appeal. This is not over. It's not right. It's just not right.' She shushed him sharply as she tried to work out what the judge was saying. She looked at the press. They seemed frozen, unsure whether to continue packing up their things or to stay and listen. They weren't quite committed either way yet, no one sat back down, but they were listening to the judge. Dana reached out her hand and gripped Susannah's wrist. She didn't seem to be breathing. The judge went on.

'These children come from every walk of life, varying socio-economic, political, religious and ethnic backgrounds. This syndrome is not picky. It affects everyone equally. The price we pay for success in the United States of America is over-work, exhaustion, chronic distraction, sleep-deprivation, toxic stress.

'I am sorry to say that this case is not unique. This will not be the last time we encounter this kind of tragedy. This is going to keep happening for as long as we insist that parents, children, families, *people* come second to profit and wealth. Nor will the problem be solved by the handing down of a custodial sentence to the defendant.'

Susannah felt something turn over in her mind. She didn't dare to hope but she felt like a huge weight was lifting as the judge continued.

'And so, I have decided that I will not be imposing any custodial sentence here today.'

Journalists who had been packing away notebooks and iPads, shrugging on blazers, gathering their belongings stopped what they were doing.

Dana's eyes were glittering with tears.

'What does this mean?' Susannah asked her. 'I thought mandatory sentencing meant it was mandatory. Is she going to suspend the custodial sentence? Can she do that?'

Dana held her hand up to silence Susannah.

'Furthermore, it is my opinion that the court has not seen convincing evidence presented here over the past week to prove *beyond doubt* the charges brought by the prosecution. I have no choice but to invoke a judgement *non obstante veredicto* and reverse the decision of the jury. I therefore find the defendant Susannah Rice not guilty of all charges.'

Dana grabbed Susannah, hugging her tightly. John joined in from the seat behind, piling on as if Susannah had scored a winning goal. Susannah felt like a rag doll. She could hear the uproar of the court. The shouts from the public gallery fell on her like arrows.

'This is a disgrace!'

'She killed her baby!'

Susannah's hands went to her head, and her shoulders hunched as if she was protecting herself from actual physical blows.

'Can she even do this?' Susannah asked Dana.

'She can,' said Dana. 'It's rare, but it's legal. Listen.'

The judge was banging her gavel, shouting for order.

The jury looked miffed. They thought their authority was final. One woman objected, 'But we found her guilty!'

The judge addressed the jury directly.

'This is not an indictment of your performance as a jury. You have performed your duty and made your judgement accordingly but I cannot support it in law because the evidence presented here, in my opinion, does not prove the charges and I cannot therefore risk setting a precedent in law when I know that this will not be the last time this kind of case comes before my courtroom.' She took a breath. 'I thank you for your service. You are excused from jury duty for the next three years.'

One of the men in the back row muttered, 'I took a week off work for this? Why have a democracy at all?'

The courtroom erupted again. There were skirmishes within skirmishes, legal teams grappling with the sudden turnaround, papers being collected by the armful, journalists making a note of the turnaround. Rogney was even more outraged than the jury at the idea of a judgement going against his finely formed morality.

'Your Honour! Your *Honour!*' Rogney had sat in stunned silence throughout the judge's speech, a look of utter disbelief on his face, but he finally snapped into action. He protested loudly and wildly. 'The jury has spoken. This is the United States of America! Dr Rice has been found guilty by a jury of her peers. Who are you to set aside what a jury has decided in law? This is unprecedented!'

Anything might happen. Susannah was not familiar enough with the law but she felt as if the verdict could just as easily flip back to guilty if Rogney argued hard enough. Could it? Could he appeal? But it appeared that the case really was at an end and so was the judge's appetite for Rogney's histrionics. She snapped her gavel and glared at Rogney.

'Counsellor Rogney, I have not finished. Over the past week I have heard plenty of judgement, shaming, speculation and the bending of facts to fit a certain distasteful narrative about mothers in our society.'

Susannah couldn't believe her ears. She looked at Dana who was smirking at Rogney's dressing down. She gave Susannah a smile. Susannah didn't dare to believe that this was actually happening. She listened to the judge.

'I've heard a lot about what a mother should and shouldn't be, how the good ones behave, how bad ones dare to take an interest in their careers. Indeed, I found myself asking throughout this trial, if Dr Susannah Rice were a *father* rather than a mother, would she have experienced a different line of questioning in this courtroom? Would she even be on trial? I understand that my esteemed colleague Judge Margaret Parker saw fit to send this case to trial but based on the quality of evidence you presented in this court, Counsellor Rogney, you have done that judge a disservice.' She paused and then her eyes met Susannah's. Her voice softened and for a moment, it was as if they were the only two people in the room.

'Dr Rice, I am sorry for your loss and that you have had to endure the extra distress that this trial must have caused you and your family. This case is dismissed. You are free to go.'

The gavel came down with a final snap.

Chapter 58

Adelaide and Julie didn't even say goodbye to each other but ran for their respective media vans, tweeting the news as they ran: *#HotCarMom found #NotGuilty as judge overturns jury verdict.*

Adelaide lacquered on heavy lip gloss as Luke popped the cap off his camera. She threw a fuschia jacket over her blouse and furiously brushed blusher on her cheeks. She smoothed her hair and breathed slowly, tried to hold on to the key points of the story in her head; no script planning could have prepared her for the morning's events. *Shock overturned verdict, hot car death, motherhood on trial, guilty jury verdict, righteous judge.*

She heard Jimmy's voice from the studio through her earpiece.

'Coming to you, Adelaide, in two minutes. Out of these commercials . . .'

The light on the camera went red and an automatic part of Adelaide began to speak.

'There were dramatic scenes in courtroom 22 in the southern district of Manhattan today as Justice Ruth Donnelly overturned the jury's *unanimous* verdict of guilty in the Dr Sue trial. The jury found Dr Sue guilty of the involuntary manslaughter of her baby girl, who died of heat stroke when Dr Rice accidentally left the child in her car last June.'

Adelaide took a breath, swallowed hard to keep her voice steady. She saw the images of the car park scroll in her mind, the images that Rogney showed in the courtroom, Zane in the ED that day, Curtis in their bathroom. She saw herself speaking to the camera.

'However, in a shock move, Justice Donnelly overturned the judgement by invoking a rare point of law. She said she had not seen evidence to convince her that what had happened to Louise Rice was anything more than a tragic accident and as a result of that she was overturning the jury's verdict.'

Susannah, John and Dana emerged from the courthouse and every reporter broke off their live report to strain their microphones towards Dana. Adelaide squeezed sideways through the scrum. Susannah and John stood side by side, just behind Dana's right shoulder, as she made a statement on their behalf. She was brief. She thanked people for their support. She urged people to invest in sensor alarms for their children's car seats. And she included the details of a website to lobby the motor industry and local representatives to introduce these alarms as standard. The website was called the Baby Louise Foundation. *Of course it is*, Adelaide thought.

Adelaide watched Susannah standing beside John on the steps of the courthouse as their lawyer read their statement. Her arm ached as she reached as far as she could between two journalists' heads, sticking her microphone as close as she could to the lawyer's mouth. She caught Susannah's eye, and smiled. When Dana was finished, Adelaide turned back to the camera.

'We'll bring you more details on this story throughout the day. I'm Adelaide Gold for CNN News.'

Chapter 59

Susannah stared vacantly into the wall of reporters and photographers that hung on Dana's every word. For the first time since Louise had died, she felt lighter. The sadness, the gnawing grief was still there but the self-loathing, the hatred, the bullying she had pummelled herself with since Louise's death felt diluted. The judge's words 'not guilty' were unambiguous. The judge believed it enough to overturn a jury verdict. Maybe Susannah should believe it too. Maybe it hadn't been her fault. Maybe the whole thing had been a terrible accident. Maybe it really could have happened to anyone.

As Dana wrapped up her speech, Susannah ignored the shouts of photographers and journalists for comments. Adelaide Gold was there, front and centre, giving her a smile of solidarity but Susannah just put her sunglasses on. They were the $400 Gucci ones. She didn't care what the news reports had to say about that now. She walked as quickly as she could towards the waiting car.

The journalists and cameras followed her like a single mass of lava flowing after her. Once in the car, their cries were muffled, the noise of their fists and cameras and microphones knocking against the windows. Susannah was trembling. John crushed in after her saying, 'Please, just drive' to the driver.

Once the pack of journalists receded behind the car, John turned to look at Susannah. There were tears in his eyes.

'I'm so relieved, Susannah. For a minute there I really thought I was going to lose you.' He hugged her tightly.

She squeezed his hand. She was still in shock. She couldn't believe this part of the nightmare was over. Was it actually over? Silence settled between them again and they listened to the burble of the car radio, barely audible but providing an invisible screen of privacy for their conversation.

'I just can't imagine my life without you and Emma,' John said. 'I'm so glad you want a fresh start.'

Susannah closed her eyes. He had misunderstood her. She did want a fresh start. She just hadn't made it clear enough that she wanted a fresh start on her own.

Chapter 60

Adelaide spotted Julie and waited for her to finish recording her own piece to camera before they retreated to the diner.

They crossed the street together. Julie was talking quickly the whole time. Adelaide could tell she was excited.

'That was really something. I've never seen anything like that!' she said. 'It was like something out of a courtroom drama. Guilty! Not guilty! My God!' She was quiet as they pushed through the door of the diner and sat down in their booth. 'Still, it seems strange to me that her baby is dead and it's nobody's fault.'

Adelaide's nerves were standing on end. She could not be more anxious if she had been on trial herself. She was not in the mood for Julie's high-handed judgement. She scrutinised the menu. She realised all of a sudden she was exhausted. The adrenalin was leaving her body. She rested her elbows on the formica table and leaned her forehead in her hands.

Adelaide knew she and Julie differed on a lot of important things. It was easy to forget for the most part, but from time to time, it found its way to the surface.

'It was an accident, Julie. The definition of an accident is it's nobody's fault.'

Julie raised her eyebrows defensively.

'Well, I'm sorry. I didn't realise you were the secretary of the Dr Sue fan club.'

Adelaide realised she was making it personal. But this *was* personal. Adelaide looked across at the bank of booths opposite them, the anonymous faces, calmly eating their food, drinking coffees, discussing small things, work deals, presentations, potential dates, last night's argument, oblivious to Adelaide, oblivious to the emotional high-wire act she had been performing since she started working on this story.

The air between Adelaide and Julie was unpredictable, staticky. Adelaide still wasn't sure if they might have an argument or if the moment might pass. Julie switched topics to safer ground.

'I've just been put on the triple familicide trial down in Florida. I mean, Jesus, shouldn't there be some workplace union rules about this? If you get one baby death you don't do another one for at least a week? Tell me you're going to be there too?'

Adelaide softened and nodded.

'Yeah, can you believe it? No rest for the wicked.' Her smile didn't reach her eyes.

'What say we head down to Miami a couple of days early, try to unwind a bit? Hit a spa by day, a club or two by night?'

'Appealing as that sounds, I think I'm going to stay put, take a couple of rest days.' Adelaide watched the sous-chef through the slot between diner and kitchen, the slice of light like a television screen. He moved back and forth at the hot plate, concentrating on the food.

'To be honest, I've found this story the toughest one I've ever worked on. I think I just need a bit of down-time before I head back into it. How do you keep going with these stories, Julie?'

Julie smiled a sad smile, like she knew where Adelaide's thoughts were leading her, the decision she had already half-made while covering this trial. Julie shrugged.

'I go to the spa for the day, then I go to a club, get drunk and I try not to think about it.'

Adelaide nodded. She tidied the little sachets of sugar and assorted sweeteners into piles then packed them neatly into the sugar-bowl, tried to make them uniform, failed. 'I just don't think this is the kind of journalist I ever meant to be. I want to make people's lives better.' She knew she was not going to Florida. She knew she was not going to work on another single story that would tear her apart from the inside out. She was going to contact her old editor in the *Times*. He had said the door would always be open for her. Maybe it was time to push that door.

'Please don't leave me,' Julie said. 'I'll have no one to talk to. And, apart from your one transgression with the professor, you have been the most consistent and loyal wingwoman I've ever had.'

Adelaide laughed, the froideur that had stiffened her moments ago, now dissipated.

She mopped the last of her pancake in the maple syrup, forked it into her mouth and drained her coffee cup.

'I'd better get back to the van. I've got to edit my packages for tonight.'

'Okay. Me too. I'll get this,' Julie said.

'Thanks,' Adelaide said.

As she left the booth, Julie said, 'See you in Miami?'

Adelaide smiled but shook her head.

'No. No, I don't think you will.'

As Adelaide left the diner and walked back past the windows, she saw her own reflection, and smiled.

Chapter 61

As the driver turned into her neighbourhood, Susannah realised she didn't want to go home. Going home was going back to her old life and that life was dead to her now.

She climbed the steps to her house, a cool tinge on the late-autumn breeze as she entered the house's shadow. She turned the key.

Emma shouted, 'Mommy!' and came running down the hall to Susannah. 'Mommy you're home!'

Susannah bent and clasped her to her, hugging her tightly. She hadn't been sure that she would get to do this today. She took in the artificial strawberry scent from Emma's hair. Christina must have given her a bath this morning. Christina walked out into the hall, smiling. There were tears in her eyes.

'I heard the news on the radio. I'm so pleased.'

Susannah stood up and Christina took the

opportunity to hug her briefly, diffidently, but Susannah was touched by the physical gesture.

'Thanks, Christina, I think we're just going to let the news sink in. You might as well take the rest of the day off.'

Christina smiled and collected her things. 'There's a casserole in the fridge.'

'What would we do without you Christina, thank you so much, for everything.'

Susannah leaned her back against the door.

'You must be exhausted,' John said. 'Why don't you rest on the couch? I'll look after Emma.'

Susannah smiled weakly.

'Thank you but I think I'd like to be with her,' she said. 'I didn't think I was coming home today.'

After a day of cuddles, movies and colouring unicorns with Emma, John heated up the casserole that Christina had made and they ate dinner together, as a family.

After Emma was asleep, John and Susannah sat on the couch watching TV. Susannah was grateful for the distraction, so that she wouldn't have to talk to him about the future. Night closed in and she turned on the lamps, to chase the darkness out of the corners of the house.

Chapter 62

When Adelaide arrived at Vicolo's that night, Michael was already at the bar, a glass of white wine in front of him. The place was old-school Italian. She opened the door and an old-fashioned bell above her head announced her entrance. Michael looked up as she walked towards him, her footsteps conspicuously loud on the hardwood floor.

'Hi,' she said, standing uncertainly in front of him.

'Hi.' He smiled then. 'I saw the news. That was quite dramatic. Not guilty is the right verdict, I think. That poor woman.'

'I know. Actually, I met her, in the diner, just before court this morning. She recognised me and we ended up talking,' Adelaide said as she took off her coat and pulled out a stool. Its legs scraped loudly across the floor.

'Wow, what did she say?'

Adelaide felt her throat go dry.

'Well, we talked about ... it's actually what I want to talk to you about.'

He gave her a quizzical look.

'You're being very mysterious.'

She looked around the restaurant.

'Let's move to a booth down here,' she said. 'Come on, it'll be more private.'

He stood, told the barman they were moving and ordered a drink for Adelaide.

He carried their drinks to the booth. Adelaide hadn't eaten since brunch and the first sip of wine went straight to her head.

She reached for a breadstick as she started talking.

'Just over ten years ago, my life was very different to what it is now. I was married, I had a baby ... my baby,' she paused. Was she really going to say this? She looked up at the ceiling and forced the words out.

'My baby died.'

She dragged her gaze down to meet Michael's. His eyes were wide, his hand covering his mouth.

'My husband died too.'

Michael's other hand came up and covered her hand. 'Adelaide, oh my God, I can't believe it. I'm so sorry. I don't know what to say ...'

Michael's face was one of utter incomprehension and pain. Now that she had told him the worst part she felt she could breathe again.

'It's okay. It's fine. You couldn't have known. But you were right to sense that I was hiding something, holding something back because ... I was. It's just not something I have been able to talk about – to *anyone*, really – since it happened.'

'This case must have been so difficult for you to work on.'

She nodded, 'It was. Susannah Rice was the doctor on call the day my baby was brought to the emergency room.'

Michael dropped his hands and they banged down on the table. 'Oh my God, that is ... *insane*.'

She nodded slowly, aware of the insanity of the coincidence.

'That's why this whole case has been ...' She splayed her fingers searching for the right term, 'just so, so difficult to work on and just really emotional too.'

'Adelaide, I ... I don't even know what to say. I can't even begin to imagine how you reported on this story for the last six months. But what happened to your baby and your husband? I'm sorry. You don't have to answer that.'

'No, it's okay,' she said. 'My baby ...' she paused, stuck on his name. '*Zane*, he just stopped breathing. They said it was a crib death. My husband, Curtis, killed himself a year later. I think he blamed himself. That was nine years ago now. And there hasn't been anybody since, not until ... you.'

She smiled weakly at him but couldn't hold his gaze.

She didn't want to look at Michael. Didn't want to see the details registering, the horror, the fear that she knew came with being so close to news like this. People just wanted to get away from it as fast as they could. So she kept her eyes down, sipped her wine, straightened her cutlery.

She swiped a quick look at Michael's face. It was completely crumpled. She looked back at the table until she heard him speak.

'I had no idea. I'm so embarrassed that I put pressure on you the other night. Jesus, I can't believe I did that.'

She gave him a half-smile, and dismissed his embarrassment with a quick and emphatic shake of her head.

'Michael, it's okay. You didn't know.' She reached her fingers across the table, squeezed his arm. There was that crackle of electricity again.

'Moving on from all that, dating someone new, it still feels like very scary territory to me. I just don't know if I'm brave enough to give anything new a go or if I'm emotionally strong enough . . . ' She puffed out a few little breaths of air, as if she had been holding it all in while she talked. 'Not to mention the fact that you might want to change your mind after hearing all this,' she smiled.

A waiter came by. They both scrambled for their menus.

'I'm so sorry, I haven't even looked. Can you recommend something? Your special?'

The waiter was distinctly unimpressed.

'The special is hake.'

'Great! I'll have the hake!' Adelaide said, desperately grateful not to have to concentrate on words, descriptions of food. Michael ordered the *spaghetti alle vongole*.

When the waiter was gone, he looked at Adelaide in awe.

'How have you managed to cover this story? Has it not been torture?

'It has been so triggering,' she said, pressing her fingers to her temples. 'And I didn't expect it to be. Can you believe that,' she said laughing, and her laugh let a lot of the tension out of her body. Michael smiled kindly.

'I really haven't wanted to address my own experience at all,' Adelaide said. 'And it's been easier than you might imagine actually to push it away, living the way I've been living, working all hours, travelling a lot, working with people who don't know me, don't know about my past . . . until I got put on this story.'

She sat back as their food arrived.

'Up until today I hadn't told anyone about it. Julie doesn't even know. But when you and I spent the night together the other night, it just brought up so much . . . *emotion*,' she said, opening her hands like tiny explosions. 'I just felt like those kind of emotions I was feeling were too powerful, too much for me. But

I've realised, thinking about it over the last few days, if I want to be with someone – in that way – again, it's not going to be worth it unless it involves those kind of feelings.'

She didn't really know what else to say so she kept her mouth shut.

'If it helps, I'm really scared too,' Michael said.

She laughed. 'It does help. It really helps.'

He leaned towards her. He was inches away from her face now and she dared to look straight at him. He touched her face tenderly and she got that jolt again, straight through her centre.

'I'm so sorry about everything you've gone through, Adelaide.'

He kissed her softly and it was like pulling a cord, taut through her body.

Chapter 63

Susannah woke up, still on the couch. John was curled up next to her. What had woken her? A cramp in her stomach, a cool feeling between her legs. She got up from the couch and went to use the bathroom. When she pulled down her underwear, she was shocked cold to see a small blood stain. The discovery was as unexpected and confusing as if she had laid an egg in her underwear. She pulled her pants up quickly, as if by doing so she could un-see the stain, undo the happening.

She went back to the couch.

'John, John,' she tried to keep her voice calm. 'I'm bleeding.'

He shifted himself up on his elbow.

'What? Where?'

He was groggy, confused, but when he took in her expression he understood immediately and was on his feet. Under her instruction, he helped Susannah to lie down, and stuck two cushions underneath her ankles, elevating her legs.

'Shouldn't we go to the emergency room?'

She felt an urgent need to vomit and made it to the bathroom, a hot pain cleaving her in two. She wept and gasped as the pain radiated through her body.

'Okay, we're going to the hospital,' John said. He got a blanket, put it over Susannah and lifted her as if she weighed nothing. There was blood on the floor now where she had been lying. He put her in the car and went back for Emma, carrying her, still sleeping, in her own little blanket. They drove to the hospital together, husband, wife, daughter, a family once more, bound by everything they had been through. Susannah stared numbly out the window at the dawn light edging up from behind the buildings, like a filter being turned up on the city.

At the hospital, they were led to a room off the main maternity waiting area.

'I've never been here,' Susannah said. How had she never even noticed this room before? It was a small waiting room, discretely tucked underneath a stairwell, away from the swollen main waiting area. The women in here were subdued, quiet, they seemed almost drugged. They murmured into phones, finding euphemisms for words that were too difficult to speak.

Susannah was taken to a private room and the

attending obstetrician came in wheeling a tray laden with apparatus. She didn't speak, didn't even say hello. Susannah, used to getting down on one knee, making direct eye contact with her patients and explaining in a loud, clear, slow voice exactly who she was and what she was going to do, was unnerved by the fact that this doctor didn't even acknowledge her.

'Please sit on the bed, then shuffle down until you are at the end and place your legs in the stirrups.'

Susannah did as instructed. She felt more like a dog or a cat in a veterinary surgery, than a patient.

When the doctor removed the speculum, it was covered in blood. Susannah saw it as betrayal. How could her body turn on her like this?

The doctor clattered the speculum into a metal kidney bowl, and without a word, made to leave the room. Susannah stirred out of her shock. 'Excuse me, wait! Can you tell me what's happening?'

The doctor looked surprised, then irritated, but sighed and said, 'Bleeding in pregnancy is most indicative of miscarriage but we'll need to scan you first.'

Susannah let out one huge sob that surprised even her. John squeezed her hand. It was only then that the obstetrician thought to sympathise.

'I'm very sorry,' she said in a perfunctory tone and left the room. The scan confirmed her worst fears. There was no heartbeat. She would have to deliver the baby. The nurse who prepared her for the labour ward was kinder. 'Hopefully we'll see you back here again very soon,' she said, but Susannah knew she would not be back.

The miscarriage operated as an indelible line drawn underneath Susannah and John's marriage. It severed whatever delicate ties remained. She had agonised about splitting up with John when she was pregnant but now more than ever she knew that leaving was the right thing to do. The relationship had always been dysfunctional. They had just been too busy to notice. She had bounced into the marriage with a broken heart and under the increasing volume of her desire to have children. John was a decent man, and he deserved someone to love him.

Susannah just wanted to be herself again and all she felt now was a kind of neutral good will towards John. She knew they would be happier apart and Emma would have a healthier upbringing if her parents were not married. She had to rebuild herself, rebuild her life, from the ground up. She had been given a second chance. Like scorched earth, it was time now to re-seed, to grow again.

Chapter 64

Two years later

Emma ran through the school gate. She was in first grade now, 'a big girl,' as she was fond of telling Susannah. She was laden down with her schoolbag on one arm, her school sweater clamped under her elbow, her school tie slightly askew. Her hands gripped several sheets of art paper.

'I made a beautiful picture for you, Mommy. This is you, this is me, this is dada, this is Abbie and this is Baba Loulou in the clouds and this is our other baby. See, Baba Loulou is looking after him in heaven! And I drew a love heart here for you, Mommy.'

'Oh, it's beautiful,' Susannah said taking the picture. Painful as it was, it was also touching to see.

Susannah gathered up the drawings, the bag, the

sweater in one hand and took Emma's hand with her free hand.

'Do you have to go back to work today, Mommy?' Emma asked.

'I sure do,' Susannah said, 'but I have just enough time to go by the ice cream stand in the park on our walk home.'

'Yaaaaaay!' Emma screamed and skipped on ahead of Susannah.

Despite her losses, Susannah felt lucky. She was lucky to have Emma. In fact, it was miraculous that she had had children at all.

Spending more time around Emma over the last two years had brought them closer. Life felt more like her idea of what a normal life should be. Work was good. She still worked as much as ever but she had reworked her schedule and had put down a few boundaries so that now it fit around her life. She worked every second weekend – the weekends John and Abbie took Emma – and on the alternate weekends, she and Emma spent the entire time together doing exactly what they wanted. Dance class, babycinos, swimming, the playground, soft play, nature walks in Gramercy Park. Sometimes they went all the way to Central Park.

And if she was honest, life was easier now with John gone. Divorcing John had been the right decision, it had liberated her. The weight of worrying about being a good wife, worrying about her marriage, fell away like a sandbag. She was no longer tormented wondering about why their relationship didn't feel quite right. It had never been quite right. John was married to Abbie now – his third wife – and Susannah got on with her own life as a mom, and a doctor, and she realised that she loved being both.

Wednesdays were her favourite days now. She finished her clinic at two thirty, picked Emma up from school and took her to her swimming lesson. Afterwards, in the changing room, Susannah slowly towelled Emma off, adding some powder to her skin, combing the tangles out of her matted hair. There was a heartbreaking pleasure in the simplicity of the actions, in the task of taking care of her child. At 5 p.m. she would be back in work for a long evening shift while John gave Emma dinner and put her to bed but it was worth breaking up her day to experience this joy of being a mother. This is what she had been missing out on. She didn't want to stop working, refused to accept that she couldn't be a doctor *and* a mother, but she realised after the trial that she wanted to change the way she engaged with both of those roles, to make sure she got the best of them.

Life was almost relaxed now, in a way she had never imagined it could be. Susannah had let go a lot too. When she took Emma to the soft-play area now, Emma buried herself in plastic multicoloured balls and Susannah only reapplied hand sanitiser twice.

Since Louise had died, Susannah had been contacted by so many people. She knew now that what had happened to her was not a one-off. She knew that apart from the forty cases a year where babies died, there were hundreds of near-misses, accidents waiting to happen. Slowly, she began to forgive herself.

Slowly, life started to feel familiar, normal even. At night she would read a story to Emma, and then watch something on TV, read a research article in a journal, before falling into bed.

She had a routine now. She finally had balance.

On the couch that night, she checked her emails before bed. Her heart stopped. Ralph Lyons. She hardly dared to click on it, then hated herself for letting him *still*, after everything she had been through, have this power over her when he probably just wanted to ask her opinion on a patient.

She clicked the email. It was a long, rambling email. Was he *drunk*? She felt her anger rising. Why was he bothering her now, after all this time?

She read on.

I realised a while back, after I heard that you and John had divorced, that I was harbouring something. I was thinking about you a lot. I realised we were really great together. I've never felt that connection with anyone else since. I regret every day that I ended things, that we didn't get married, have a child together. Please, if you still feel anything for me, call me.

Love,

Ralph.

Susannah's eyes widened. *Love!* He had never used that word once in all the time they had been together. He couldn't even use the word 'girlfriend', never mind 'love'. How *dare* he disturb her hard-earned peace of mind like this. The nerve of that man.

She knew that he had never loved her when they were together, and he certainly didn't now. He only loved himself. She carefully moved her curser to the trash icon, and clicked on it. But it wasn't enough. She went into her deleted items folder, selected the email again, and clicked 'Delete Forever'.

Good riddance, Ralph.

The next day, after dropping Emma to school, Susannah stopped by the canteen in the hospital. She picked up a copy of the *New York Times* from the table next to her. She no longer feared picking up the newspaper. She only featured in print now if she had a new book out, which she had done last year. After her name had been cleared, she had renegotiated her publishing deals and published her most successful book yet – *Parenting and Failure*. Susannah opened the *Times* and discovered an article about moving on after grief, written by Adelaide Gold. Susannah often wondered what had become of the journalist Adelaide Gold. She had disappeared from the TV news soon after Susannah's trial had ended. Accompanying the article was a picture of Adelaide, smiling, standing behind a stroller with a beautiful baby girl sitting in the seat, and ... was that the professor from the trial? Susannah read the photo caption underneath the picture: 'The journalist Adelaide Gold pictured here with her partner, Professor Michael Thomas, and their six-month-old baby daughter, Aisha.'

Funny how things work out, Susannah thought, smiling. She felt unreasonably happy for the journalist.

Words from the past echoed through her mind. 'You have to make a decision to be happy.' That's what Adam had told her in one of their long-ago therapy sessions. 'After a tragedy like this, you actually have to decide you are going to be happy. Otherwise, you *never* will be. I know it feels wrong, like you are disrespecting the memory of Louise, but trying to be happy in your life as it is now, is not disrespecting her. In fact, it is the opposite – you're honouring her.'

It hadn't made sense to Susannah at the time, but looking at the photograph of Adelaide and the peace in her expression, Susannah thought she could feel the grief that had nested in her heart for so long dislodge and take flight. She realised Adam was right. She had to decide to be happy. She owed it to Louise, and to

Emma, and to herself, to make the most of the second chance she had been given. As she listened to the background noise of the hospital – the low hum of voices, the beeping of monitors and machinery, the shouting of orders – Susannah realised with hope that she felt like herself for the first time in years.

Acknowledgements

I would like to acknowledge several sources that were of particular help in researching this book: Gene Weingarten's 'Fatal Distraction' (The *Washington Post*, March 8, 2009), Amber Scorah's 'A Baby Dies at Day Care, and a Mother Asks Why She Had to Leave Him So Soon' (*New York Times*, Nov 15, 2015) and Dr Sally E Shaywitz's 'Catch-22 for Mothers' (*New York Times*, March 4, 1973). Also, Janette Fennell's website www.kidsandcars.org, Reni Eddo-Lodge's *Why I'm No Longer Talking To White People About Race* (Bloomsbury; 2017), Austin Channing Brown's *I'm Still Here: Black Dignity In A World Made For Whiteness* (Virago; 2018), Ta-Nehisi Coates's *Between The World And Me* (Text Publishing Melbourne Australia; 2015), Ijeoma Oluo's *So You Want To Talk About Race* (Seal; 2019) and the journalism of Candice Brathwaite.

Thank you to my agent Marianne Gunn O'Connor for seeing potential in this story and in me. Thank you to my editor Darcy Nicholson and Sphere Books for being so passionate about this book from the very beginning. Thank you to Callum Kenny, Thalia Proctor, Sophie Harris, Kirsteen Astor, Jim Binchy, Breda Purdue, Elaine Egan, Siobhan Tierney and Ruth Shern and all the editorial, sales, marketing and publicity teams at Sphere and Hachette Ireland.

Thank you to my dear friends Aoife Kelleher and Hugh Rodgers, Ruth Murphy, Helen Murray, the Medeans Mary Carton and Lynn Millar, Rosanna Bravar, and Zbyszek Zalinski. Thank you Cormac Kinsella and Sinead Dunwoody, Caroline Sheedy, Yvonne Hogan, Thomas Kelly, Joanna Smyth, Dani Gill, Elaine Feeney, Emily Cullen, Rachel Andrews, Aoife Barry, Anna Carey, Susan Daly, Sinead Gleeson, Sarah Maria Griffin, Ger Holland, Siobhan Kane, Darren Kennedy, Jackie Lynham, Judy Kavanagh, Aine Lyons, Mary Watson and Morag Prunty. Thank you to Patrick Dempsey, Susan Battye and Bríd Higgins Ní Chinnéide. Thank you Grainne Faller, Karen Browne and Ann Keane, and to the Galway Writers' Workshop for very early encouragement. Thank you John Boyne, Marian Keyes and Liz Nugent.

Thank you to my family, the Coffeys, the Walshes, the Lappins and the Fahys. Thank you to my mother, Enda, I miss you every day, and to my dad Sean and my brother John for unconditional support. Thank you Jacinta Hannon for everything you do for us.

Finally, thank you to Henry, Arthur, Edith and Frieda – I am so lucky to be your mother – and to David, my husband, for making everything possible.